"Fancy us meeting like this," he said, his tone sarcastic. "I see it as one of those meant-to-be things."

Maci glared at him. She'd be damned if she was going to let him stroll down memory lane. Their past was off-limits.

"Yes, fancy that." She heard the defiant note in her tone as their eyes met.

The effect was galvanizing.

Maci sucked in her breath, and he cursed. Later she didn't know who turned away first. At the time, she didn't care. For her own self-preservation, she couldn't have looked at him another second. "Look, I know this…us…is awkward, but—"

"I thought about trying to find you."

Her heart skipped several beats and she tried to avert her gaze, but found that she couldn't. "Holt—"

"Holt, what?" His tone thickened. "Don't say what's been on my mind for two years."

"Stop it," she muttered tersely, leaning closer as though fearing someone would hear their conversation. "I told myself I wouldn't let you dredge up the past."

"Too late, honey. The past has slam-dunked us both."

Also by MARY LYNN BAXTER

WITHOUT YOU
PULSE POINTS
HIS TOUCH
LIKE SILK
TEMPTING JANEY
SULTRY
ONE SUMMER EVENING
HARD CANDY
TEARS OF YESTERDAY
AUTUMN AWAKENING
LONE STAR HEAT
A DAY IN APRIL

Watch for Mary Lynn Baxter's newest novel

EVENING HOURS

Available October 2005

MARY LYNN BAXTER

IN HOT WATER

ISBN 0-7783-2142-8

IN HOT WATER

www.MIRABooks.com

Printed in U.S.A.

To Warren and Wayne Elledge
for all their invaluable help.
Thanks, guys!

Prologue

She knew she shouldn't be dancing so intimately with a complete stranger.

And she shouldn't be enjoying it, especially when there was no music. But she was. His strong arms and callused hands were like nothing she'd ever experienced.

Still, this was crazy behavior. She'd come on a mission to this Jamaican paradise, but it wasn't to get involved with a man.

"You feel so right in my arms," he whispered against her ear.

Each touch, each caress made her burn inside.

He chuckled. "Cat got your tongue?

"Yes." Her breathing quickened. "I mean no."

He laughed even as he pulled her closer, their bodies swaying in the light breeze. In the distance, she could hear the ocean raising as much havoc as her heart.

She had seen him the first day she and her three friends had arrived on the island. He had intrigued her immediately. He wasn't classically handsome. His shoulders were broader and his arms more muscular than those of any man she knew. His abs were cut to perfection. Rugged was an apt description. She figured that was what had aroused such a wild streak in her.

Character lines had been etched into his tanned face by the sun and wind, and coupled with his blond hair and blue-green eyes, his looks were captivating.

When their eyes first met, she felt an electrified attraction between them. Whenever their paths crossed afterwards, that intensity made her stomach quiver.

Earlier in the evening at a cabana party he'd asked her to dance to a slow, erotic tune. She'd gone into his arms without hesitation. After remaining there through several songs, he'd grabbed her hand and said in a low voice, "Let's walk."

They had strolled barefoot along the water's edge until he'd stopped and pulled her again into his arms. Now, as they continued to dance to imaginary music she was powerless to stop him.

"You're not supposed to be thinking," he whispered into her ear.

The warmth of his breath sent chills down her spine. "I'm not."

"No," he whispered again, stopping in the middle of the make-believe dance and pushing her to arm's length.

She looked at him, held his gaze, and felt her heart beat loudly in her chest. "Why is that?"

"Because only feelings are allowed." He grabbed her hand and pulled her in step with him. "It's a night of magic."

The raspy tone of his voice affected her as much as the touch of his hand clasping hers tightly.

"I don't know you," she said, her gaze resting on his profile.

"That's okay."

"Is it?" Her voice wavered.

He stopped, turned her to face him, then tipped her chin up. "Forget about the world. Just think about the moment and how you feel."

"I don't even know your name."

"If a name is what you want, call me Stan."

"I'm Mildred." She couldn't believe she had outright lied, but then she didn't believe his name was Stan either.

"Mildred it is," he said in a low voice.

She shivered, though the ocean breeze was warm against her skin. "This…is crazy."

"I'm crazy about you," he countered.

In the moonlight she could see his chiseled features and his deep-set eyes, eyes that seemed to penetrate right through to her thoughts.

She licked her dry lips. "That's not possible."

"Anything's possible tonight," he rasped. "Don't fight yourself. Don't fight me."

She closed her eyes, struggling to get control of her wayward emotions. If only she hadn't had that last drink. Perhaps, then, she wouldn't have left her friends partying at the cabana and taken a midnight stroll on the beach with a perfect stranger.

"Hey," he said, "you're thinking again."

She felt his finger trace the line of her jaw before running it along the inside of her lower lip.

Her breathing became erratic. His touch left her feeling hotter than she'd ever been.

"I want to kiss you," he whispered, his hand now trailing down her neck and onto her collarbone.

Her head lolled back like a flower on a weak stem as his hand found its way to a breast. "Please."

"Please what? Kiss you? Touch you?"

"Yes to both." Her words came out in a gasp.

His hand slipped under her halter top and rubbed her breasts. She couldn't breathe or talk.

"Perfect," he whispered, lowering his mouth to hers.

His lips gently cajoled hers, but then she whimpered; his kiss belied such raw, aching hunger that she nearly collapsed against him.

As his mouth continued to cover hers, he sank to his knees and took her with him down onto the wet sand.

"I want you more than I've ever wanted anyone." His voice was so hoarse she could barely understand him.

His words didn't matter. Nothing mattered except the feel of his hands removing her top, his mouth suckling her breasts and his teeth gently nibbling at her nipples. Locking her hands on his head, she held him close, reveling in every sensation he aroused.

"I want to see all of you," he said, pulling her upright.

He removed her shorts and panties and cast them onto a dry, sandy part of the beach.

Standing like a dazed nude statue drenched in the moonlight, she watched as he peeled off his own clothes. She gazed upon his flat, muscled stomach only a moment before looking downward.

He was big and hard.

Desire spread throughout her body. She must have made a satisfactory sound in her throat because he made a strange sound of his own before grabbing her and kissing her again.

"Do you want me as much as I want you?"

She could only moan.

And anticipate.

And soak up the frantic need escalating between them.

"Answer me," he demanded in a guttural tone.

"Yes" was all she could manage, especially after his hand cupped her hot mound and two of his fingers pressed and probed her insides, making her wet.

Again she felt like collapsing, and again they sank to their knees. Using the wet sand as a bed and the water lapping around them as cover, he lowered himself over her, then spread her legs.

Unable to utter even the smallest of sounds, she reached for his throbbing erection and guided it into her. With a deep groan, he penetrated her.

Her eyes widened as she realized how large he was inside her.

He paused long enough to whisper, "Are you okay?"

"Yes, oh yes," she said through gritted teeth, clutching at his back, beckoning him to come more fully inside her, to invade her, to fill her, to give her all to him.

Now.

As if he could read her mind, he ground into her and began pounding her with a force akin to the surf pounding against the beach. She wrapped her legs around his buttocks and felt the silent screams of pleasure bounce around her head as her heart begged for more. She wanted more.

* * *

He didn't know when he'd been this tired. But then he'd worked hard at beating up on his body this morning.

First, he'd run five miles on the beach, which was like running in a straitjacket, then he'd lifted heavier weights than usual in the compact but ample sized gym onboard his sailboat.

Now as he made his way into the outdoor café at the luxury hotel, he realized that his stomach gnawed from lack of food. His overzealous workout had used up what energy he'd had stored.

Still, he shouldn't be here. He should have already set sail. He hadn't planned on hanging around the island another day, because he had other places to go, other fish to fry, and because a buddy of his had agreed to meet him in a couple of days for some deep-sea fishing. Yet here he was pulling out a chair in a crowded corner of a café.

So why was he lollygagging?

Her.

He was hoping that he would run into Mildred. He smirked at the thought of her name. It was no more Mildred than his was Stan. But he wasn't complaining.

He'd take her any way he could get her and under any name, too.

She was a little hottie.

"May I take your order, sir?"

He'd ordered and the waitress hurried off. Holt perused his surroundings. Instantly, his stomach clenched and he sat up straighter. He couldn't believe his luck. There she was, though not alone. She was with the same three women who had accompanied her to the party. His stomach tightened as he realized his luck had just ended.

What had he expected? A woman with her assets wouldn't be alone. If she hadn't been with other women, she would've been with a man. No matter. Who she was with or what she was doing was certainly none of his business.

He told himself that last night had been a one-time fling.

She had been lovely in every way imaginable with striking black hair, blue eyes and alabaster skin that was enhanced by a dusting of natural color on her cheeks. Of course, he'd been in the company of more beautiful women than he cared to name. Yet none had affected him like she had.

One look at her and he'd been down for the count.

Had it been her lush, tantalizing lips or her huge eyes that had danced with secrecy when she'd looked at him that had completely unsettled him? Or had it been the whiff of perfume he'd breathed when she'd first passed him? Or her traffic-stopping smile? He decided it had been her entire body, the way all her curves connected in just the right places.

"Can I get you anything else?"

The sound of the waitress's voice brought him back to reality and after answering no he gazed back at the woman, leaving his breakfast untouched.

He'd never been married to anyone or anything except his work, but he'd slept with his share of women. He'd never quite had as cursory a one-nighter like last evening. But that woman had turned him on faster and more furiously than anyone he'd ever known.

She still did. Just looking at her made his insides

burn. He shifted his position for fear someone might see his obvious hard-on.

Fearing, too, that she might spot him staring at her, he forced himself to eat a few bites of the omelet he'd craved moments ago. Now his craving lay elsewhere. His appetite for food gone, he again stared at her.

This morning she was dressed in another pair of shorts and a different halter top that exposed the lightly tanned cleavage between her well-endowed breasts. Remembering how it felt to touch and taste her, he could hardly remain in his seat.

So he stood up. Telling himself he had nothing to lose he took two steps toward her when his cell rang. Cursing, he reached for it at the same time she turned and spotted him. Their eyes locked and he sucked in his breath and held it, waiting for a sign of acknowledgement.

Nothing.

She looked straight through him as if she'd never laid eyes on him. His blood turned to ice. He had figured she was too good to be true. Now he knew it. His cell rang again and, turning away, he barked into the receiver.

One

Two years later

The disinfectant smell of the O.R. seemed more tainted than usual with the metallic odor of blood. Added to the normal tension surrounding a difficult surgical procedure was an almost tangible panic among the assistants to Seymour Ramsey, the tall, silver-haired doctor who alone appeared unaware of the frantic beeping of various monitoring devices. The only visible sign that he might be concerned was the profuse amount of perspiration that saturated his surgical cap and face.

"Doctor, are you all right?" A nurse's voice broke the tense silence.

Seymour swore under his breath and turned a glassy-eyed look at her. "Yes, dammit. And don't ask me that again."

The nurse muttered, "Yes, sir." But the rigid set of her jaw and the sudden flush in her cheeks revealed her desire to say much more, especially when she stole a glance at the other members of the surgical team.

No one responded to her silent plea. They all continued with their assigned jobs.

A few minutes passed before the anesthesiologist announced, "His blood pressure is dropping, Doctor. He can't afford to lose much more blood."

The assisting surgeon glared at Seymour, "What the hell—"

"Just shut up, Chastain." Seymour's tone was as harsh as his words. "I know what the fuck I'm doing."

Silence once again reigned over the room as the nurse mopped Seymour's wet brow. She jumped slightly when he growled, "I just need one more minute."

"Better make it a fast minute," the anesthesiologist countered as he watched the rapidly falling blood pressure of the man on the table. "I'm doing all I can here," he added with a horrified look on his face.

Moments later, Seymour stepped back and jerked off his mask. "There. It's done." He cast a glance toward his fellow surgeon. "Sew him up."

Seymour stalked out of the O.R. into the doctor's lounge where he immediately leaned over the sink, turned on the faucet and splashed cold water on his face. He sensed rather than heard someone approach from behind him. He looked up and saw Chastain's face in the mirror. Seymour whipped around, slinging droplets of water on the other doctor. "What do you think you're doing? You're supposed to be closing my patient."

"He's in no hurry, Seymour." Chastain's tone matched the cold fury in the older surgeon's eyes. "He died right after you walked out of the room. He lost too much blood."

"Shit. Shit. Shit." Seymour pounded his fist on the edge of the sink.

"The family's in the waiting room," Chastain said in an accusatory tone. "You'd best go talk to them. They've already waited a long time."

Minutes later, Seymour shuffled toward the waiting area where the three members of the Dodson family sat, their hearts registering in their eyes.

"Doctor Ramsey?" Michael Dodson rose, fear in his voice. "How's Dad? Is he—"

Seymour forced himself to face the younger man. "There's no easy way to say this, son. Your father didn't make it. I'm sorry—"

"But what happened?" Michael asked in a screeching voice as his mother and sister broke into hysterical sobs and moans. Michael advanced until he was within touching distance of Seymour, his stance threatening. "You said he'd be all right."

Seymour stepped back, then began trying to explain, but words failed him. He mumbled something about blood pressure.

"Sir," Michael interrupted, "you're not making any sense at all. In fact, you're slurring your words. What's wrong with you? You're acting crazy." he said incredulously. "Don't tell me you operated on my father in this condition."

Seymour rubbed his forehead. "I did no such—"

The sentence was never completed. Seymour's eyes rolled back in his head and he hit the floor.

Two

The heat was sweltering.

Maci had taken that into consideration earlier when she'd slipped into a peach-colored sundress and a pair of strappy sandals.

Summer in south Louisiana was notorious for its combined heat and humidity, but this year both were setting records daily. She couldn't seem to get cool no matter where she was.

Despite the cold air pouring out of the air-conditioning vents, Maci found herself perspiring. Maybe that was because she was upset. Since she and Seymour married a little over two years ago they had rarely disagreed.

That had changed after she had learned of her husband's secret dependence on prescription drugs. Lately she'd been at her wits' end as to what to do about it, especially after he'd lost a patient and friend on the operating table.

Only after that tragedy did Seymour admit he'd

blacked out while talking to the family and that both he and the incident were under investigation.

Once she had gotten past her stunned horror, Maci hadn't wanted to know the dirty details associated with his vile habit. Instead, she had pleaded with her husband to seek help immediately. She feared for his well-being as well as that of his patients.

During the past three weeks, Maci had thought he'd kept his promise, but then last night, for the first time ever, Seymour had come home on a drug-induced high. He'd previously hidden the effects of the drugs from her and the rest of the world, but now his habit was known, he no longer seemed to care about covering it up.

That fact alone caused her to confront him. "How dare you come home in this condition?"

"I don't know what you're talking about, my dear."

"You damn sure do," she lashed back. "Now that I know what you're up to, it's obvious you're high."

"You're wrong."

"Don't insult me, Seymour. I may have been gullible in the past, but no longer."

He smiled a cherubic smile. "You're getting yourself all worked up for nothing, my dear." He paused, his grin still in place. "I don't know about you, but I'm calling it a night."

Maci's insides shook with anger, but she knew she was fighting a losing battle. Once her husband dug his heels in, there was no way she could penetrate his steel facade.

She was now at a loss as to how to reach Seymour. Their personal relationship and home life would soon suffer. Maci feared that if Seymour continued down this destructive path, the man she'd married would be lost to her forever.

Again she knew he needed professional help.

Maci paused in her thoughts and peered at her watch. Seymour was due home from the hospital any time now to join her for a late breakfast. She hated to admit it, but she wasn't looking forward to seeing him.

"Mrs. Ramsey, Jonah's about to go down for his nap."

A smile transformed Maci's strained features when she glanced at Liz Byford, her son's nanny. "I'm right behind you."

When Maci walked into the nursery, her baby, almost entering into the terrible twos phase, was bouncing up and down in his bed and grinning.

"Hey, big boy, what are you doing?"

"Down, Mommy," he cried, reaching out his arms.

Maci gave him a bear hug, then a kiss on the cheek. "It's time for your nap."

He shook his head. "No, Mommy, no."

"Yes, Jonah, yes." She grinned. "How about I hold you and read you a story?" This was a tried and proven trick to get him to sleep.

His grin widened and his bouncing increased.

"Whoa, there, tiger. Mommy can't lift you unless you settle down."

"I'll eat my lunch while you're with him," Liz said, blowing the child a kiss before closing the door behind her.

Maci lifted Jonah out of his bed, nuzzling him on the neck. He smelled so good, felt so good, she wanted to squeeze him into her. And she did for a second. Then he started squirming.

"Book."

"That's right," she said, sitting in the rocker and grabbing his favorite nursery rhymes. "We'll read this together, squirt."

Five minutes later, Jonah was sound asleep, but Maci continued to rock him, loving the feel of him in her arms.

Her gaze rested on his perfect little features and tears misted her eyes. He looked so much like her it was uncanny. Yet he had the Ramsey build. When he grew up—she smiled inwardly at that coined phrase—Jonah would be tall and thin.

In her mind her son would make a statement in this world. She would see to that. He was the love of her life. And the purpose for her life.

She was blessed that Seymour felt the same way. He, too, doted on Jonah. Thinking of her husband removed the smile and tossed her thoughts back into chaos. How could she reach him? Holding her eyes steady on this precious child for whom they were both responsible made her grief and fear more potent.

Seymour had to get help. He had to beat his problem. It was imperative that he set an example for his son who would soon look to him for guidance and trust. A chill darted through Maci and she shivered. As though Jonah sensed her unrest, he jerked.

"Shh," she said in a soothing tone, pushing a soft strand of wispy hair off his forehead. "It's okay."

Once he was sleeping soundly again, Maci wondered how she could have been so stupid or so incredibly naive. Both apparently applied.

Could his downfall partially be her fault? She admitted she hadn't been Seymour's mate in the true sense of the word.

She didn't believe in trust, especially when it came to trusting men. Despite her warm, sunny personality and her love for people, Maci harbored a bitterness for the opposite sex fostered by her father and her ex-fiancé.

When Will Grayson had learned literally hours before their wedding that Maci's father had lost his millions on bad investments, liquor and women, he walked out on her without a backward glance.

To this day, she saw no reason to forgive the man who had left her at the altar. Her father, however, was a different matter. She had tried to forgive him for his betrayal, especially now that he was dead. But she'd never been able to totally put that pain aside. Some days the hurt was as strong as the day it had happened during the summer of her sophomore year in college.

At the time, however, she had patched her broken heart as best she could and gone on with her life. She'd worked her way through school as an interior designer while taking care of her mother who had been stricken with Alzheimer's.

During those years of hardship, her social life had been nonexistent. Only once had she agreed to attend a charity ball given by a client. There she had met Dr. Seymour Ramsey, a man twenty years her senior. He had been instantly smitten with her and wouldn't leave her alone. Finally, he had worn her down after promising to love, honor and cherish her while at the same time resurrecting her previous life of wealth and luxury.

That had been a deal she couldn't pass up. While she hadn't loved him with passion, she had loved him.

She'd certainly been bowled over by his attention. Seymour had turned on the same charm that had helped catapult him, a young man from the wrong side of the tracks, to the top of his profession. Maci had sensed he was a decent man who wanted to make a home with her.

Being "in love" was no longer high on Maci's priority list. Seymour understood, having told her he'd take her any way he could get her.

Two weeks after taking a Jamaican holiday, Maci had married Seymour despite the teasing from her friends that she would be joining the "trophy wife's club." Maci had known better. In their own way, she and Seymour had formed a bond based on mutual respect and admiration.

She had signed a contract that entitled her to a certain amount of money for every year she remained married to him. Once that fact hit the gossip mill, her friends had upped the ante on their teasing.

She had taken it all in stride since that contract had been so important to Seymour, which she understood. She'd had no quarrel with him wanting to protect his investment and his pride. What no one knew was that she'd had no intention of touching the money for her own use. Instead, she'd put it in trust to care for her Alzheimer-stricken mother as long as she lived.

The fact that shortly after they had exchanged vows Maci had found out she was pregnant had served to strengthen her and Seymour's marriage. They had both been delighted. Her life then settled into a normal routine. She had thrived on her role as expectant mother and wife of Doctor Seymour Ramsey, convinced she had everything she'd always wanted.

And while she'd concede their marriage was far from perfect and probably unconventional by most standards, it had worked for them.

Until now. Until his abhorrent habit had come to light.

Maci's heart faltered as she leaned down and kissed her baby on the forehead, holding him a bit tighter, careful not to disturb his sleep.

The consequences of what Seymour had done could be forever life-changing. They had already been life-altering.

If her husband failed to get control of his problem, then she… Maci refused to think about that. Seymour *would* mend his broken life and emerge a stronger, healthier individual. She had to hold on to that thought. Anything else was too painful to pursue.

Jonah stirred again prompting her to place him in his crib. That done, Maci glanced at the Waterford clock on the table and realized that Seymour should have already been home. She knew Annie, the housekeeper, had their brunch ready. And so did Seymour. Maci frowned, trying not to panic. Most of the time her mind was her own worst enemy.

Still, she couldn't settle the disquiet that accompanied her downstairs. After passing Liz who was on her way back to Jonah, Maci made her way into the breakfast room. She was startled to find her husband.

No one would ever guess Seymour's secret by looking at him.

His charming demeanor and handsome features persuaded many to believe in him.

He was tall and lean with silver hair that showed no signs of thinning. His deep-set green eyes seemed to smile when he did. But his pride and joy was his body. He kept it in tip-top condition by working in their gym at home as well as one at an exclusive country club.

"You're just in time, my dear." Seymour smiled and pulled out her chair. "Annie's just about to serve us."

"I didn't know you were home," Maci said inanely, feeling herself staring at him, looking for signs that he was using again. She couldn't believe such horrible terminology popped into her mind much less applied to any part of her life. The idea seemed to sully everything around her.

If Seymour noticed her reaction, he didn't let on. Instead, he smiled and asked, "How's my son?"

Clearly he wanted to pretend nothing out of the ordinary had happened, even though they had had the sharpest disagreement of their marriage. Momentarily her temper flared, but she held it under wraps. Maybe his way was the best way. Holding a grudge definitely wasn't the answer.

Maci released a sigh. "He's great, as always."

"I started to come up, but Liz told me you were rocking him." Seymour shrugged. "I figured he'd be asleep."

Maci sat down and the buxom housekeeper served their food. After taking a sip of almond-flavored tea, she glanced at Seymour. "How was your morning?" she forced herself to ask, still having difficulty pretending everything was normal.

Seymour touched his mouth with the white linen napkin, then smiled. "Fine. Another normal surgery day. One stacked on top of the other. How 'bout you?"

"Same here. I called on a new client who I think will turn into a gold mine. Shortly, I'm headed to Bobbi's."

"How's that project coming?"

Maci played with her chicken salad. "Down to the wire, actually."

Bobbi Trent was her best friend turned client. As a divorcée, she was trying to adopt a baby. Maci felt driven to get Bobbi's house refurbished before the agency called her to say that they had located a child for her.

"I just wish you wouldn't work so hard."

"I know," she said softly but with determination. "You also know how important it is for me to keep my independence." Especially now, in light of the circumstances, she was tempted to add, but didn't. There was no point in fueling an already simmering fire.

"You're right, and I'm sorry, my dear. There's no point in my belaboring the point. Besides, I just want you to be happy."

"I am, Seymour. Or at least I—"

The chiming of the doorbell aborted her sentence.

"Are you expecting anyone?" Seymour asked.

"No. Are you?"

He shook his head just as Annie appeared in the doorway, a perplexed frown on her face. "I'm sorry to disturb you," her eyes turned to Seymour, "but there are two gentlemen here who insist on speaking to you."

Putting down his napkin, Seymour stood. "Tell them I'll be right there."

"Don't bother, Doctor, we decided to come to you."

The taller of the two men had made that declaration and now strode over to Seymour. He had a stern look on his face.

"And who are you?" Maci demanded, furious with their blatant intrusion and total lack of manners.

"I'm Detective Greg Johnson," the short, stout one said. "And this is my partner, Detective Oscar Ford." They both flipped open their badges.

Maci was glad she was seated as every muscle in her body weakened.

Johnson's gaze whipped to Ramsey. "Doctor, we have a warrant for your arrest. The charge is criminally negligent homicide in the death of your patient, Grant Dodson. Cuff him, Ford."

Maci gasped in shocked horror at the same time Seymour's tanned skin turned deathly white.

Three

Keefe Ryan looked like what he was—a socially inept attorney. He was short, bald, wore black-rimmed glasses and there was nothing attractive about him or his personality. Maci had always considered him to be the most boring man she'd ever met.

Yet when he walked into the police station, she had never been so glad to see anyone. She would never think ill of Keefe again.

In the process of being led out of the house by the two officers, Seymour had barked an order for her to call his attorney. She had waited until she was on her way to the station to do so. By then her mind had cleared somewhat, and she could punch in Keefe's number on her cell phone.

He appeared now as composed as ever, dressed as impeccably as ever, though she knew he wasn't. Maci had observed a little tick in Keefe's right cheek when he was under stress and that tick was present as he made his way toward her.

Maci had been told to take a seat in the outer lobby and that the chief would be with her shortly. So far, shortly had not come, giving her plenty of time to observe the police station. This afternoon there was a lot of activity. Phones rang while officers and other personnel scurried about. Although she had received several curious glances, no one had bothered to speak to her or ask if she wanted or needed anything.

She couldn't believe she was here. The horrendous circumstances made the situation even more demoralizing.

When the press learned of this...

"Maci, what the hell is going on?"

She turned her attention back to Keefe. She had never heard him say anything that resembled a curse word. But then she'd never seen him this flustered. His features were pinched and he was out of breath.

Despite the fact that Seymour could be overbearing at times, he and Keefe seemed to have a genuine friendship. While Keefe handled mostly taxes, he had at one time practiced some family and criminal law. So he wasn't completely out of the loop when it came to helping Seymour. Maci never doubted Keefe had Seymour's best interest at heart. If he wasn't the one for the job, he would find someone who was.

"Seymour's been arrested," Maci said, hearing the tremor in her voice. She hadn't bothered to tell Keefe what was going on beforehand. She had simply told him that Seymour needed him and to meet them at the police station. She'd hung up with Keefe still asking questions.

Keefe's face now drained of its remaining color. "That's preposterous."

"It's a fact," she countered flatly.

"Are you all right, my dear?" Keefe cleared his throat, then peered down at her, concern mirrored in his eyes. "Of course, you're not. Forget I asked that."

"I'm fine," she said, which was a lie. She was anything but fine. She was sick all over. She clutched at her stomach.

Homicide?

Her wealthy, charismatic husband accused of such an abominable deed was not possible. Only it was possible, or she wouldn't be sitting in an obscure corner of this godforsaken place.

"You just stay put while I get this mattered straightened out," Keefe said without further ado. "Then we'll all be on our way home."

"Thanks, Keefe," Maci said, fighting back tears. How could this be happening to her well-ordered world?

Hopefully Keefe could indeed make this nightmare go away.

Moments later Keefe returned, his face as grim as hers. Her heart faltered. Perhaps gaining her husband's immediate release wasn't going to be as easy as Keefe had thought.

"The chief wants to see us both."

Maci stood on unsteady legs, yet when she walked into the rather austere room, she held her head high and her shoulders back. She intended to conduct herself with dignity, and she expected the same from the tall, thin-faced man who was looking at her through narrowed eyes.

Chief Ted Satterwhite introduced himself, then beckoned for both of them to sit in the leather chairs in front of his desk. "Can I get you something to drink?" he asked in a deep, hoarse voice indicative of bad sinus drainage.

Both Maci and Keefe politely declined, then Maci asked, "Where is my husband?"

Satterwhite pulled out a big handkerchief from his back pocket and wiped it across his nose before answering, "Waiting to be questioned by the detectives. He's been read his rights, and has requested that his lawyer be present."

"Is that necessary?" Maci asked, thankful he didn't outright blow his nose. She tried to keep her disgust from showing.

"That's procedure, ma'am." He pushed back from his desk and crossed a leg over his knee. "That's how we do things in this department. By the book."

"I'd like him to go before the judge this afternoon," Keefe said in a huffy tone as though he resented being talked down to.

"All in good time, Mr. Ryan."

"Chief—"

"The judge will hear the doctor's case in the morning."

"That's unacceptable," Keefe declared with a flare of his hand.

Maci groaned, especially when she saw the chief's features tighten.

"Acceptable or not, that's the way it is." Satterwhite's tone had gone from cool to cold.

His face suffused with unnatural color, Keefe opened his mouth as if to argue, but ultimately ground his jaws together. Maci felt him look at her.

Ignoring Keefe, she faced the chief. "May I please see my husband?"

Satterwhite took his time unfurling his gangly frame to full height. Bastard, Maci thought. He was in his element, lording his control over them. Maci fought the urge to lash out at him, to ask him if he knew who he was toying with.

After all, everyone knew the Ramsey name carried weight in this town. While that hadn't always been the case, it was now. Her husband was no longer thought of as the downtrodden boy who had defied the odds and made good, but rather as a renowned surgeon. He'd built a stellar reputation in the medical community throughout the entire state of Louisiana. And here in his hometown of Dayton he'd used his wealth and power to the greater good.

Seymour wouldn't tolerate this method of treatment. But that was before he'd been accused of causing his patient's death, Maci reminded herself. A negligent homicide charge could relegate him to the bottom of the scum barrel in a heartbeat.

"That can be arranged," Satterwhite said at last, coming from behind his desk. "Follow me."

When they walked into the room where Seymour was held, Detective Johnson acknowledged their presence, then left. The chief followed shortly, leaving Maci and Keefe alone with Seymour.

For a moment, a thick, heavy silence prevailed.

"Are you all right?" Maci asked in an unsteady voice.

"I will be, when I get the hell out of here." Seymour's eyes darted to Keefe. "I'm assuming you can do that."

Keefe blew out a long breath. "I can't until morning."

Seymour swore.

"Keefe's doing all he can, Seymour," Maci pointed

out in a calm, soothing tone, hoping to defuse the volatile situation.

"Then it's not good enough," Seymour shot back.

Another awkward silence fell over the room. Maci bit down on her lower lip and looked at Seymour. He appeared tired and drawn, yet restless and hyper. Control was what fed him, what made him the man he was, and now that he wasn't in control, Maci knew he'd be jittery.

Or was he simply acting like a common street junkie who was in the throes of coming off a drug high?

Maci's stomach hated the path her mind had taken, but she couldn't avoid the hard cold facts, not when they were being rubbed in her face.

Her husband was a drug addict, and according to the law he was accused of homicide.

"Satterwhite is not someone we…you want to tangle with right now," Keefe said. "You have to know that."

"I refuse to stay in this stinking hole overnight."

Maci crossed to her husband and touched him on the arm. "Don't do this to yourself. Spending one night—"

He shook off her hand. "I'm not some common criminal, and I resent the hell out of being treated like one."

"They are accusing you of homicide, Seymour," Keefe said in a low, even tone. "What do you have to say about that?"

"Dodson's death was not my fault."

Maci eyes widened.

Seymour's smile was humorless. "See, my own wife doesn't believe me."

"That's not true," Maci snapped, feeling her face flush. "If you tell me you're not responsible—" Her voice faltered, and she cleared her throat.

Seymour stared at her for a long moment, his expression unreadable. Then he focused on Keefe. "What are the exact charges against me?"

"I haven't had time to read the report," the attorney responded. "I only know what Maci told me."

Seymour hit the palm of his hand on the tabletop. "Go talk to that prick Satterwhite then read the report. I don't trust him as far as I can throw him. That redneck's got it in for me, and he doesn't care who knows it."

"I sensed the same thing, Keefe," Maci said, easing down into a straight-backed chair at the table.

"I'll be right back." Keefe's tone was clipped.

Once he had left the room, Maci stared at her husband, noticing the strain weighing heavily on him. "I'm so sorry about this." Her thoughts jumped to Jonah and she ached to hold him tightly right now.

"Tell me you believe me."

"I want to, Seymour," she said, feeling her eyes mist with tears, "but remember I've seen you high and it's not a pretty sight."

"Okay, so I was using when I operated on Grant, but I had full control of my faculties, for god's sake. I would never do anything that asinine. You have to know that."

"I do, but—"

Keefe interrupted her when he reentered the room.

"The charges stand as Maci described them," Keefe said, tossing the folder down on the table, then sitting down. His gaze settled on Seymour. "Suppose you sit down and tell me your side."

Seymour didn't sit. He just began talking. "There's really no side. The man bled to death through no fault of mine."

"So you're taking no blame at all?" Keefe's tone was incredulous.

Seymour's hard gaze didn't waver. "None whatsoever."

"Are you denying you were on drugs at the time?"

"No. Like I was telling Maci, I admit I had taken some pills, but I knew exactly what I was doing with that knife."

"Passing out and slurring your words in front of the family doesn't support that, Seymour," Keefe said with low-key honesty, "especially since they know exactly the level of drugs ingested."

"I agree with Keefe," Maci said, her gaze also unflinching on her husband, watching closely for some glimmer of remorse or something that would indicate he was the least bit sorry.

Nothing.

She flinched. When had Seymour become so calloused to the loss of human life? Had she been so caught up in her own life and that of Jonah that she'd failed to notice yet another dark side of her husband?

Maci couldn't believe this was the same man she had married, who seemed to adore both her and Jonah, who lavished them with time and attention. Something was terribly wrong somewhere.

"How long have you had this nasty little habit?" Keefe asked.

"Since I had the accident that tore up my back."

Maci sucked in her breath. That accident, which had been a car wreck, had happened several years before she married him. Surely, he'd hadn't been addicted for that long.

"You mean you were hooked before you married me?" Maci barely choked the nasty words out of her mouth.

"Hooked is hardly the right word, my dear," Seymour said with disdain. "Was I using drugs to help my back? Yes, and I still am. But I'm in control of the situation, not the other way around."

Maci didn't know how to respond, so she didn't say anything. She felt like she'd been hit in the stomach with a brick. Apparently so did Keefe as his face seemed to have taken on a greenish tint.

"Make no mistake, Keefe," Seymour said with conviction, "I'm not going down for this."

"If that's the case, then I'm certainly not your man. I suggest you find the best criminal attorney possible and hire him."

"I agree."

Keefe's gaze didn't waver. "Do you have someone in mind?"

"Yep."

"Tell me who to call," Keefe responded, "and it's a done deal."

"My oldest son."

Maci stared at Seymour in shocked silence.

"Holt?" Keefe asked, clearly taken aback.

"That's right," Seymour said. "You told me I needed the best, and he's the best."

"But, Seymour, that doesn't make any sense," Maci pointed out, her mind reeling. "You haven't seen your son in years."

And she had never seen him. Not before she married Seymour or after. In fact, it was hard to remember that Jonah wasn't Seymour's only child. She had no idea what Holt Ramsey looked like. No pictures of him appeared anywhere in the house.

She knew very little about what had caused the estrangement between father and elder son, but she suspected a lot. Seymour had refused to discuss the issue with her, which she could understand. Suicide was a tragic and touchy subject.

What she did know was that Holt was a single attorney who rarely practiced his profession, choosing rather to spend his time on his sailboat. She had gleaned this information from the housekeeper who had been in the family when Seymour was married to his first wife. Annie had also told her that Holt blamed his father for his mother's suicide. Since the housekeeper doted on the elder son, she still bemoaned the breach between her favorite men.

"Maci's got a point," Keefe said in a strained voice. "With all the bad blood between you and Holt, what makes you think he'll help you out now?"

"He'll come, all right." A strange glint appeared in Seymour's eyes. "If nothing else, he'll use it as an opportunity to exact his pound of flesh."

Four

He had no one to blame but himself. In the future, he would check his caller ID before he answered. Damn Marianne for giving out his number. He'd have to remember to speak to her about that.

Swallowing a frustrated sigh, Holt Ramsey stared at the sky and counted to ten while Keefe droned on, trying to make his case. The second after he had said hello, Keefe had rushed into the reason for the call and he hadn't stopped yet. He hadn't so much as taken a breath.

"Keefe, give it a rest," Holt interrupted, his patience having long evaporated.

"Trust me, I'm aware of the situation between you and your father," Keefe continued as though Holt hadn't spoken.

"Hey, hold it," Holt said, no longer willing to let Keefe steamroll over him. "Time out. Look you're wasting your time. You've done your job. You've related Seymour's tale of woe to me. All you have to do is tell him I'm not interested. Voilà! You're off the hook."

"Holt, please, hear me out," Keefe pleaded. "Since you have a reputation for being one of the best criminal lawyers around, you're the logical choice. More than that, your father needs you."

"Yeah, right."

"I know—"

"You don't know jack, Keefe."

Holt heard Keefe's gasp, but he didn't care. "I've heard all I need to hear, and I don't know how to say it any plainer. I don't care what Seymour needs or doesn't need."

"How can you say that?"

"Easy."

"He's your father, for god's sake," Keefe stressed. "Have you no shame?"

Holt gritted his teeth and swore silently. "It's only because I respect you that I'm even still on the line. But I'd advise you not to push your luck."

"Under the circumstances," Keefe hammered on, "I don't see how you can take such a hard-nosed attitude."

Holt heard the pleading note in Keefe's voice, but he ignored it.

"There's nothing else I can say to make you change your mind?" Keefe's harsh sigh filtered through the line.

"Is that a question, Keefe?"

"Yes."

"Not a thing. Tell my father he made his own bed and that I'm going to take delight in watching him wallow in it."

Keefe slammed down the receiver.

Holt in turn flipped the lid shut on his cell. Frustration and anger churned inside him and he knew it was time to make use of his gym. His favorite stress reliever was his punching bag. Hitting it repeatedly would definitely do the trick.

A smirk altered Holt's tight features. It would certainly be better than heading for the jail, jerking up his old man and punching the crap out of him.

He despised his father so much that he knew he could do it.

But he wouldn't. Holt walked to the bow of his boat and felt the warm breeze on his hot skin. Any time he thought about Seymour, his entire body reacted violently. He knew that for his own good he should let that hate go, that carrying it around would eventually eat him up.

It was starting to now. He grasped the railing and swore. If he never saw his father again, he'd be happy. He'd been certain Seymour felt the same way. So what had made him change and ask his son for a favor?

Fear.

The gut-wrenching, twisting kind. That would be unacceptable in Seymour's world where everyone lived according to his rules and regulations. The thought of spending a day in prison, much less years, must be driving him insane.

Holt's smile twisted into a sneer. Good. If Seymour was convicted, he'd get what he deserved. What goes around comes around. In his father's case, this philosophy was proving to be true, and in a way Holt had never thought possible. Hooked on prescription drugs. He just couldn't believe it. His father and drugs just didn't mix. Seymour's modus operandi was that he controlled everything; nothing controlled him.

It had always been that way. Even when Holt was a

young child Seymour had wanted to control every part of his son's life, just as he'd controlled Holt's mother.

Only Holt had rebelled and oftentimes bested his father, especially when he shot down Seymour's dream of his son following in his footsteps and becoming a surgeon. Instead, Holt had opted to become a criminal defense attorney. He had gone to work for a famous firm and done far better than even his wildest expectations until his mother's death and a severe case of career burnout sent him off into uncharted waters on his sailboat.

And he hadn't regretted a day he'd turned his back on his career and his father.

Holt wondered what had made Seymour slip into the gutter. Perhaps his young trophy wife was giving him trouble. Perhaps she'd decided to ditch him for a man her own age. Just the thought had probably sent his old man into a frenzy. Or perhaps his trip down Drug Lane had nothing to do with the second Mrs. Doctor Seymour Ramsey. Perhaps she'd turned out to be the wife of his dreams.

Holt couldn't care less.

He'd never even seen the woman much less met her. Since Holt maintained an office in Dayton where he took on clients from time to time, news of his father always reached him.

Anything that pertained to the Ramsey family was big news. Unfortunately, that included him whenever he was in town. He'd been told by his friends that pictures of Seymour's second wedding and the subsequent events had been splashed all over the pages of the daily paper.

Holt had counted his blessings that he'd been nowhere around, that he'd been on one of his long jaunts in and around Canada. If he'd been in the vicinity, he might have done something he'd regret, and Seymour hadn't been worth that.

Seymour had ceased to mean anything to Holt when he'd divorced his mother years ago simply because she no longer pleased him physically or mentally. Six months later Lucille Ramsey had taken her own life by shooting herself in the stomach. A day before her death, she had told Holt she still loved his father, that she would always love him.

That declaration had devastated Holt.

After the funeral, he had severed all contact with Seymour. That had been years ago. How many years? He had no clue. He didn't care. All he knew was he hadn't forgotten or forgiven his father and that he could no longer bear the sight of him.

Holt shook his head trying to clear it. He squinted his eyes against the sun's harsh glare and peered at the magnificent sail that billowed in the breeze. A sense of peace momentarily replaced the anger that had raged inside him.

Still, he strode down into his gym and battled it out with his punching bag. Later, after showering and swigging down a beer, he sprawled on the sofa and closed his eyes.

Only he couldn't sleep. Images of his mother's face swam before his eyes. He squeezed them tighter, willing his mother away. It was as if he could hear her whispering softly to him, telling him what she wanted him to do.

"No, I can't," he muttered out loud in an agonized voice. *"I won't."*

* * *

Everything appeared normal. Maci actually pretended her life was back to the way it was before Seymour's arrest. But when she walked out the door and into the media scrum, Maci got a severe reality check.

Moments like that made her fear her life would never be the same, especially if her husband went to prison. Disregarding that unwelcome thought, she looked up from the set of house plans in front of her and wiggled her shoulders. She'd been working for several hours on a kitchen for a new client, and she was tired.

But her fatigue went much deeper than a sore neck and shoulders. Since Seymour had been hauled off in handcuffs, she hadn't slept a wink. The fact that he'd been released on his own recognizance two days ago hadn't helped.

Seymour, however, didn't seem to have the same problem. Earlier at breakfast he'd eaten his omelet with his usual healthy appetite which prompted her to ask, "You really aren't worried, are you?"

He put his fork down and looked at her. "Not in the least."

"Well, I am," she countered.

"I know you are, and I'm sorry, sorry for the pain I've caused you and Jonah."

"What about yourself, Seymour? Even if you get out of this mess, your arrest is bound to have an impact on your practice." Her voice rose an octave. "A man is dead."

Seymour's cup stalled halfway to his mouth, and his eyes narrowed. "I'd rather not have a replay of the past few days, Maci. I'm trying to get on with my life and my practice."

Frustration surged through her. "And just how is that possible when every time we walk outside, bulbs flash in our faces and hurtful questions are thrown at us?"

"I'm sorry about that, too, but this will pass. In a few days, someone else's life will be under the microscope."

"Meanwhile, you're going to go on with yours as usual."

"Absolutely. And I suggest you do likewise."

"It's not that easy for me, Seymour." She paused with a deep sigh. "The thought of you—"

"That's not going to happen," he said in a stern, harsh tone.

"Maybe not, if you'd consider looking for another criminal attorney." She refused to back down and play the feebleminded mate without a thought of her own.

"That's not necessary. I'm certain Holt will be here."

"How can you be so sure, especially when he gave Keefe an emphatic no? Shouldn't you at least have a contingency plan?"

"You worry too much, my dear." Seymour wiped his mouth and then stood. "I'm going to the office. Give Jonah a hug for me. I'll see you this evening."

He leaned over and pecked her on the cheek. "Oh, I've invited Keefe for dinner. Please inform Annie."

Maci didn't move once he was gone. Anger and shocking disbelief threatened to engulf her. When had Seymour gotten so arrogant? Were the drugs responsible for this haughty and unrepentant attitude? For all their sakes, she prayed Seymour was right and that his son would show up and clear his father's name. If Holt was the crackerjack attorney Seymour and Keefe said he was, then he would be their savior on earth.

Suddenly, Maci felt the urge to see her son. Jonah seemed to be the only thing that grounded her. When she walked into his room, Liz rose and smiled at her before glancing at the child who was sound asleep on a pallet. "He just conked out."

Maci squatted, then leaned over and grazed Jonah's apple-red cheek with her lips before standing to full height. "That's good. We played long and hard last night."

"Ah, so you let him stay up late?"

Maci gave her a sheepish grin. "Actually, I'm guilty of two infractions. I let him sleep with me."

"I bet he loved that."

"We both did," Maci responded, settling her gaze back on her baby. "I just don't want the little bugger to think it's going to be an every night thing."

Liz's eyebrows rose, but she didn't say anything.

"I'll check in with you later on today. I'm off to see a client. Call if you need me."

"You know I will," Liz said, an uncertain look crossing her face.

"What?" Maci prodded, sensing there was something else on Liz's mind. "Hey, don't ever hesitate to ask me anything, especially if it pertains to Jonah."

"I'm not sure I should take him out today, like to the park, for instance."

A frown marred Maci's unblemished features. "You shouldn't. That pack of media wolves outside will probably attack you as well. No way will I put Jonah or you through that abuse."

"Is…is Dr. Ramsey going to be all right?"

Again Maci heard the reluctance in her voice, and

while she didn't want to talk about the dreadful situation, she had no choice. Liz had become part of the family shortly before Jonah's birth, following a slow and in-depth search for the right person to help care for her son. The young woman, who had yet to marry and have a family of her own, had turned out to be a jewel. Maci knew she owed her an explanation.

"Let us pray that he is," Maci said at last. "As of two days ago, he was released on his own recognizance, and that's a positive thing." She couldn't bring herself to say that he was out of jail.

"He's such a nice man. I can't believe this is happening to him."

"Thanks for your concern, Liz. Just keep us in your thoughts, and take care of Jonah. That will help us as much as anything."

"You can count on that. Those people with the microphones and cameras don't scare me." Her tone was defiant.

They do me, Maci almost said but didn't. "That's the attitude. I'll see you both later."

On her way downstairs Maci smelled the strong aroma of fresh coffee. She peered at her watch. She had time for another quick cup. Food, however, was out of the question. She hadn't eaten anything since Seymour's arrest anyway.

Once she reached the sunny breakfast room, Annie brought her a cup of coffee. Drinking leisurely, Maci stared out the window, taking in the beautifully manicured rolling lawn. Flowers splashed the lush greenery with vivid color.

She loved this place, loved the grounds and the old

colonial pillared house that Seymour had purchased long before he married her. She had refurbished it to suit her tastes with Seymour's encouragement. He had told her the renovations were long overdue. Maci had been relieved as she and the first Mrs. Ramsey had nothing in common when it came to interior design.

"Mrs. Ramsey, you have a call. It's Mrs. Trent."

"Thanks, Annie." Maci reached for the phone, grateful her favorite client and friend chose that moment to call. "Hey, Bobbi, I was just on my way to see you."

Thank God, she had her work to keep her mind occupied.

"Keefe, may I get you another drink?"

"No thanks, Maci. I'm fine."

"I'd like another one," Seymour said with a smile. When Maci hesitated, he raised his glass to her, his eyes mocking. "Never mind. I'll get it myself."

Maci ignored him and smiled at Keefe. "I hope dinner was to your satisfaction."

"Oh, absolutely," Keefe said in a slightly flustered tone. "Your housekeeper outdid herself."

"Actually, it was Maci who made the shrimp dish," Seymour said. "My favorite, by the way."

Keefe returned the favor with a smile. "Well, as I said, it was delicious."

"When I have the time, I love to cook."

A silence fell over the study for a long moment, then Keefe set his drink down and cleared his throat. "Seymour, has it dawned on you yet that Holt is not coming?"

The doctor placed his drink on the mantel before leveling his gaze at his attorney. "Did you hear from him?"

"No."

"Enough said."

"No, it's not," Keefe rebuked in a blustering tone, only to quickly modify it when color surged into Seymour's face.

Maci knew Seymour was agitated that Keefe had crossed him. But she was glad the attorney had done so since she hadn't made a dent in Seymour's armor at breakfast. Maybe together she and Keefe could talk some sense into him.

"I'm telling you, we need to call another attorney," Keefe stressed. "Jack Little—"

"Not interested." Seymour leaned his head back, drained his glass, then plunked the glass down on the bar and promptly refilled it.

Maci winced. She feared her husband was replacing drugs with alcohol as he'd overindulged every night since his brief incarceration.

"All right, Seymour, you're the boss," Keefe said with obvious displeasure.

"That's right." Seymour took another sip, then turned to Maci. "How about I make you a drink? Your coffee cup's empty."

Maci shook her head. "No, thank you." Then to Keefe, "Is there a chance that Seymour could be convicted?"

"More than a chance. It's a real possibility."

"Dammit," Seymour lashed out, "don't discuss me like I'm not here."

The chiming of the doorbell forced a silence.

Maci stood, turning toward the French door of the study as it opened. At first, Maci thought her eyes were playing tricks on her, that the man who stood there with his hands in the pockets of his shorts was a figment of her imagination.

"Holt," Seymour exclaimed, dashing across the room, hand outstretched. "I knew you'd come." Even though his hand was ignored, the gleam remained in the doctor's eyes when he swung around and faced Maci and Keefe. "See, I told you my son wouldn't let me down," he added in a gloating tone.

Maci remained upright by sheer force of will. Yet when she tried to open her mouth to speak, she couldn't. Her throat, along with her entire body, seemed paralyzed.

"Maci, meet my son and your stepson, Holt."

No. God, no. It couldn't be. She swallowed a mournful cry. The man she'd made passionate love to on the beach in Jamaica and her stepson couldn't be one and the same.

Only they were.

Five

"Maci, are you all right?"

She heard Seymour's question, but she couldn't answer. Her throat was so tight that no air could get into her lungs. The room spun and she feared she would faint.

Digging her hands deeper into the leather-backed chair, Maci forced herself to smile, all the while feeling as if her composure might crack under the pressure of this shocking encounter.

"Maci, what the hell's wrong with you?"

Seymour's harsh tone broke her out of her catatonic state. "I'm actually not feeling well," she responded in a halting tone.

Seymour frowned his disapproval.

"But I'll be fine," she added on a rushed note, keeping her gaze averted from Holt Ramsey.

"Why don't you have a seat, Maci?" Keefe said in his gentle tone. "Forgive me for saying so, but you don't look well."

Maci smiled her relief as she took his suggestion, holding her gaze steadfast on Keefe's nondescript features, seeing him as a safe harbor.

"Holt, my boy, what can I get you to drink?" Seymour asked with exuberance.

"Nothing." Holt's tone was clipped.

Seymour's brows shot up. "Why not?"

"This isn't a social call."

Seymour muttered under his breath and then fell silent.

Maci concentrated on smoothing a wrinkle out of her capri pants as distraction from the alarming thoughts going through her mind. A voice screamed inside her telling her this wasn't fair. No one deserved two cruel twists of fate in a row.

"It's good to see you, Holt," Keefe said into the daunting silence before walking over and extending his hand.

Maci watched the exchanged handshakes but still couldn't bring herself to look at Seymour's son. Even thinking the word stepson was impossible.

"Likewise, Keefe," Holt said in his low, rough-edged voice. His sexy voice.

Maci drew in a shuddering breath. This couldn't be happening. Maybe if she blinked a time or two, he would disappear. Instead of blinking, she actually looked in Holt's direction. He hadn't disappeared, nor was he a figment of her imagination.

There he stood rock solid, and looking more gorgeous than he had two years ago with his fabulous head of blond hair and his blue-green eyes staring at her as though he'd seen a ghost. If anything had changed, he'd gotten browner and leaner, which made him seem taller.

His was the commanding presence in the room. The other two men seemed to have shrunk.

Once she looked at him, she couldn't take her eyes off him. He'd had this same effect on her in Jamaica. Her stomach was in a knot and she still felt dizzy.

"Did you sail here?" Seymour asked.

"No." Holt's tone was clipped.

"Then I'm assuming you'll be staying here," Seymour said, breaking the second long silence. "With us."

Holt shrugged. "That depends."

Maci saw her husband's lips stretch into a thin line. "On whether you help me or not."

Holt uncoiled his frame from against the door. "That's right."

"Sit down," Seymour urged, gesturing toward a winged back chair. "We have a lot to discuss." He turned to Maci. "I'm sure Holt's ready for something to drink. Are you up to making him one?"

"Don't bother," Holt said, his eyes finally finding hers.

Maci held her breath. The physical attraction that had electrified her in Jamaica was still there, and from the look that jumped in Holt's eyes, he felt it, too. She swallowed and shifted her gaze, her blood drumming in her ears. Seymour must never guess she and Holt had a past. Panic washed through her.

"I'm so glad you're here," Keefe said in a nervous tone. "Your father desperately needs you."

"That remains to be seen." Holt's tone was harsh with cynicism.

Seymour flushed, and his eyes narrowed on his son.

Maci knew he was having a difficult time keeping the lid on his temper. In fact, she was surprised that he had.

Groveling was not Seymour's style. But if Holt's attitude prevailed, that was exactly what her husband was going to have to do.

Unless Seymour decided Holt wasn't worth the effort.

Maci's breathing faltered again, this time for a different reason. Seymour couldn't go to prison. He just couldn't. If Holt was the key to stopping that from happening, then he had to be persuaded to stay.

But how could she handle his constant presence? She couldn't. That was the bottom line.

"Why did you come, then?" Seymour asked after taking a gulp of his scotch and water. His eyes never wavered from his son.

"I have my reasons."

"Fine," Keefe interceded quickly. "We won't argue with that as long as you stay and hear us out." The attorney didn't bother to keep the guarded eagerness out of his voice.

"Look, son, I know—"

"Save it," Holt cut in brutally. "It's too late for that."

Seymour's eyes flashed. "Okay, you're here, and I'm grateful. Having said that, your attitude sucks."

"Take it or leave it."

Maci's gaze bounced between father and son while the air in the room crackled with tension. Her heart was hammering so hard she feared everyone could hear it.

"I'll take it," Seymour muttered.

Maci watched as relief settled over Keefe's features. She, however, didn't share it. And not because of her and Holt's past, but rather because of Holt's present relationship to Seymour.

Holt's attitude did indeed suck. Under that circumstance, how effective would he be in representing his father on a murder charge? And why would he want to?

The answers to those questions weren't readily apparent, so Maci would have to attempt to answer them later. While Keefe filled Holt in on the details of the case, Maci watched Holt's reaction closely. Nothing was forthcoming. His features remained stoic, his eyes unreadable, and his thoughts hidden.

When Keefe finished, Holt turned to Seymour. "How long have you been hooked?"

"I'm not hooked," Seymour declared in a huff.

"Yeah, yeah." Holt's tone was bitter. "That's what they all say."

"I resent you comparing me with the average street junkie," Seymour fired back in anger.

Keefe cleared his throat, trying to defuse the mounting hostility. "Let's stick to the facts, shall we?"

Maci let out a breath. "Maybe this evening isn't the time to discuss this. I mean—"

"I know what you mean," Seymour said, facing her, his tone mollified. "But I'd rather know if I have to look for another attorney." He turned back to Holt.

Holt spread out his hands in a sweeping gesture. "For your sake, that would be a wise choice."

"Is that a no?" Seymour demanded.

"I didn't say that."

"Then what are you saying?" Maci asked, then momentarily regretted butting in. This was between father and son. But it also involved the entire family. The stakes were high for her and Jonah as well. If Seymour were convicted, there would be definite repercussions for her and her son. "Either you agree to help him or you don't," she added on a defiant note.

"Well put, Maci," Seymour said without looking at her. "So can I count on you?"

"For now."

"I need more assurance than that," Seymour said. "I need your word that you won't bail out on me, like—"

"If you complete that sentence, you'll regret it." Holt's tone was low and menacing.

Seymour shut his mouth, though he glared at Holt.

Not a pretty situation, Maci thought, biting down on her lower lip to steady it. Whatever had gone on between them must have been nastier than she'd thought. That left her to wonder again why exactly Holt had returned.

"So can we count on you?" Keefe asked, breaking the tension as his gaze swung from Holt to Seymour.

"Please," Seymour added in a muffled tone.

Maci stared at her husband, shocked at the pleading note she heard in his voice. She had never seen Seymour in such a state or heard him reach the point of begging. Trying to ignore the fear coursing through her, she held her breath and waited for Holt's reaction.

He walked deeper into the room. "I'll need to know the rest of the story."

"Are you really back in town?"

"Yes, Marianne, I'm really here."

"So I guess I'd better get to the office first thing in the morning. Right?"

Holt heard the excitement in her voice even if he was sure it was lacking in his. "That's why I'm calling."

Marianne Foster was the perfect employee. A bona-fide paralegal, she preferred to spend most of her time as a wife and mother of two teenagers, a job that kept her hopping. She agreed to work for Holt when he did return to town, and he paid her handsomely for her standby services.

"Everything is ready and in tip-top shape."

"I know that," Holt interrupted. "I have every confidence in you. But you know that, too."

"Still, it's always good to hear," she responded a trifle breathlessly. "And to have you back."

"Later then," Holt said with more abruptness than he intended. If Marianne had a downside, it was her inability to control her tongue. She loved to talk more than anyone he'd ever known.

"Uh, are you here to work? Like try a case?"

Realizing he'd missed his chance to end the conversation, he added reluctantly, "Looks that way."

"That's great. I'm really eager to get back to work myself. Too much of my kids can be a bad thing."

"I understand," Holt said for lack of anything better to say.

"Will you be defending anyone I know?" she pressed.

Holt tried to hide his irritation. "My father."

He heard her sharp intake of breath. "Dr. Ramsey."

Her response wasn't a question, so he didn't treat it as such. "One and the same."

"I'm so sorry about what happened to him."

"Thanks." Holt's tone was terse.

Having obviously picked up on that, Marianne said on a rushed note. "Again, it's good to have you back."

Once he was off the phone, Holt walked to the window in his old bedroom and stared into inky blackness. He didn't need daylight to visualize what was out there. As always, the grounds, covered with flowers, would be impeccably groomed. There wouldn't be a stray leaf in sight no matter how hard the wind blew.

He thought about stepping onto his balcony, but it was still hotter than hell due to the humidity. He supposed he wasn't used to this climate anymore; that was why he always felt so sticky, like he needed a shower.

Actually what he needed was several cups of chicory coffee, stout enough to make the hairs stand up on his chest. That might get him motivated.

He had no intention of going to bed since he knew already that sleep wouldn't come easily. So much was going on inside his head that even if he tried to drown his woes in a bottle of expensive bourbon, he'd be wasting his time.

He rubbed the back of his neck trying to uncoil muscles that had tensed into one big jumble of nerves.

He had Maci to thank for that.

Admitting that did little to relieve his anxiety. He still could not reconcile the shock of walking into that room and stepping on a loaded stick of dynamite. It had taken every ounce of willpower he possessed to maintain his composure.

Yet seeing was believing. There she'd sat in the flesh looking as appetizing as she had the first time he saw her. All her best features were as he remembered: a gorgeous body with shapely legs and a tight ass, skin like white velvet, deep-set black eyes, apple-red lips and short black hair that would complement any man's pillow. She was actually more appealing than he recalled.

Having a baby had ripened her body.

Blood surged into his groin and he grimaced. He'd had no intention of ever coming back to this house or seeing his father again, much less help him beat a murder rap. Now, after learning who "Mildred" was, he sure as hell didn't want to be there. Remaining was actually an insane proposition.

Yet here he was. Committed.

He wished he hadn't left his sailboat in Florida and flown here. Now he was expected to stay in the mansion, in his old room, too near to her.

He had never forgotten that night in Jamaica and had thought seriously of trying to find her numerous times, only to convince himself she was happily married with no possibility of a repeat performance of their time together.

Well, she was married all right. And she was his stepmother.

Holt muttered a double expletive. The little hottie from the night was now his stepmother. Go figure. He laughed a harsh laugh. Stranger things have happened, he guessed. Just not to him.

Once their eyes locked in that room for even a brief second, it was all he could do not to cross the room, jerk her into his arms and kiss her until the breath left her.

If he'd read her right, she had wanted the same thing.

So much for wedded bliss, he told himself, almost choking on another bitter chuckle. It wasn't too late to tell his father to go to hell, he reminded himself, then walk out the same door he'd come in.

He even took that first necessary step when he again heard that sweet, soft voice pleading with him to stay. He balled his fists and stood his ground.

Now all he had to do was convince himself his weakness had all to do with his mother and nothing to do with Maci. He knew better. His staying had everything to do with her.

Admit it, Ramsey, he told himself. You're fucked.

Six

"Liz, if he isn't better in a little while, I'll call the doctor."

"I don't think that will be necessary, Mrs. Ramsey. The little fellow's just teething."

Maci rubbed her son's back as his head lay cuddled against her neck. It was all she could do not to squeeze the life out of him. He smelled so good, felt so good, she never wanted to let him go. He was her sanity now that the rest of her life was in utter chaos.

Liz had sent word down that Jonah wouldn't stop crying. Maci had immediately excused herself and gone to be with her son. While she wasn't glad her baby was upset, she had been glad of an excuse to escape. She didn't think she could have borne the explosive atmosphere in the study much longer.

"Are you all right, ma'am?" Liz asked.

"I just hate to see Jonah so fussy," she said, ignoring Liz's concern.

"Jonah will be fine," Liz said with confidence. "The

last time he was teething the doctor said to give him some baby Tylenol. I'll get it and give it to him if he needs it later."

Maci nodded, then realizing that her son was fast asleep, she laid him in his bed, then kissed him gently. "Sleep tight, my precious," she whispered, feeling unbidden tears sting her eyelids.

Moments later, safe in her room, Maci sagged against the door. She had made it to her suite in record time for fear she would accidentally bump into Holt.

Nervous and upset, Maci placed her hand over her mouth. She was going to be sick.

Scurrying to the bathroom, she emptied the contents of her stomach. She patted her face with cold water, brushed her teeth, then peered into the beveled glass mirror. Her reflection told her she looked awful. No color bled through her cheeks. She doused her face with more cold water. The queasiness, however, remained even after she eased onto the chaise longue and closed her eyes.

Holt's face seemed plastered on the back of her eyelids. She sat upright, her heart continuing to pound at a rapid clip. Two long deep breaths in succession calmed her.

This madness couldn't go on. She had to find a way to get control of her splintered emotions. She hadn't planned on ever seeing "Stan" again. The thought of crossing his path on a daily basis was unthinkable.

Making her way to the cabinet that hid a juice bar, Maci made a cup of peppermint tea and then rested once again on the chaise.

After several sips, her stomach, along with her

nerves, settled. Maybe now she could figure out how best to handle this latest debacle.

There was no best way.

Until now she had managed to banish the memory of that night in Jamaica. She sometimes even believed that the hot night of passion in a stranger's arms had merely been an indulgent dream.

Once she and her friends had arrived back home, the pace of her life had increased to a frantic pitch. Seymour had insisted they marry at the mansion and forgo plans to leave town. He didn't want to wait.

After the stunt she'd pulled in Jamaica, Maci hadn't wanted to return there, so she agreed, realizing that settling down without further incident was the best thing for her. Two weeks later she and Seymour had repeated their vows, surrounded by close friends.

She'd only been married six weeks before she began to suspect she was pregnant. She had told Seymour right away; to her surprise he'd been overjoyed.

What she hadn't told him was that the baby might not be his. The idea that she could be having a stranger's baby had devastated her. After days of agonizing over that real possibility, she decided she had no recourse but to tell Seymour the truth, though she knew that deed could bring her brief marriage to an abrupt end.

"We need to talk, Seymour," she had told him one evening in the study.

He had peered at her over the rim of his drink and smiled. "My, my but you look so serious."

"I am serious."

"You're okay, right?"

"I'm fine," she said, unable to look him in the eye.

"Maci, what's wrong?"

She released a sigh. "It's something that happened—"

He held up his hand, his features hardening slightly. "I'm not interested in hearing confessions."

She was taken aback. "But—"

Seymour interrupted again. "What happened before we got married is your business not mine. I'm not comfortable discussing my past. Therefore, I don't want to hear about yours. End of conversation."

Taking the coward's way out, she had been relieved. By law, Seymour was her baby's father, she had told herself, further justifying her actions. Proving otherwise would serve no purpose. It would only do irreparable harm to everyone involved. Besides, she'd been convinced she would never see her lover again.

Nonetheless, guilt from withholding her confession gnawed at her until Jonah was born. Once she held that miracle in her arms, however, she stored that reckless incident in the most private part of her heart and went on with her life, more convinced than ever that her digression would never be revealed.

The possibility that it might be now was most frightening.

Maci's stomach lurched again. What if Holt suspected Jonah could be his? That thought numbed her with such terror that she feared she'd lose her mind.

Maybe he wouldn't stay. Maybe he wouldn't be able to remain in such close proximity to his father. Or maybe she would be the force that drove him away.

Her conscience suddenly pricked her and she felt selfish. She should be thinking of her husband's welfare and what was best for him. If Holt was the answer to

Seymour's needs, then she should welcome him with open arms. Under different circumstances, she would have, having often wondered how she could broach the subject of his estranged son.

That was before she knew who he was.

But whether Holt stayed or not was his call. Right now, she sensed he would bolt. The sight of her couldn't have made his day. To say he'd been stunned was too understated. She had seen a glimpse of the same raw shock she felt mirrored in his eyes. He'd seemed to recover more quickly, replacing that rawness with a cynical contempt aimed at his father.

But she knew she had read him right when he refrained from looking at her after that one time their eyes had locked. Her instinct had told her that had been intentional.

As she finished her tea, Maci heard a tap on her door. For a moment, she froze, fearing who was on the other side. Then feeling foolish for such an irrational thought, she said, "Come in."

"How's Jonah?" Seymour asked, making his way into the room, stopping only when he reached the midway point.

At the mention of the baby's name, she smiled. "Just fussy because he's teething."

"Hopefully by now he's settled."

A short, but heavy silence followed his words. Maci wanted to fill it, only she didn't know quite how. She hated this awkwardness that existed between her and Seymour. The wedge between them seemed to grow wider each day.

"Did you and Holt resolve your differences?" she asked, bridging the gap of silence before it lengthened.

"For now," he said in a harsh tone, rubbing the back of his neck.

"I'm sorry," she said. "I know you were counting on more."

Seymour shrugged. "I still haven't played all my cards."

Maci thought that was an odd thing to say, but she didn't pursue it. She hadn't been privy to what had taken place between father and son early on and she didn't suspect her asking questions now would change that.

"I hope you don't mind having a guest for a while."

"Would it matter if I did?"

He gave her a strange look. "No, not in this case."

Feeling that awkwardness deepen, she forced a calm to her tone. "But of course I don't mind. If he can help you, I want him here." She turned away so that he wouldn't notice that her eyes failed to back up her words.

"For sure he can help me. Holt and I might disagree on everything else, but I'll have to hand him his just deserts—he's a crackerjack attorney."

She forced a smile. "Maybe this tragedy will allow you two to patch up your differences."

"I doubt that." Bitterness lowered Seymour's voice. "His mother stands between us and always will."

"That's too bad."

"That's the way it is, and I've accepted it." Seymour paused and walked toward her. "It's certainly nothing for you to worry about. As I've already told you, the past is the past and not to be reopened. Besides, I have another son, thanks to you, who's not going to disappoint me."

"Let us pray," Maci said lightly.

He smiled. "Prayer has nothing to do with it. I'm going to see that he follows in his old man's footsteps."

Jonah might have something to say about that, she almost blurted out. But since that decision was a long way off, she didn't see any reason to start an argument by disagreeing.

"I know this mess has been hard on you," Seymour said, "but rest assured our lives will be back to normal soon."

For some reason that statement, reeking of smugness, irritated her. "I know you say Dodson's death was an accident—"

"It was," Seymour cut in sharply.

"Still, I don't understand how you can take no responsibility or feel no remorse."

"How do you know I don't?"

"Well, do you?"

"No. The death was accidental."

"Still, a man's dead."

"He isn't the first patient I've lost nor will he be the last."

Maci massaged her temple. "That sounds so—"

"Callous," he said, finishing the sentence for her.

"Yes, that's a good word."

"That may be. But like I've maintained all along, I was in complete control of my faculties, which absolves me."

Was there no end to his arrogance?

Suddenly, Maci stared wide-eyed at the man who was her husband and saw him with clear objectivity. She didn't like what she saw. The man with new creases around his eyes and less hair on his head, the man she'd pledged to love and honor until death parted them, no longer measured up.

In fact, she felt like she no longer knew him.

Perhaps she never had. Perhaps the magic of who he

was and what he could offer her had been so dazzling, she'd been blinded to the truth.

"What's wrong, darling?" Seymour sounded contrite. "You look like you just saw a ghost."

He was within touching distance of her now, watching her with a glint of desire in his eyes.

Every nerve in her body rebelled as he reached out and touched her face with the back of his hand. It was all she could do not to flinch.

"It's been too long since we made love," he said, his tone having dropped to a husky pitch.

"Seymour—"

He smiled, only that smile didn't reach his eyes. "Don't tell me you have a headache."

His intention was to tease, she knew, to lighten the tension circling them. It didn't work. She couldn't bear for him to touch her. Hiding her feelings was her only option.

"I really do have a headache," she murmured.

His look was one of disbelief; then his hand fell to his side. "You're serious." He made a flat statement.

"Yes," she whispered, moving out of his reach.

His features blanched and his mouth tightened. "Another time, then."

With that he turned and walked out the door.

Maci's fingernails dug into her palms while tears dampened her eyes, but she refused to give in to any further weakness. She would deal with her disintegrating life with her head up and a smile on her face.

Even if it killed her.

Seven

Despite the cloying early-morning heat, the garden was lovely. Maci could always count on the flowers to boost her sagging spirits. Today was no exception.

After inhaling the sweetly scented air deep into her lungs, she sat down on a wrought-iron cushioned chair. She took two sips of her cup of hazelnut flavored coffee while her gaze tracked a butterfly whose wings were lavender and black. It amazed her that such a delicate creature could spread its wings and mindlessly fly, fly, fly. Only after it flew away did Maci take a breath, realizing she'd been mesmerized by the butterfly's actions.

She hadn't slept much last night, and she felt listless and tired, not at all like herself. Before Seymour's arrest, her energy level had been unending. Now the drastic changes in her well-ordered life had robbed her of any spare stamina.

Jonah's fussiness had continued into the night, and he'd wanted her, not Liz, to rock him. That was exactly what she'd done, and didn't regret one minute of it.

Still, she had a lot on her plate today, and if she didn't snap out of her doldrums, she wouldn't get anything done. She was due to spend the day with her friend Bobbi, working on her house.

Maci sipped her coffee. In the past the thought of plunging into her work would have sent a rush of excitement through her. In fact, she would have been hustling to grab a bite to eat before meeting a client. That sense of excitement had diminished along with her energy.

Damn Seymour.

Guilt descended over Maci. She should be backing her husband, not condemning him. But after their conversation last evening, Maci's feelings were more confused than ever. She wanted to believe Seymour, that what had happened on the operating table had truly been an unavoidable accident, that he had gone exactly by the medical book, and that despite all his efforts the patient still hadn't lived.

But she couldn't ignore that he'd been under the influence. Letting Seymour touch her in an intimate way after she glimpsed his arrogant denial was repugnant to her. Her rejection had angered and hurt him, she knew, but she couldn't help it. If she had it to do all over again, she would do the same thing.

A shudder went through her as she pictured Holt's face. She trembled at the thought that *his* presence in the house could have had anything to do with her reaction to Seymoure.

No, of course, it hadn't, Maci reassured herself, swallowing the knot of panic in her throat. Holt Ramsey's appearance was simply a bad nightmare that had raised its head to haunt her again.

Yet she hadn't been able to get him out of her mind. She'd gone upstairs with his features etched in her mind, and there they had remained all night.

Shock.

That was what it must be. The shock of seeing him again and under such bizarre circumstances was rattling her clear-sightedness. Anyone would react the same way. Still, Maci knew that as long as Holt was in the picture, nothing would be the same.

"Mind if I join you?"

Maci nearly jumped as she swung around and saw Holt sauntering toward her. *Of course, I mind,* she screamed silently. If she had wanted to utter those words, she couldn't have. His unexpected appearance this morning was almost as big a shock as seeing him last night.

He paused, a hand resting on the chair across from her. For a second, her gaze fell then lingered on the slender, tanned fingers, fingers that had touched her so intimately. A tiny earthquake struck the center of Maci's being. "Would it make a difference if I said no?"

A brown eyebrow quirked as his hand seemed to tighten around the iron. "Are you saying that?"

"No, I mean—" Maci's voice played out when she realized she sounded like an idiot or worse. Her stomach did a somersault. She wanted to react to that, but the urge not to let Holt know he unnerved her was stronger so she sat in stoic silence and stared at him as he yanked out a chair.

The scraping sound invaded the quiet. At least the noise would drown out the heart she could almost hear thumping in her chest.

Holt was dressed in much the same attire as last evening, with the exception of his choice of pants. Khaki Docker slacks had replaced the causal shorts that had displayed his tanned thighs and legs to perfection. The T-shirt was the same, only yellow instead of beige. Made of a clingy knit fabric, it wrapped around his broad shoulders, raised biceps and six-pack abs as if it had been glued on.

"Mmm, coffee smells good," he said in his low, raspy voice, his gaze turning to an extra cup on the tray. Too bad Annie had added an extra cup.

No doubt, he was hinting for an invitation to join her and would probably help himself.

"What if I don't want company?" Maci forced the words through her cotton-dry lips.

"You should've spoken sooner," he said, the hard glint in his eyes pinned on her. She fought the urge to squirm like a bug under a microscope. But she didn't. Again, she refused to let him know that he unnerved her.

"Fancy us meeting like this," he said, his tone sarcastic. "I see it as one of those meant-to-be things."

Before she could find a suitable comeback, he latched on to the empty cup and filled it with coffee.

Maci glared at him. For a second she felt like slapping his hand like an errant child. She'd be damned if she was going to let him stroll down memory lane. Their past was off-limits.

"Yes, fancy that." She heard the defiant note in her tone as their eyes met.

The effect was galvanizing.

Maci sucked in her breath, and he cursed. Later, she didn't know who turned away first. At the time she didn't care. For her own self-preservation, she couldn't have looked at him another second.

"So how did you and dear old dad hook up?"

His tone now tainted his smile.

She swung her head back around but refrained from looking directly at him. "That's none of your business."

His smile burgeoned into a grin. "You're right, it isn't."

"Look, I know this…us is awkward, but—"

"I thought about trying to find you."

Her heart skipped several beats and she tried to avert her gaze but found she couldn't. "Holt—"

"Holt, what?" His tone thickened. "Don't say what's been on my mind for two years."

"Stop it," she muttered tersely, leaning closer as though fearing someone would hear their conversation. "I told myself I wouldn't let you dredge up the past."

"Too late, honey. The past has slam-dunked us both."

"We can pretend it never happened."

"Sure we can."

She flushed and looked away.

Seconds passed.

"You're right, this isn't about us."

She swung back to face him. "You're right, it isn't. It's about your father."

His features darkened.

"You despise him, don't you?"

He snorted.

"I know you blame him for your mother's death, but—"

"I don't want to discuss my mother with anyone," he interrupted harshly. "Least of all you."

Her flush deepened, partly from anger and partly from embarrassment.

"This isn't going to work, is it?" he asked, his voice weary.

"No, it isn't," Maci responded. "All the more reason for you to leave by the same door you came in."

"And miss out on all the fun of watching you play out your role as the money-grubbing little bitch—"

Maci launched to her feet, her eyes firing. "How dare you say that to me?"

"I dare say anything I want."

She ignored his rebuttal. "You don't know anything about my and Seymour's relationship."

He shrugged. "You're right, I don't. But I know what I see."

"And just what is that?" she lashed back, then regretted the question. But it was too late to take it back. How had this happened? She'd had no intention of entering into a verbal slinging match with him. Yet that was exactly what she was doing.

"A younger woman who married an older man for his money."

"That's not true!"

"Oh, really. Why else would you marry a man so much older than you—a good-looking woman like you? You could have any man you wanted." Holt paused as if to let his words penetrate. "We both know you're not frigid."

"Enough!"

He merely shrugged.

"This isn't going to work," Maci said more to herself than to him.

"Are you telling me to leave?"

"What if I am?"

He rose. "Suits me. I'd much rather be on a boat sailing into the wild blue yonder, than defending my father."

"Then tell Seymour you're out of here."

Holt laughed without humor. "Not on your life, sweetheart. If you want me gone, then you tell him."

"You bastard. You know I can't do that."

"Sure you can," Holt drawled, then paused as if to make a point. "If you're prepared to answer questions as to why *you* want me to pack."

Maci quelled the urge to smack him again, then was appalled by the depth of her feelings toward this man.

"And we both know you're not prepared to do that."

Sparks flew from her eyes. "Don't bet your life on that."

"What I'm betting is your husband's."

This time she flinched, then whispered, "Why are you doing this?"

"What?" he asked with childlike innocence. "Making you face the truth?"

"Acting as though you hate me."

"I don't hate you," he countered with ease. "I don't have any feelings toward you one way or the other."

"That's a bald-faced lie." Maci refused to back down. "But since I really don't care how you feel, I'm going to let it slide."

"That relieves my mind."

Ignoring him, she continued, "Look, I don't want Seymour to know about us. To do so would serve no purpose. Surely you can understand that."

He seemed in no hurry to respond which fueled her

anger even more. He was enjoying himself at her expense. He enjoyed watching her on the hot seat.

"What's it worth to you for me to keep my mouth shut?"

Maci sucked in her breath, reeling against the pain that shot through her. "You bastard," she spat, then turned and walked off, praying the tears that blurred her vision wouldn't cause her to stumble.

Would he ever learn to control his tongue? Holt wondered. He had been baiting his father's young wife, intentionally jerking her chain, and he'd enjoyed it. Or so he'd thought. But now that she'd stormed off, he was having second thoughts. He felt like kicking himself for acting like the bastard she'd called him.

More than that, he wished he could start the conversation all over again. His demeanor and choice of words would certainly be different.

Sweat dotted his upper lip and forehead. Frowning, he pushed the half-drunk cup of coffee aside and peered at a blue sky that seemed as never ending as Maci's long legs.

A groan split his lips. Still, the image of her wouldn't go away. When he had walked outside on the veranda and seen her, he'd frozen for a moment and simply watched her, lapping up her beauty just like he would a scoop of homemade vanilla ice cream.

In the dancing sunlight, her dark hair had shone like new money, all short and stylishly tousled. Her sleeveless peach-colored dress was also short, nowhere near reaching her knees, thus exposing those incredible legs. Sexy but classy. Even clothed, she could melt his insides as if he had just stepped in hot asphalt.

With her sitting there, drumming one perfectly manicured hand on the table, another around the cup, staring off into space, it was all he could do not to leap on her. Face it, he told himself, he still had the hots for this woman.

Yet he hated the sight of her. He hated himself more for wanting her.

He had to stop thinking about her as a woman he'd made love to once upon a time. That wasn't going to be easy, especially when unbidden snapshots of her naked on the sand, her breasts, plump and juicy in his hands, her legs spread, welcoming his throbbing erection, suddenly flashed through his mind.

Shaking his head, Holt lunged to his feet, muttering several expletives.

She was his father's wife, and he'd best remember that or stop threatening to get the hell out of Dodge and do it. He was tempted more now than he had been last night.

His head pounded like someone was using it as a punching bag. He got up and made his way to his vehicle.

The sooner he took care of business for his mother's sake, the sooner he could sail away. That was the day he was living for. Starting right now, he would count the days.

The hell with that; he'd count the minutes and the hours.

Eight

"You're still here, I see."

"For now." Holt couldn't hide his disdain for Seymour, so he didn't try.

"You look like hell," Seymour said, narrowing his eyes on his son.

"I could say the same for you, but I won't."

The conversation started just as Holt imagined it would when Annie told him Seymour wanted to see him. He'd been about to leave to go to the police station.

Holt had put off this second encounter as long as he could, taking more time in the shower and dressing. But like he'd told himself, the sooner he took this case and ran with it, the sooner he could sail away. That strategy had gotten him in gear quicker than anything else.

"I was hoping we could get through this without exchanging insults."

Holt gave his father a sardonic smile. "Then don't insult me."

Seymour released a harsh sigh. "I can't for the life

of me understand why you can't forgive and forget. Dammit, I'm your father."

Holt's stomach coiled into a knot. "Whoa. Memory Lane is closed. I suggest you keep that in mind when we're together."

"In other words, I heed or you walk."

"That's about the size of it."

"You're a real bastard, Holt."

"Like father, like son, I guess." Holt shrugged.

"Do you want some coffee?" Seymour asked in a tired tone.

His father looked exhausted, Holt thought. And old. Yet that defiant glint remained in his eyes and in the way he carried himself. But the lines in his face seemed to have deepened and his hands shook slightly, a result Holt figured, from his drug use.

"Holt, I asked you a question."

"No coffee for me."

"Suit yourself. I'm having some."

Holt watched as Seymour not only poured himself a cup out of the silver coffeepot that Annie had brought in, but brought back a small bottle of bourbon from the bar and proceeded to lace the coffee with that.

"Are you a drunk as well as an addict?"

Seymour muttered a curse as he glared at Holt. "While you're under my roof, I demand you show me respect."

"If you earn it, you'll get it. And drinking at this time of the morning isn't going to earn it."

"You just don't understand," Seymour responded in a clipped tone.

"I understand that if you don't straighten your act up, they'll put you under the damn jail instead of in it."

"I'm paying you big bucks to see that doesn't happen."

"I'm an attorney, not a miracle worker." Holt paused and made his way deeper into the room. "As for money, I don't want one red cent from you."

Seymour looked him up and down, the curve of his mouth bordering on a sneer. "Well, from the look of you I'd say you need it. I've never seen you so unkempt, so without pride."

Holt clenched his jaw to keep from retaliating. They could stand there and hit each other with barbs until doomsday and nothing would change. Seymour was losing control even though he refused to admit it. And control was what made his father tick. Since Holt didn't see him relinquishing rule without a fight, he'd have to ignore his little power plays.

Until Seymour tried to control *him*, that is. Then he'd nail him.

"Put the bottle away and pour the coffee out," Holt said, with steel behind his words.

Seymour glared at his son. "I won't have you dictating to me, dammit."

Holt didn't flinch. He merely held his gaze steady.

"Oh, all right," Seymour muttered, shoving the cup aside.

"Were you drinking when you operated on Grant Dodson?" Holt questioned.

"Of course not," Seymour snapped. "I would never take a drink before surgery."

"But drugs are okay?"

Seymour's face turned so red that Holt thought it might explode. "That's different. I was just easing the pain in my back."

"So you still maintain your complete innocence?"

"Without reservation."

"Well, I can tell you right now, the odds are stacked against you."

Seymour narrowed his eyes on Holt. "If I didn't know you and your sense of ethics, I'd say I'm a fool for trusting you."

"That's a chance you'll have to take."

Their eyes met for a long hostile moment.

"So what's your plan?" Seymour asked into the silence. "I want to be kept in the loop."

"You know that's not my style. When I think you need to know something, I'll tell you. Meanwhile, I'll do my job."

"That's unacceptable."

"That's the way it is."

"If you're planning to use this unfortunate accident to bring me to my knees, to try and make me pay for—"

"Put a plug in it, Seymour," Holt interrupted. "You're not fit to mention my mother's name."

Color flushed into Seymour's face, but he didn't say anything. He merely clenched his teeth so tightly, his jaw quivered.

"I'm out of here," Holt said. "Before I go, I think it'd be to your advantage to be on your best behavior since the press is all over this like stink on stink."

Seymour stiffened. "I don't need you to tell me how to conduct myself."

"From where I'm standing, you damn sure do."

Holt sat behind the wheel of his SUV rental, trying to calm his temper before tackling the chief of police.

If he'd thought that defending his father was the ultimate insult, having to be around Maci, his stepmother, was more difficult. "Can it, Holt," he muttered to himself, stepping out of the vehicle, feeling the heat from the concrete rise up and envelop him. This weather was another reason his temper was on a short fuse. He didn't appreciate air conditioning with his shirt plastered to his skin.

Patience, he told himself, walking into the station.

Five minutes later he found himself sitting across the desk from Ted Satterwhite, which had surprised him. He hadn't expected to have such easy access to the chief, even though they had known each other since elementary school. Attorneys didn't usually get such good treatment and he'd doubted he'd be an exception.

"So what can I do for you, counselor?"

"Other than touching base with you after a lot of years, I'd like a copy of the charges against my client."

"That can be arranged."

"I don't suppose you want to tell me your secrets." Holt kept his tone blasé, willing to play a game of cat and mouse with good old redneck Ted. One never knew what might come of that.

"I'll tell you mine if you'll tell me yours. Is that the deal?"

"Works for me."

Ted shrugged. "At this juncture, we have none."

I'll bet, Holt thought. Obviously, Ted wasn't going to play along.

"By the way, thanks for seeing me," Holt said. "Maybe we'll actually get through this with as little bloodletting as possible."

"Maybe so," Ted drawled, leaning back in his chair.

Holt stood.

Ted's eyes drilled him. "Are you sure you know what you're doing?"

"No," Holt admitted with unvarnished honesty.

"At least you got the guts to tell the truth." Ted's scrutiny deepened. "All that bad blood between you and the doc is certainly no secret."

"Didn't think it was." Holt purposely spoke in a rendition of his own drawl.

"I have to tell you, though, he's going down for killing that fellow."

"We'll see," Holt said in a nonchalant tone.

Ted pushed his gangly body to its full height, which made him tower over Holt who was over six feet himself.

"I'd like to think this won't get ugly." Ted rubbed his slightly grubby-looking chin. "But if it's a street fight you want, the D.A. is sure capable of giving it to you."

"Has he—or maybe he's a she—ever won a case against a doctor?"

Ted seemed taken aback, then his expression hardened. "I don't rightly know."

"Sure you do." Holt spoke with confidence. "And the answer is no."

Ted didn't so much as stumble in his reply. "There's always a first time. When you read the arrest report, you'll see why I'm so confident."

"I know what it says. I just wanted a copy for my files." Holt smiled. "By the way, how's Beth and the boys?" He couldn't believe he'd failed to ask that already.

Ted's grin was genuine. "Great. Maybe you'd consider coming to dinner one evening."

"Maybe I will." He paused. "I'll be back in touch."
A smirk curled Ted's lips. "I'm sure you will."

"So how did it go with Satterwhite?"
"Easier than taking candy from a baby."
Holt smiled at Marianne whose fair complexion accentuated the freckles across her nose Holt often teased her about while she rebutted that they were angel kisses.
"Huh," she said in a huff, "I wouldn't trust that redneck as far as I could throw him."
"Well, you should know. If my memory serves me correctly, you two were once sweet on each other."
Marianne's pert nosed wrinkled in distaste. "Only for a week."
Holt chuckled. "Whatever."
"I'm serious. You shouldn't trust him."
"Hey, do I look like I just fell off a watermelon truck?"
Marianne flushed. "Of course not. I didn't mean to imply you had."
"At ease. I was just ribbing you. And I have been out to pasture for a while."
"That doesn't mean you've forgotten how to kick butt."
"We'll soon see, won't we?"
Arriving at his office after leaving police headquarters, Holt found that Marianne had everything in order. She'd even pulled the folders from pending cases that had been updated and placed them on his desk, along with law books pertaining to cases on doctors.
"What's first on the agenda? Or do you know yet?"
"Read the actual police report, then go from there."
"Oh, before I forget, a reporter from the paper stopped by and wanted to talk to you."

"I hope you told him to take a hike."

She grinned. "Not in those exact words, but he got the message."

"I hope so. Talk about losing my cool. That would do it."

"That's why I'm not stepping out of this office. Just in case he tries to sneak back in."

"Thanks."

"By the way, it's good to have you back."

He smiled, but it was short-lived. "Don't get too used to it. As soon as I can, I'm sailing back off into the wild blue yonder."

Her thin mouth curved downward. "I'll enjoy you while I can."

Holt turned to the police report, but instead of seeing the printed words, Maci's face flashed across the screen of his eyes.

Blinking, he muttered a curse just as the door opened and Marianne stepped inside. "You'll never believe who just dropped in."

Maci. His heart raced at the thought. "I don't want to guess either," he said tersely.

"Mrs. Grant Dodson."

For a moment, the name didn't register. He must've looked blank because Marianne gave him one of her looks. "Dr. Ramsey's friend who died on the table. She's his wife."

"Sarah's in the office?"

"That's what I just said."

He stood. "Send her in."

"Are you sure?"

"Hell no, but what choice do I have?"

"I can tell her you're not here."

"I think it's a bit late for that. Besides, I have to face her sooner or later."

"Done," Marianne said before sweeping out of the room.

Holt didn't bother to sit back down. Seconds later Sarah Dodson, a formidable opponent under even the best of circumstances, walked across the threshold, her mouth stretched pencil-thin.

"I'm proud of you young man for having the balls to see me."

In spite of himself, he smiled. "Hello, Sarah."

Nine

"You look like you've been rode hard and put up wet."

"Thanks, friend," Maci replied drolly. "That's not exactly what I needed to hear."

"Ah, even on your worst days, you're still gorgeous. And I'm pea-green with envy."

"Stop it," Maci admonished with a grin. "You've got a lot going for you, too."

Bobbi rolled her big blue eyes. "Sure, all one hundred and fifty pounds of flab."

"Once the baby arrives, that excess weight will come off." Maci gave Bobbi a brief hug. "You'll see. Trust me, I know from experience."

"You're being kind, and I love you for it. But we both know better. I'm a short tub of lard, and I don't see that changing at this stage in my life, baby or no baby."

"Speaking of baby," Maci asked, "have you heard anything?"

"Not a word, but then you should know that. After me, you'll be the first to hear the good news." Bobbi paused and gestured with her hand toward the plush sofa in the great room. "Hey, come on in and sit down. I didn't mean to keep you in a holding pattern at the door."

Maci chuckled. "Hey, I'm not company, so don't treat me like I am."

"Of course, you're not company. Before we get started on the house, let's have a cappuccino, shall we? I need to catch up on what's going on with Seymour."

Maci felt her features tighten.

"Sorry," Bobbi said. "I didn't mean to hit on a nerve."

"That's the beauty of our friendship. I can be myself with you. I don't have to pretend that life is a bowl of cherries when it's not."

"I know this mess is taking its toll on you. I think—no, I know—you've lost weight, and you didn't have any to lose."

"I'll be fine."

Bobbi made a face.

"I will. You know I'm a survivor. Just like you."

"You're right about that. Still, I'm sick that it happened. In fact, I still can't believe it. I thought doctors were untouchable."

"I know that, but not in this case. When he passed out in front of the patient's family and slurred his words, his behavior raised necessary suspicion. Finding enough narcotics in his blood to choke a horse compounded matters.

"I keep telling myself this is all a nightmare," Maci said, "and that I'll wake up and everything will be back to normal."

"Sit before you collapse," Bobbi demanded, pointing to the sofa. "I'm going to run and make our concoction. I won't be long."

"Let me help."

Bobbi shrugged her pudgy shoulders. "Sure, why not?"

Although Maci trailed her friend into the kitchen, she ended up standing by while Bobbi operated the cappuccino machine. When two cups were brimming with the frothy liquid, Bobbi placed them on a tray with a plate of muffins.

"Yum, those look good," Maci said, eyeing the sweets with a smile.

"I ran by the bakery early this morning with you in mind."

Maci's smile widened. "Good girl."

"You want to indulge in here or back in the living room?"

Maci nodded toward the breakfast nook, a spot that she had already redecorated. "Here, of course."

"Of course." Bobbi's tone was teasing. "I should've known you'd want to wallow in your success."

Maci laughed out loud, and it felt good. Since Seymour's arrest, there had been little spontaneous laughter in her life. Even around Jonah, she found it hard to be lighthearted.

With Bobbi, laughter was as much a part of her as her chubbiness. The trials and tribulations of life never seemed to get her down, though she'd had more than her fair share. During the time Maci had known her, Bobbi had divorced a physically abusive husband and made another life for herself.

She and Bobbi had met at a charity function that raised money for a local adoption agency. Maci was on the board, and Bobbi's application to adopt a child as a single parent—no easy feat—had been pending. Yet it had finally been approved.

Bobbi was now awaiting a call telling her about her son or daughter. Maci had done her best behind the scenes for Bobbi. She never doubted her independently wealthy friend would make an exceptional parent, and she didn't want her overlooked simply because she was unmarried.

"What's going through that mind of yours?" Bobbi asked once they were seated across from each other in the glassed-in breakfast nook that overlooked the garden. "When you're this quiet, it spooks me."

"I was thinking about your house," Maci said with obvious guilt over the little white lie.

"You're fibbing, but that's okay. I'll let you off the hook until we've polished off the goodies."

"I've been working on sketches for your bedroom and the guest suite."

To date, Maci had refurbished Bobbi's great room, dining room and breakfast nook. Their plan to take one room at a time was working, but Bobbi had wanted the entire house finished before the baby arrived. Unfortunately, Maci wasn't certain that would happen. Suppliers and contractors often ensured that the wheels of remodeling moved as slowly as the wheels of government. That was how she'd justified the delays to Bobbi.

"My, but you've been busy even under duress."

"That was my intention."

"I can't wait to see what you've come up with."

"I'm kind of nervous. You know renovating this old house has been my biggest challenge yet. So in a way you're a guinea pig."

Bobbi smiled. "With your talent and what I've seen so far, I'm happy to be your guinea pig."

Maci blew the foam on top, then took a sip. "Yikes, that's still hot."

"Give it a minute, though hot doesn't bother me." Bobbi backed up her words by taking a healthy sip from her cup before leveling her gaze on Maci. "Let's talk, shall we?"

"I thought that's what we were doing."

"About you. Specifically."

"My brain's on overload." Maci broke off a piece of the blueberry muffin and fiddled with it, all the while looking at Bobbi, a lovely woman with her bobbed off jet-black hair and porcelain skin.

"No wonder, with what you've been through," Bobbi said.

"You don't know the latest," Maci said in a forlorn tone, the blueberry muffin suddenly having lost its appeal.

Bobbi's thick eyebrows rose. "What now? I didn't think anything could get worse than Seymour getting arrested. I figured everything from then on had to be uphill."

Maci didn't quite know how to tell her friend about Holt, but she had no choice as Bobbi had seen him in Jamaica and had seen her dance with him. What she hadn't been privy to was what happened on the beach in the middle of the night. No one but she and Holt would ever know about that. Still, she had to cover her tracks, something that was as distasteful as it was dangerous.

"Just spit it out, okay," Bobbi said, her gaze penetrating. "It's not Jonah, is it?"

"No, he's fine, just cutting teeth."

"Atta boy. Now back to you."

"Do you remember the guy that I danced with in Jamaica?"

Bobbi's eyes flared brighter than the sunshine pouring through the glass. "Do I ever. He could eat crackers in my bed any day, as the saying goes. Stan was his name, right?"

Maci hesitated, searching for the right words.

"Why on earth are you thinking about him?" Bobbi frowned, helping herself to another pinch of muffin. "And after two years?"

"Because I saw him again."

"Oh, really." Bobbi grinned. "Well, he sure had the hots for you. For a while there, I thought the favor was returned."

Maci felt color rush into her cheeks.

It didn't escape Bobbi. "Hey, are you having an affair? With him? Is that what this is all about? If you are—"

Maci was horrified and it showed. "No, I'm not having an affair. You know better than that."

"Well, I thought I did, but things happen. Anyhow, I never figured out why you married Seymour to start with."

"Don't go there, Bobbi. Please."

For once, Bobbi looked chastised. "I know. I don't process before I speak, which never fails to get me in trouble. But enough about me. So where did you see this hunk again? God, if he looked you up after all this time, how cool is that?"

"Bobbi," Maci said in a rebuking tone.

"Sorry, I'll keep my mouth shut until you're finished."

"The guy's name wasn't Stan."

"Oh."

"It's Holt."

Bobbi shrugged. "So it's Holt."

"Holt Ramsey."

Maci waited with her heart in her throat for the tiny missile to hit Bobbi's brain and soak in, knowing that when it did, she'd be stunned.

"Did you just say what I think you said?" Bobbi demanded, slack-jawed.

"Yes, I did."

"The guy is Seymour's son?" Bobbi's tone was incredulous.

Maci nodded.

"Holy shit."

Maci managed to find enough air to chuckle in spite of the stress she felt. "It's your reaction that made me laugh, not the situation," she explained.

"You don't have to tell me that."

"So what is going on?"

Maci tried to make Holt's appearance seem a matter of course. Although she had replayed the moment he'd sauntered into the room a thousand times, the shock never lessened.

Talking about it now made her stomach hurt, especially in light of the confrontation she and Holt had had earlier. She was still spinning from that and had yet to sort through the consequences associated with it.

"You mean to tell me that he's an attorney who's going to represent his old man."

"It looks that way."

"That's un-fucking-believable."

"Bobbi," Maci exclaimed, pretending to be shocked at Bobbi's unladylike choice of words.

"Don't give me that. You know I call it as I see it."

"I won't argue with that," Maci said in a shaky voice.

"So did Holt say anything about knowing you?"

"God, no," Maci said before she thought.

"Why not?" Bobbi's question was as blunt as her tone.

Again, Maci felt her face flush. "I…we just didn't think it would be a good idea."

"Is there a Mrs. Holt Ramsey lurking in the shadows?"

"No. That I know for sure."

"I can't imagine that hunk staying footloose and fancy-free."

Maci merely shrugged, hoping to discourage her friend from delving further into Holt's business.

"So you two have talked privately?" Bobbi pressed, her tone obviously suspicious.

"This morning, as a matter of fact, though it wasn't a very pleasant conversation. He and Seymour have an old ax to grind. His mother's suicide is at the root of it. It's obvious Holt is bitter and holds a deep-seated grudge.

"That shouldn't bode well for him defending his father."

"My thoughts exactly, though Seymour is hell-bent on him doing just that."

"Holt must know his stuff then," Bobbi said, then grinned. "Not only is he hot stuff, but he knows his stuff."

"Funny."

"It made you smile, didn't it?"

"I'm sorry I haven't been very good company."

"Hey, with all you have on your plate, I'd be hiding in a dark closet, whimpering."

"Baloney. You don't know what it is to play the shrinking violet."

"Neither do you, so don't start now."

Maci gritted her teeth. "I don't intend to, but until Seymour is either vindicated or—" She broke off.

"No need to go there either. I get the picture." Bobbi seemed to pause deliberately before asking, "Meanwhile, what about your stepson?"

"What about him?"

Bobbi shrugged with a devilish glint in her eye. "I just figured he's the type who might like to play grab ass with daddy's trophy wife."

Maci kicked her friend in the shins.

"Ouch!"

"That will teach you to watch your mouth."

"Will not. So answer me. What if sonny boy makes a pass at you?"

"Bobbi, stop it."

"Well, life around your place won't be dull, that's for sure."

You don't know the half of it, Maci thought, a sense of dread chilling her blood.

Ten

"You're a little showoff. Did you know that?"

Jonah grinned, toddled toward Maci, then flung himself into her arms, wetting her face with slobbery kisses.

She laughed as she hugged him. "My, but those taste good."

Though it was stifling even in the shade, she had given in to Jonah's fretting and brought him outside. Her intention had been to remain under the covered portion of the veranda, but that had gone awry. Jonah wanted to run and chase a stray cat in the grass. Like it or not, she'd had to tag along.

But enough was enough. Her blouse and capri pants were sticking to her skin. She had slathered Jonah and herself with sunscreen before taking a step out the door. Early afternoon was one of the hottest and most dangerous parts of the day, yet she didn't have the heart to force him back inside. She decided instead to settle for the next best thing.

"Come on, sweetheart, let's go find some shade. Both of us have had enough of the sun for a while." She hoisted him onto her side, the smell of jasmine wafting her senses.

Jonah squirmed in her arms. "Down, Mommy."

"Not yet, son."

"Kitty." He pointed where the cat had scurried into the nearest cluster of bushes.

Smart kitty, Maci thought with a smile.

"Kitty, kitty," Jonah called.

"Kitty's gone bye-bye for now."

"Kitty gone," Jonah mimicked.

"That's right. But that's okay. You and me, buddy, are going to have some juice."

Jonah grinned, kicking his legs against her thighs in excitement. "Juice."

"And thanks to Annie, you have your choice—grape or Kool-Aid."

He tried to say Kool-Aid only to end up butchering it so that Maci laughed and gave him another hug.

"Down," Jonah ordered once they had reached the porch and he'd seen the goodie tray that Annie had left them. "Cookie."

"In a minute." Maci put him down. "First, we have to clean your hands." Having said that, she reached for the package of wipes the housekeeper had also left on the tray. Maci was paranoid about germs. Seymour often accused her of wiping the top layer of Jonah's skin off.

"All right, big boy, your hands are squeaky clean."

Before she could serve them, however, her hands needed attention. Actually, that wasn't all. She eyed the splashing fountain several yards away, suddenly wishing she could take her son and jump right in, letting the water cascade over them. Anything to cool off her clammy body. She unbuttoned the top three buttons on her blouse, feeling a trickle of perspiration run down between her breasts.

"Okay, we're ready for the fun part, our picnic."

"Can anyone join?"

At the sound of Holt's deep, seductive voice, Maci swung around, her stomach twisting with sudden emotion. Dear Lord, what was he doing here? It didn't matter. She had to stop letting him rattle her every time he was near.

But that was easier said than done, she realized, conscious of how she must look—like a wilted flower with her blouse molding her upper torso as if it had been glued on. What if he noticed her nipples that had sprung to life when she heard his voice?

Defensively, her hand went to her throat as if to cover herself. But she knew she was wasting her time. No telling how long he'd been standing there looking at her before she knew it. With her breath still caught somewhere in her throat, Maci removed her hand, though she continued to stare at him as if the fleeing cat had confiscated her tongue.

She hadn't seen Holt in two days, which she had counted as a blessing. Avoiding another altercation like the other morning was uppermost in her mind, especially since he appealed to her baser senses.

In his frayed shorts, T-shirt and holey tennis shoes he looked like he was about to board his sailboat.

"I wish you'd stop sneaking up on me."

Holt cocked an eyebrow at the same time as a laid-back smile eased across his lips. That was when she noticed his gaze was fixed on Jonah, who for once was content to sit on the pallet beside her, seemingly captivated with one of his toys.

"Good-looking kid."

Maci slipped a protective arm around Jonah's shoulders, then smoothed a strand of unruly hair. "He is, isn't he?"

"Looks like you."

"Is that a compliment?" she asked, then wished she hadn't. She didn't care about his opinion one way or the other.

"For sure."

She didn't know if it was his words or his penetrating gaze that sent the color rushing into her cheeks and tension stiffen her spine. Either way, it didn't matter. She lowered her head.

"Are you going to offer me some juice?"

She raised her eyes to meet his as he plopped down on the pallet close to Jonah who grinned up at him and said, "Hi."

"Hi, yourself, kid."

"Juice?" Jonah responded, crawling to the tray.

Maci placed her hands around his waist, stopping him. "Whoa there, fellow. Let Mommy get it. You'll have it all over the place."

"Cookie," Jonah said, pointing at the platter of goodies.

"How 'bout I take care of serving us?" Holt asked.

Us.

That tiny word sent shock waves through Maci. She

could not only smell the faint aroma of his cologne and see the thin lines tracking through his tan, but it was his incredible thick eyelashes that held her captive.

Only when he reached across to tousle Jonah's head did she move out of harm's way. The glinting look he gave her told her he knew exactly what she was doing. When she raised her chin in defiance, a slow smile spread across his lips.

She caught her breath.

"I'm not going to touch you."

He spoke in such a low rumble that at first she wasn't sure she had heard him right. Besides, the look in his eyes overrode anything he might have said.

"Mommy, cookies."

"Sorry, fellow," Holt responded in that same low, rough voice.

Still, he didn't turn away from her quickly. In his eyes she saw contempt replace desire.

"How 'bout two cookies?" he finally asked. "One for each hand?"

Jonah gave Holt an answering grin as he reached greedy little fingers toward the sugar cookies and latched on to them.

"Hey, kid, you know a good thing when you see it."

Maci wanted to respond, but she couldn't. It was as though she was having an out-of-body experience, watching Holt serve her son.

"Next comes the juice," Holt added, pouring a cup partly full, then holding it up to Jonah's mouth.

It was only after Jonah choked that Maci took charge. She grabbed him and sat him in her lap, patting him gently on the back. "It's all right, sweetheart."

Once his coughing fit had passed, he extended his hand back to Holt. "Cookie."

Holt chuckled and reached for the tray.

"Oh, no, you've had enough," Maci said, refusing to look at Holt. Maybe if she pretended he wasn't there, he'd go away. She wanted him as far away from her and her son as possible. Any idiot could see how he felt about her. And she was no idiot.

Desire and hatred were waging a war inside him.

She knew which would win.

"He just got strangled," Holt said. "He's okay."

"Since when did you become an expert on children?" she lashed back.

He held out his hands in fake surrender. "Excuse me for speaking out of turn."

Silence fell between them. Jonah broke it when he began to fret. Maci had just finished bathing his face with another wipe when Liz made an appearance.

"Perfect timing," Maci said, gladly letting the nanny take Jonah. "It's so hot he's getting fussy."

With a nod in Holt's direction, Liz disappeared with Jonah who was in the process of holding out his arms to Maci and shedding crocodile tears.

"Mommy will see you shortly." She blew him a kiss. "You be a good boy for Liz."

Once child and nanny had disappeared inside the house, the silence became heavier.

"I was out of line the other morning," Holt said without preamble.

"Is that an apology?"

"Do you want one?"

"No. I don't want anything from you."

"Not even to get your husband off the hook?" His smile was cynical.

"You know I want that. Why do you purposely misconstrue everything I say?"

"I didn't realize I did."

"Well, you do."

She averted her gaze and waited for him to speak. When he didn't, she faced him again, and noticed his eyes were focused blatantly on her breasts that remained molded to her bra. He slowly lifted his head.

His brazen scrutiny electrified her senses, but the spell was broken by the buzz of a bumble bee flying around her head. She waved nervously, almost glad for the distraction.

"Be still," Holt ordered in a soft, but sharp tone. "He won't bother you."

Remaining in one spot was not easy, but she did it, though her heart was beating wildly in her chest.

"See, it's gone."

Maci went weak with relief. "Thanks."

"That wasn't so hard, was it?"

"What?"

"Thanking me."

His comment infuriated her. Suddenly everything about him infuriated her. She wanted to get away from him without giving him the satisfaction of knowing how much he got under her skin.

"Look, I'm going inside."

"I want to talk to you."

"What about?" Her tone was leery.

"Seymour."

"Has something else happened?"

"Yes and no."

"That doesn't make much sense."

"Hear me out and it will."

She forced herself to relax, reaching for a glass filled with ice that was now mostly water. After taking a drink, she said, "I'm listening."

"I read the official charges today?"

"And?"

"The deck appears pretty stacked against him."

"Can you unstack it?"

"Maybe."

"That's not exactly what I wanted to hear."

"Just how dependent on drugs is my father? You of all people should know that."

"Only I don't. I was clueless until a few months ago. After I found out, of course, I begged him to get help. He promised he would, and I assumed he had."

"He lied." Holt's tone was harsh and blunt.

"Apparently so."

"Dodson's widow came to see me this afternoon."

Maci's eyes widened. "Oh, no."

"So you know her."

"Everyone knows Sarah."

"She and the rest of her family want Seymour behind bars."

A sick feeling washed through Maci. "Since they had been so quiet, I thought maybe they—" She broke off and placed her arms across her chest.

"They what? Had forgiven dear old dad?"

Her eyes flared against his sarcasm. "That's not unheard of, you know."

"From where I sit it is."

"Do you think she'll sue for money?"

"Probably, but not because she needs it. It would be to prove a point. She doesn't want Seymour operating at all, to protect others. She doesn't even want him in jail. She'd like his license revoked so that no other patient or family would be at his mercy."

"Have you told Seymour?"

"Nope. You're the first to know."

"So all this could get uglier?" Maci rose to her feet, feeling tears prick the back of her eyes.

"A lot." Holt rose as well, putting him in touching, smelling distance of her. She drew in a deep breath and backed up. His eyes followed her.

"I'm going inside."

The seconds pounded as their eyes held each other's.

He cleared his throat, then said brusquely, "I think that's a good idea."

Eleven

"How is she today?"

Debbie King, Maci's mother's live-in sitter, gave a semblance of a smile. "About the same, I'm afraid. She's resting."

"I'll just take a peek at her, then go."

"Oh, please stay," Debbie said in a slightly anxious voice.

Maci gave a start. "Has something happened with Mother that I should know about?"

"No." Debbie's sheepish smile brightened her dull features. "I just tried out a new cookie recipe, and I wanted to share."

Maci answered her smile, thinking again how lucky she was to have such a caring person tend to her mother. Debbie was a widow with one grown son. She needed someone herself. With Hannah, she seemed to have found her niche.

Debbie was short, plump and gray-haired, with the perfect laid-back personality to attend to someone in her mother's condition. On most days, Hannah's care required the patience of Job and more.

"So do you have time?"

Maci forced enthusiasm. "By all means. I rarely pass up sweets." She didn't have the time, but she wouldn't hurt this dear lady's feelings for anything.

"Good. Have a seat and I'll be right back."

"Need any help?"

Debbie shook her head then disappeared. Maci eased down on the sofa in her mother's new but modest home and let out a sigh. When it came to visiting her mother, she warred between love and hate. She couldn't stay away, of course, yet each time she saw Hannah in this state she felt the sting of an open wound.

Her mother had been diagnosed with the dreaded Alzheimer's so many years ago that it was sometimes difficult for Maci to remember her as a normal mother who took care of her child rather than the reverse.

No matter how painful these visits were, Maci would never forsake Hannah who early on had been a devoted, loving mother before being struck with the curse that stole her mind.

Deep down, Maci blamed her father for her mother's descent into that abyss of darkness. It was after his desertion and betrayal that Hannah began showing signs of memory loss. Maci was convinced the pain and shock of losing her husband and her lifestyle all at once was too much for Hannah. Yet she had hidden her grief well and had never inflicted her heartache on her only child.

Maci would be forever grateful that her mother had still been well when Maci's fiancé had literally left her standing at the altar. Her mother had been a tower of strength. Now, Maci was determined to return the favor. Marrying an older man for affection, mutual respect and security rather than passionate love had been the price she had paid.

Again, she had no regrets. Knowing that the trust fund she'd established would guarantee her mother was looked after around the clock was a great comfort and blessing. No matter what happened to Maci and Seymour, there was now enough money in the fund to take care of Hannah for as long as she lived.

Thinking she heard a noise coming from her mother's bedroom, Maci got up and went to the door. She cracked it, then peeped in. Hannah was indeed asleep, an afghan thrown across her legs. Her arms were lying across her chest.

For a second, Maci's heart skipped a beat. She looked so peaceful, like she was dead. On closer observation, Maci could see her chest moving up and down. Fighting off a profound sense of sadness, she eased the door shut and made her way back to the sofa.

Debbie had returned with a tray laden with coffee and cookies. "Is she still sleeping?" she asked in her soft, sweet tone.

"Like a baby."

"Sleep is what she needs most since she doesn't get much of it."

Maci didn't respond until after she'd accepted a cup of coffee and sipped on it. "Mmm, that's good. Flavored, right?"

"Yes, but I'm not sure with what. You like it?"

"It's really good." Maci reached for a cookie she didn't want and took a bite. "This is delicious, too," she added, washing the cookie down with another drink of coffee.

"I hope Mrs. Malone will eat some."

"Don't you think it's time you called her Hannah? After all, I consider you part of our family."

Debbie's face lit up again, showing her delight. "You have no idea how important that makes me feel, not having much of a family of my own." Her voice broke.

Maci had never seen Debbie's son, but she didn't want to. It was obvious he didn't care about his mother. Even Debbie had admitted as much, often telling Maci she didn't know where she'd gone wrong in raising him.

"I'm just so grateful at the kindness and patience you show Mother." Having said that, Maci reached over and squeezed Debbie's hand.

Afterward, they sat quietly munching on the goodies.

"Speaking of kindness," Debbie said, severing the silence, "you're showing yours by indulging this old woman when I know you have other fish to fry."

"You don't worry about all those other fish." Maci reached for another cookie. "I wouldn't have missed sampling these morsels for anything."

"Just in case you might want to make some for your family, they are called mud-pie cookies."

Maci groaned and rolled her eyes. "With all the gooey chocolate and caramel mixed together, that's an appropriate name, especially when I can feel the fat collecting on my hips."

Debbie flapped her hand. "Honey, you could eat those till doomsday and still not be fat."

"Well, we both know that's not going to happen."

Debbie chuckled but then turned serious. "There is something I wanted to bring to your attention."

Maci snapped to it. "What's Mother done now?"

"Nothing bad really. I even hesitate to say anything to you about it. In fact, I'd decided not to. It's just one of those situations where you don't know whether to laugh or cry."

Maci wasn't in the least offended by that statement because she knew just how true it was. Many times she had laughed in order not to cry. She had learned that from an Alzheimer's support group she had attended shortly after Hannah had been diagnosed.

"Tell me."

"She's got it in her head that Pedro's been sneaking into her bed at night and touching her."

Maci stared at Debbie in horrified silence.

"Look, I'm sorry I said anything. I should've kept my mouth shut."

"Of course, you should've told me. I want to know everything about Mother. She hasn't said anything to Pedro has she?" Maci was aghast, her thoughts centering on the shy yard man who was a faithful employee.

"Not that I'm aware of, though I have left her on the patio for short periods of time while Pedro is nearby trimming hedges."

"Where on earth did something like that come from?" Maci asked more to herself than to Debbie.

"It's part of the disease."

"Of course, it is," Maci said, "and I know that. It's just that when she says those off-the-wall things, I still react with dismay."

"Bless her heart."

"Maci!"

Both Maci and Debbie swung around in the direction of the voice. When she saw her mother standing wild-eyed in the door to the family room, Maci leaped to her feet. Hannah didn't often call her by name. Most of the time Hannah didn't appear to know who she was.

"Hi, Mother," Maci said, going to her and giving her a soft hug.

Since the disease had taken over her body, her mother seemed to have shrunk. Where once she had been a robust and striking woman, she was now thin and pale. The most upsetting factor, however, was the vacant look in her eyes. That got to Maci more than anything else. For all intent and purpose, her mother was gone.

"Mother, I'm so glad to see you," Maci said.

Hannah merely looked at her, then took her by the hand and led her down the hall. Even after they were sitting on the love seat in Hannah's bright and cheerful sitting room, Hannah continued to cling to Maci's hand. "You have to take me away."

"Why is that?" Maci asked in what she hoped was a soft, reassuring tone.

"She hasn't fed me in three days."

Maci's heart wrenched. "Are you talking about Debbie?"

"That woman in there."

"Are you hungry, Mom?"

"She's starving me." Hannah spoke in a conspiratorial tone.

"Shh, it's okay." Maci used her free hand to circle her mother's frail shoulder and pull her against her side. "I'll get you something to eat."

"No." Hannah shook her head violently, her eyes open as wide as they would go. "I don't like her."

"Why? Debbie's a nice lady, and she loves you very much."

Hannah merely looked at her with those vacant eyes, locked her arms across her chest, stared into space and began humming.

With a heavy heart, Maci stood, realizing that her mother had retreated back into that black void where she dwelled most of the time. After caressing Hannah's cheek, Maci leaned over and kissed her in that same spot. "I'll see you later, Mother. I love you."

Struggling for a decent breath, Maci made her way back into the family room, then into the kitchen where Debbie was busy puttering.

"Is she okay?" the sitter asked.

"She's rocking herself like a baby." She saw no point in telling Debbie what her mother had said, though the caregiver wouldn't be shocked by the accusation. Paranoia went along with the disease.

"I'm so sorry," Debbie said, her features softening on Maci.

"Me, too." Maci cleared her throat. "Look, would you make sure Pedro understands that she can't help herself, just in case she's said anything to him?"

"You don't worry about that for one minute. Consider it taken care of."

Maci gave Debbie a silent hug, then grabbed her purse and walked outside. Under any other circumstances, the glare from the intense sunlight would have blinded her.

But today her eyes were too full of tears.

Twelve

"What did Vince say?"

Marianne paused in the doorway to Holt's office and grinned. "You want his exact words."

"Fire away."

"Okay. 'Just who does that s.o.b. think he is?' Referring to you, of course."

"Of course." Sarcasm colored Holt's tone.

"There's more," Marianne went on, her entire face lit up by one big grin.

"You're enjoying this, aren't you?"

"You'd better know it. When you're in town and in this office, there's never a dull moment."

"Get on with the rest of the story," Holt said, "if you must." He was unable to curb his impatience and it showed.

"Okay. And I quote again, 'If he thinks I'm going to ask how high when he says jump, he's sadly mistaken.'"

"He'll be here." Holt spoke with confidence.

"That's what I thought, too," Marianne responded, still grinning.

"Meanwhile, I want you to prepare a file on the Dodson family as well as my father."

Marianne frowned. "Too bad the widow is out for blood."

"That's the way it is. We'll take the hits as they come."

"Do you think she's going to file a civil suit against Dr. Ramsey?"

"Probably."

Marianne wrinkled her nose. "That won't be good."

"No, it won't. But again, we'll just have to take one hit at a time and deal with it."

"Which means you may be around a lot longer than you planned."

"I know," Holt said in a terse tone.

Marianne leaned against the doorjamb. "I still can't believe this is happening, that you're having to defend your father against a homicide charge."

Holt's patience was gone. "I know you mean well, but—"

"Uh, right. I need to get to work and let you do the same."

"You got it," Holt quipped with unusual bluntness.

Grinning again, Marianne reached for the door and closed it behind her. Holt let go of a frustrated breath. Marianne would talk the horns off a billy goat and back on again. Thank goodness she didn't take offense at his putting her in her place when needed. Still, he wouldn't trade her for anyone else.

Holt looked at the stack of law books that he had yet to touch. Getting back in the saddle was going to be tougher than he'd imagined. He gazed out the window at the bright sunlight with a growing sense of restlessness.

In his mind, he could envision the ocean sparkling like highly polished diamonds in the sunlight and feel the sea breeze caress his skin. He couldn't forget the fishy scent of salted air that tickled his senses.

He turned away with a pang of longing kicking him in the gut. Freedom.

A few days ago he'd taken his ability to indulge his wanderlust spirit for granted. Now stuck in town, in his office, his independence seemed forever gone.

The only thing he wanted with the same passion as his sailboat was Maci. He snorted. What a comparison, but it was the truth. Every time he saw her, the ache in his groin increased. It was all he could do to keep his hands to himself. But he knew he had no other choice.

She was as forbidden to him as the fruit had been to Adam in the Garden of Eden.

"I'd ask what's going on in that head of yours, but since it's empty I'll refrain."

Realizing he was no longer alone, Holt turned a startled look to the door. His private detective friend, Vince Hillyard, was slouched against the frame.

Even though it had been a couple of years since he'd seen his buddy, Vince hadn't changed much. Just the girth around his middle had grown bigger. But since Vince topped almost six-five he could easily handle the few extra pounds. Big, robust and bald was his overall image, though his bare head rarely showed because he was never without his Stetson.

Holt stood, feeling a grin spread across his lips. "I could say the same for you, but I won't."

"I told myself and Marianne I wasn't coming."

"So she said, but I knew you couldn't stay away."

"Your smug ass sucks," Vince said with a slight curl to his lips.

Holt pitched his head back and laughed, then walked toward his friend. "It's good to see you." Instead of shaking hands, they embraced briefly, then stepped apart.

"Ditto, only I'm sorry it's under such circumstances."

"So you know." Holt's sentence didn't end with a question mark.

Vince's bushy eyebrows shot up "Who doesn't?"

"Sometimes I forget the small-town mentality."

"Not all of us here have that luxury."

Holt smiled again at the sarcasm lacing Vince's statement. "Hey, take the load off." He gestured toward the plush chair in front of his massive desk. "I'd offer you a beer only it's too early in the day."

"Says who?"

This time Holt's brows shot up. "You wanna beer? I have a full fridge."

"Nah. I need a clear head to deal with you."

"So you'll help me out?" Holt asked.

"Depends."

"On how much I'm willing to pay you."

Vince grinned, displaying stained, uneven teeth. "Now we're on the same page."

"You always were a greedy bastard," Holt responded with a smile.

"And proud of it, too."

"Would you take an IOU? I'm actually short of cash."

"Bullshit."

Holt chuckled. "I'll see what I can do."

"Just dig up one of those coffee cans full of cash you keep buried."

"Already done that."

"What you're telling me is that you intended to return to civilization, even if this hadn't happened to Seymour?"

"That's right. When my funds get low, I have to take several cases to tide me over."

"Must be nice."

Holt grinned at the envy he heard in his friend's voice. "It is."

"Do you think you'll ever settle down again, as in practice law full-time?"

"Don't plan to any time soon."

"I'd like to sail with you sometime."

"What about Hope and the kids?"

"The kids are grown and Hope wouldn't give a rat's ass."

Holt smiled. "So wifey's still giving you a hard time?"

"You don't know the half of it. Stay single, my friend. Just fuck 'em and leave 'em."

Holt chuckled. "Give Hope my best."

"Oh, you'll see her. She'll insist on having you to dinner."

"I'd like that."

Vince's big features sobered. "So are you really going to defend Seymour?"

"Yep, but not because I want to."

"I bet the doc finds that reassuring," Vince noted with sarcasm.

"He trusts me." Holt's tone was flat.

"He's a damn fool, then."

Holt's eyes narrowed. "You don't think I'd sell him down the river, do you?"

"Can you honestly say you haven't considered using this screwup as an excuse to finally get revenge?"

"No, I can't," Holt admitted with bitter honesty, "but then Mother's face and voice start to haunt me."

"Well, she could always keep you on the straight and narrow," Vince said, stretching out his long legs, "when no one else could, I might add."

"She never stopped loving the bastard."

"And you've never stopped hating him."

A silence fell over the room

"That's about the size of it," Holt finally said.

Vince whistled. "This ought to be the case from hell."

"It already is. Seymour and I have already tied it on a couple of times."

"So what does dear old Dad have to say for himself?"

"That he's innocent."

Vince blinked, then laughed, though the laughter had a hollow ring to it. "Arrogant as always."

"Some things never change, pal."

"I know you've gone over the charges against him with a fine-tooth comb." Vince paused and thumped his hat farther back on his head. "So what are your chances of making this go away?"

"I'm guessing fifty-fifty."

"What does Doc think about those odds?"

"He won't even entertain the idea that he's done anything wrong." Holt shrugged. "So I didn't bother to tell him."

"Wise choice."

"Now you can see why I need your expertise."

"You expect me to stop whatever I'm doing and get on this, right?"

Holt grinned. "ASAP."

"You prick."

"I've been called worse."

"Before we get to me, what about you? Have you done any probing on your own?"

"I picked up the charges from Ted Satterwhite and visited with him."

"So what have they got?" Vince asked.

"Needless to say, he wasn't forthcoming."

"Meaning they don't have much, except maybe the M.E.'s report."

"Which reminds me," Holt said, "that's something I don't have." Further proof of his shoddy work habits, he reminded himself with a grimace.

"Want me to get it?"

"Nope, I'll get it myself. The M.E. just happens to be another old buddy of mine."

"Good thing you're such a friendly bastard."

Holt grinned. "Ain't it, though?"

"Any particular place I need to start other than the hospital?" Vince asked.

"Not at the moment. The employees, especially the surgical team who worked with Seymour, are the key players here."

"Gotcha. Don't expect a whole lot from these people, but then you ought to know that." Vince eased the Stetson back on his head. "They'll be as tight-lipped as monks."

"And stick together as tight as glue."

"Let us pray that's the case." Vince's voice was hard. "Otherwise—"

Holt certainly knew the otherwise and so did his father. "That's why Seymour's so confident," he said. "He doesn't think anyone at the hospital will rat on him. Apparently they haven't."

"If he *is* guilty and his cronies do roll on him, he might as well pack his bags."

Holt nodded, his features grave. "You hit the nail on the head."

"If there's nothing else, then, I'm outta here."

"Hold up. There is something else," Holt said. "Find out everything you can about Grant Dodson and his family. He's the man who died on the table."

"Expecting trouble there, huh?"

"His wife, Sarah, came to see me." Holt told him about that conversation.

Vince whistled again. "And the beat goes on."

"That it does."

For a moment Vince hesitated. Finally he said, "You can tell me it's none of my business—"

"Then don't ask," Holt interrupted.

Vince chuckled. "You know me better than that. Gotta say what's on my mind."

"I'm waiting," Holt said with a scowl.

"I'm curious about your stepmother."

Holt's gut twisted, but when he spoke, he forced his tone to be blasé. "What about her?"

Vince's mouth curved downward. "Oh, come on, you know what I'm talking about. Your old man pulled off a coup by marrying her. She's some looker. I've only seen pictures of her in the newspaper—she's big into charities and all, you know—but in person, I have to think her sex appeal would singe the hair off a man's hide."

"So she's got a great body." Holt spoke in a nonchalant but brittle tone. "Where I come from, women like her are a dime a dozen."

"Must be nice," Vince said drolly.

Holt didn't reply, hoping his silence would encourage Vince to change the subject. He didn't want to talk about Maci. He feared he might give himself away. Also, he wasn't ready for anyone to know about their past, especially when he hadn't sorted through the ramifications in his own mind. To a large extent, he was still shell-shocked.

"I know you think she took your mother's—"

"Give it a rest, Vince." Holt's tone was harsh.

Vince shrugged where he stood. "No problem. Didn't mean to step on a nerve."

"You didn't."

"I'll be in touch," Vince said with his usual ease.

"Remember ASAP."

"Gotcha." He tipped his hat, then sauntered out of the office.

Alone, Holt suddenly felt drained and irritable. He knew why. Maci. Just mention her name, and his body went into overdrive. He got up from behind his desk and swept a hand across his neck. God, he was tired. Already. And the game was only in the first inning.

"Holt," Marianne said through the door.

His gut instinct was to tell her to get lost, which would never do. Getting control of his nerves, he said, "Yes."

She stepped inside the office, then closed the door quickly behind her.

"What's up?"

"A man's here to see you."

"As in client?"

"I think so."

"Did he give you a name?"

"Lucas Tom Sanders."

"Really?"

"You know him?"

"Yep. He's an old college buddy of mine. What does he want?"

"To talk to you about defending him."

"On what charges?"

Marianne's eyes widened, and she lowered her voice. "Capital murder."

Thirteen

Holt muttered an oath. Then he forced himself to settle down. When he'd picked up the phone and called the M.E., Pete Ashburn, who'd done the autopsy on Dodson, it hadn't crossed his mind that Pete might be on vacation.

He could either wait for the M.E. to return or send Vince to the district attorney's office to get a copy of his report. Holt drummed his fingers on the desk. Either way, he knew pretty much what it was going to say anyway, so he could wait.

Besides, he had another alligator snapping at his neck. He was convinced he'd lost what little brain matter he'd had. Maybe Maci had messed with his psyche more than he dared admit because otherwise he would've told Lucas Tom Sanders to hit the door.

Only he hadn't.

He'd listened to Lucas's tale of woe and told him he'd consider taking him on as a client.

He didn't need another high-profile case. Seymour's was enough to keep his nose to the grindstone and give him ulcers to boot. Why would he put himself through more torture? The answer was simple.

Cold hard cash.

If he was going to remain in town, he needed to make some money in order to fund another jaunt on his sailboat. And since there was no way he would take any money from his father, he had to pad his bank account by other means.

The other means could very well be Lucas Sanders. He was rolling in the green stuff. He'd inherited plenty, but he'd made millions on his own with sound investments.

But capital murder?

He wasn't sure there was enough money worth that. And Holt didn't want to work that hard. Not anymore. That was the reason he'd walked out on his upscale job and lifestyle. The pressure from both had led him to spend more time studying the bottom of a bottle than his law books. He'd known it was time to quit.

Even if he'd been excited about representing Lucas in order to get his competitive juices flowing again, he wasn't sure he could keep up the hectic pace of two complicated cases. He had downsized so much and become so laid-back that he wasn't certain his mind was as sharp as needed in order to practice criminal law.

But Lucas Tom had been so damned persuasive. In addition, he'd called in an old favor.

"I won't take no for an answer, Ramsey. I'm telling you that right up front."

"Hey, man, take a breath." Holt had forced his tone to be calm and upbeat.

Lucas smiled sheepishly. "Sorry, I forgot my manners." He paused and held out his hand. "It's good to see you, old friend."

"Same here," Holt responded, pumping Lucas's hand, "though I'd like it to have been under different circumstances."

"You and me both."

"Sit and tell me what's going on. First though, how 'bout something to drink? Coke? Coffee?"

"Coffee'll do fine."

"Coffee it is." Holt walked to the makeshift minibar where he filled two cups, handing one to his visitor.

Although they were the same age, give or take a few months, Holt didn't think the aging process had been kind to his buddy. Lucas's hair had turned a lackluster gray and deep lines scored his gaunt face. The skin seemed to sag on his thin frame. He obviously didn't spend a lot of time in the gym.

Yet his brown eyes still held a twinkle, though at the moment his eyes looked dull and almost void. With good cause, Holt reminded himself, given that he was suspected of murder.

"What's going on, Lucas?"

"The police brought me in for questioning. They think I killed my wife."

"Damn," Holt muttered.

"It's one helluva mess," Lucas said. "I gotta tell you."

"Did you kill her?" Holt asked bluntly and without apology.

Lucas didn't so much as blink. "No, I did not."

"What happened?"

"I found her dead several weeks ago around 10:00 p.m. I'm surprised you didn't read about it in the paper."

"I wasn't here. Since my homecoming—" Holt's tone was cynical "—I've been a little busy myself."

Lucas gave him a contrite look. "Man, I sure hated to hear about Seymour. He's regarded as one of the best surgeons in this area. Or was, that is. I'm sorry for you."

"That's a waste of time. And don't feel sorry for him either. Seymour made a stupid mistake that could cost him dearly."

"So you and your old man still don't see eye to eye?"

"Nope."

"But you're going to defend him, right?"

"It looks that way."

"I won't ask why."

"Smart move."

"So is it true that he's on drugs?" Lucas asked.

"You know I can't answer that or discuss it."

"Of course you can't." Lucas's tone was apologetic. "And I knew better than to ask. Besides, who am I to talk about someone else when I'm trying to keep my head above quicksand?"

"I'm glad you recognize that." Holt's drawl was sarcastic.

Lucas laughed for the first time since he entered the room. "You haven't changed either, Ramsey. You're still a cocky s.o.b., which is why I'm here. You always did have more confidence than anyone I knew."

"Thanks," Holt said, "but if you're trying to butter me up…" He let his words trail off when he saw the panicked expression on Lucas's face.

Holt squirmed. Guilt was not something he wanted to feel.

"Will you take my case?"

"Seymour already has my balls in a vise."

"Can I add mine?" Lucas asked in an almost pleading tone, though a smile toyed with his lips.

"I need the work, but another murder case is not what I had in mind."

"You might when you've heard the details," Lucas argued.

Holt's frustration was rising. "True, but—"

"I hate to remind you that you owe me."

Holt bristled. "You'd use that accident as leverage?"

"If that's what it takes to get your help."

"Dammit, there are several other lawyers who would do you a better job than me. I'm as rusty as a hundred-year-old nail."

"I'll take my chances," Lucas responded with dogged determination in his tone.

"I don't like being blackmailed." Holt gave him a grave look. "In fact, it pisses me off that you'd stoop that low."

Lucas's already pale features turned even paler. "I deserved that, I know. But I'm prepared to take whatever you dish out in order to get you in my corner."

Holt didn't respond right away but thought about exactly why he owed Lucas Tom big time. During their freshman year at the university, he, Lucas and another buddy had been involved in a fiery car crash that hadn't been their fault.

The friend who was driving had been killed instantly. Lucas had been thrown from the car and miraculously survived, while he, Holt, was trapped inside the burning vehicle. Lucas had risked his own skin to pull him to safety.

That heroic measure on Lucas's part had formed a

bond that had lasted through the years even though the two friends rarely saw each other.

"You're thinking about the accident, aren't you?" Lucas asked in a dejected tone.

"Yep."

"I'm sorry. I shouldn't have said what I did."

Holt didn't respond.

"Look, if you really don't want to or can't take me on, then I'll understand."

"What was the cause of death?" Holt asked in a resigned tone.

Lucas looked like he'd just been given a reprieve from the hangman's noose. "A broken neck from a fall down the stairs."

"Ouch."

"I know," Lucas said with emotion.

Holt blew out a breath. "Were you there when she fell?"

"Not at the time, but I had been."

"So where were you?" He paused deliberately. "At the time?"

Lucas hesitated. "Walking the dog."

Holt gave him an incredulous look. "Surely you can do better than that."

"That's the truth," Lucas responded on the defensive.

"You'd best get off your high horse."

"Look, Holt—"

"Did you tell the police you were walking your dog?"

"Yes," Lucas admitted in a weary tone.

Holt let go of a choice word.

"I know how it sounds." Lucas stiffened his shoulders. "But, again, it's the truth."

"Can anyone vouch for that?"

"No."

"That's not good."

"Tell me something I don't know," Lucas said in an irritated tone. "That's why I'm in deep trouble and need you to get me out."

"What about your marriage?"

Lucas looked blank for a moment as if the change in subject caught him off guard. "Uh, what about it?"

"Were there problems?" Holt asked, not masking his impatience.

"A few."

"That's not good enough."

"Okay, so we had more than our share. But what couple doesn't who've been married as long as we have?"

"How about elaborating on those *few* problems?"

Lucas flushed. "I was having an affair."

"Great."

Lucas's flush deepened. "I was in the process of ending it."

"Did your wife know? By the way, what is...was her name?"

"Rachel." Lucas's voice held a quiver.

Holt worked on mellowing his tone. "Did she know about the affair?"

"She knew, but when I told her I was ending it, she seemed willing to forgive and forget."

"Sure." Holt simply couldn't keep the sarcasm out of his tone.

"Dammit—"

"Hey, if you think I'm asking hard questions," Holt lashed back, "just wait until the D.A. gets you on the stand."

"It can't be much worse than I've already been through with the police," Lucas muttered down-in-the-mouth.

"Before we go any farther," Holt said, "who represented you when you were brought in?"

"It doesn't matter. When I heard you were back in town, I fired him."

"Pretty confident, huh?" Holt's tone was hard.

Lucas's mouth thinned. "No, just hopeful."

"Right."

An uncomfortable silence followed; the chiming of the wall clock was the only sound in the room.

"So are you going to represent me?" Lucas asked.

Another silence.

"Holt, don't make me grovel, please."

"If that's what you want, then I'll give it my best shot." Holt batted the air with a hand. "But know that my circuits are already on overload."

"Like I told you, I'll take you on any terms I can get you."

"Let's get down to brass tacks, then."

"Not before I get some more coffee," Lucas countered with a renewed energy in his voice and bounce to his step as he strode toward the bar.

"Help yourself."

"Okay, shoot," Lucas said, once he'd reclaimed his chair.

"I gather you're the only suspect."

Lucas heaved a sigh. "You gather right, but the cops apparently didn't have enough to hold me, so they let me go. But I'm here to tell you that one of those detectives came at me with his guns blazing, especially since there was no indication of a break-in."

"If it wasn't an accident and you didn't do it, then she had a visitor whom she knew."

"That's possible." Lucas scratched his chin. "I was gone a good while."

"Do you have any idea who would've wanted her dead?"

"Of course not. As far as I know, she had no enemies."

"Was she employed?"

"As a secretary for Bradford Investments."

"Was she having trouble on the job?"

Lucas frowned. "Not that I know of. But then, we didn't talk that much." His frown turned into a flush. "We've sorta been going our separate ways."

"So you don't know if she was upset about anything?"

"Sorry," Lucas muttered. "But what could her job have to do with her murder?"

"Maybe nothing and again, maybe everything."

"Going down that road seems like wasted effort to me."

"At this point," Holt said sharply, "nothing is wasted or off-limits."

"So you think her murder could actually be work related?" Lucas seemed genuinely stunned.

"I haven't a clue," Holt admitted. "But like I just said, we can't leave any stone unturned. Trust me, the cops won't, not when it comes to a philandering husband."

Lucas face turned a bright red, then he mumbled, "I'm not very proud of myself."

"Is there anything else you need to tell me?"

"Like what?"

Holt's gaze was direct. "Like a skeleton in the closet. I don't like getting karate-chopped from behind."

"I'm not keeping anything from you."

It was obvious Lucas took umbrage at his inquiry but Holt didn't care. He'd learned from experience that clients were seldom forthcoming with their attorneys.

"How long is this going to take?" Lucas asked on a sigh.

"To you, it'll seem like forever."

"It already does."

"Remember when you get discouraged," Holt said, "the burden of proof is on the D.A., not on us."

"Somehow that's not much comfort."

Holt shrugged. "For now, it's the best I can do."

Another tense silence followed.

Holt picked up his questioning. "What about other men?"

Lucas jerked his head up. "You mean in Rachel's life?"

"Don't play stupid, Lucas," Holt said with impatience. "Could she have been having an affair, too?"

Anger flared in Lucas's eyes then suddenly disappeared. "No. She isn't...wasn't that kind of woman. She wouldn't have ever strayed."

"So you shared the same bed?"

The red in Lucas's face deepened. "Of course."

"At least that's in your favor."

"Look, I loved Rachel." Lucas's voice shook. "I guess I didn't realize how much until...until I found her dead." Suddenly he began to sob. "I didn't kill her. Honest to God, I didn't. You've got to help me."

Holt was uncomfortable with this display of emotion. "I know you didn't."

Lucas raised his wet face. "What if—"

"If you're innocent, you won't go down for this," Holt said in a controlled tone. "Count on it."

Suddenly the phone rang, and he jumped. Marianne

would take the call, but the sound brought Holt back to reality. He moved from behind his desk and walked to the window, deeply troubled.

It wasn't like him to spontaneously accept any case, especially one where a man's life hung in the balance. His gut told him Lucas was innocent. That aside, he'd made a promise he wasn't sure he could keep.

But then, after seeing Maci again, he'd done a lot of crazy things.

Fourteen

It was late.

Maci studied her watch and gnawed on her lower lip, trying to decide if she had enough time to stop by Bobbi's and drop off a bunch of fabric samples before she met Seymour at the office. Making a side stop would be cutting it close, but she thought she could do it. Besides, if she were thirty minutes late, Seymour probably wouldn't notice.

Then again, maybe he would. Punctuality was important to him. It was for her, too, but not this evening. They were attending a charity function near his complex, and so Maci had agreed to meet him in town.

She wasn't at all excited about this shindig. She no longer sought crowds made up of false friends. She knew she and Seymour continued to be the talk of the town. Everywhere she went, she received covert looks and heard blatant whispers. Those barbs hurt.

All the more reason to attend this dinner and dance with her head held high, she told herself. While she might be under siege both inside and out, she would never let it show. She had too much pride. Tonight would be a great opportunity to display it.

She had shopped for a new dress, a designer original. Her intention was to look her best, and she felt she'd pulled that off. The lines of the ankle-length, black cocktail dress were simple—except for a splatter of beading on the strapless top that sparkled when she moved. But what had cinched the purchase had been the fit. The material hugged her body like a second skin. She looked sleek and chic.

What more could she ask for when she was trying to make an impression? Still, she had misgivings about the evening. Her heart wasn't in it. She had always been ready and willing to party, but now, following the scandal, she preferred staying at home and playing with Jonah.

Maybe a dose of her friend, Bobbi, was what she needed to perk her up. She grinned. Bobbi would advise her to tell those "so-called friends" to kiss her butt. Of course, that wouldn't happen. But the thought was comforting, nonetheless. After checking her reflection one last time in the mirror and reaffirming that she did look good, Maci walked out of her bedroom and down the stairs.

When she reached the last step she saw him.

Holt was slouched against the study door, a half-empty glass in his hand, staring at her. She hesitated at the same time her heart took a nosedive.

For the briefest of moments, their eyes met.

He looked sexy dressed in a pair of ragged edged cut-offs and a T-shirt. No shoes. Maci envisioned him on his sailboat, tall and Greek-god beautiful, but that image quickly disappeared when he shoved away from the door and eased toward her.

Even though she was on solid ground, Maci grabbed the banister for support, feeling her body heat to a full boil. From the look in his eyes, the same fire raged in him. Dear God, this was madness.

"Going out?" he asked, his covetous gaze moving up and down her body, finding a resting place on the white globes of her breasts swelling above the fabric.

"You know the answer to that," she said in a low, terse tone.

If she'd had a shawl, she would've reached for it, but since she didn't, she forced herself not to move, not to react to the overt hunger in his eyes.

"Nice dress."

"Thanks," she muttered, unable to look away.

He deliberately raised the glass to his lips, though his eyes never once wavered away from her.

"I need to go."

"You're the loveliest thing I've ever seen." His voice was low and husky and a bit slurred. But it was his eyes that she couldn't run from. They were devouring her.

Another sizzle of electricity reinforced her hold on the banister.

"In fact, you look delicious."

"Holt."

"Holt what?" he rasped, stepping even closer, his gaze unwavering.

"You've been drinking," she whispered, feeling the space narrow between them.

"So I have."

"Let me by." Her voice trembled.

"Why?"

She licked her dry lips. "Don't, Holt."

He groaned. "Do you know why I'm getting stinking drunk?"

"No," she whispered without thinking.

"Because when I'm sober I can't stop thinking about you."

Now Maci looked away. He was far too close for comfort, forcing her mind into forbidden territory that left her aching to know what it would feel like to have him actually touch her, kiss her.

Only she already knew.

She tried to dig her fingers into the hard wood for extra support. "Please." The word came out sounding like a pitiful croak. She hated herself for the weakness of her flesh when he was around.

He was her stepson, for heaven's sake.

"Please what? Touch you?"

Holt's bourbon breath caressed her cheek before she gave her head a violent shake.

"I know you want me, too," he pressed. "I see in your eyes, feel it in the rise and fall of your breasts."

"Stop it," she cried, her eyes sparking and her heart nearly hammering out of her chest. "You have no right to talk to me like that."

"Then stop looking at me like you could eat me."

Maci sucked in her breath, then did something totally foreign to her. Lifting her hand, she slapped his face, then scurried around him and out the door.

Her breath was coming in heaves by the time she reached her vehicle and got inside. She tried to start the ignition, but she was shaking too badly. She couldn't get the key into the ignition.

Cursing, Maci leaned her head back against the seat and fought for control. She couldn't believe she'd behaved in such an irrational manner. She had never ever hit a person in the face. And while Holt's comment had deserved such a response, she wished she hadn't lost her temper to that extent.

He had to leave.

That was the only solution if she intended to hang on to her sanity and her marriage. Louisiana was full of competent attorneys. Seymour would just have to find and hire one of them. Now all she had to do was tell her husband.

Without explaining why.

A short time later Maci had regained her composure and made her way into the plush outer office of Ramsey Plaza. Her outward calm was still fragile. She couldn't allow her thoughts to backtrack for one second or she was doomed. Hence, she didn't know when she was going to come up with a plan that would send Holt packing.

For the moment, however, she forced her mind to think about something generic—her surroundings.

Two hefty-bottomed lamps on tables emitted a soft glow, allowing her to view her handiwork in all its glory. The walls were painted a ravishing coral color that added warmth to the room. The seats of the wooden chairs were covered in an animal print fabric while the sofas were upholstered in butter pecan material that complemented the bold print. But it was the cushions she'd had the most fun with. They were part animal print and part tapestry, adding a richness to the room.

A scattering of plants, pictures and simple window treatments finished out the decor. This project had brought her several new clients as Seymour was always quick to point out his wife's work.

Thinking about her husband, Maci threaded her way to his private suite. "Seymour," she called out after she reached his door. It was closed.

Later, she couldn't say why she hadn't knocked before opening the door. Maybe it was the fact that it appeared as though he hadn't been expecting her.

"Seymour," she called again, crossing the threshold into the semidark room.

He was nowhere in sight. Maci frowned. Had they gotten their wires crossed about the meeting place? No. She remembered him telling her to meet him here.

Where was he?

Without a valid reason, a chill darted up her spine as the room suddenly took on a deserted, eerie feeling. Had something happened to him? Then it dawned on her. He'd probably been called out on an emergency. That would certainly account for his absence. But then he would have gotten in touch with her.

Reaching in her purse, she checked her cell phone. No calls.

She gnawed at her lower lip. Should she go to the function without him? No. If she went anywhere else it would be home. She balked at that idea, thanks to Holt. She wasn't up to another confrontation with him.

"Maci?"

She swung around, her heart in her throat. "Seymour,

you scared the wits out of me." She blinked several times before realizing that he was at least ready for the occasion, impeccably dressed in a tux, complete with cummerbund. She hadn't seen him look that nice in a while.

"Why didn't you knock?" he asked.

Her hearing perked up. Were his words slurred? Was he drunk? Or was she just being paranoid?

"I didn't know I needed to," she said, making her way toward her husband. Her eyes narrowed.

He stepped back into the shadows, triggering an alarm inside her head.

"I'm not quite ready yet," he said, turning his head, opening and closing his hands.

"Why is that?"

"You look lovely, my dear."

She ignored the compliment. "Seymour, are you all right?" She knew the answer to that question, though she shied away from admitting it.

"Of course, I'm all right." His tone had a quarrelsome ring to it.

"The fact that you're in the dark makes me think otherwise."

"I was in the bathroom."

Perfect explanation. Except that he would've still heard her.

"I'm not buying that, Seymour."

She was close enough to see him visibly stiffen, though he still kept his face averted.

"You're behaving in a ridiculous manner," he snapped. "That's not like you."

"Are you high?" She almost choked on those words, but they had to be said.

"Of course not," he snapped again, turning his back on her.

Fury raced through her. "Look at me, damn you."

"Don't you dare talk to me in that tone."

"Don't you dare treat me as if I'm an imbecile."

For a long moment, Seymour remained facing the window, his shoulder muscles tense. Then he slowly turned and faced her, his chin raised in defiance. The light was on her side. It caught him just right, leaving no doubt as to his dilated pupils.

He was pumped high on drugs.

A myriad of emotions charged though Maci, beginning with white rage and ending with irreversible disappointment.

"Have you lost your mind?" She barely recognized her own voice.

"So I slipped, sweetheart," he said in a cajoling voice, a grin splayed across his lips. "One time isn't going to hurt."

That was such absurd reasoning that it rendered her speechless.

"Look, let's forget going to the party. Hell, we can have our own right here," he suggested.

"You disgust me," she spat out, backing up.

He widened his grin and said, "Ah, now, don't be such a party pooper. As long as this little mistake stays between you and me, what's the harm?"

"You just don't get it, do you?" Tears of anger and frustration broke Maci's voice. "If you were to get caught in this state, you could spend the rest of your life in prison."

"Nonsense."

She simply didn't know how to respond to that kind of inane reasoning, so she didn't even try.

"You're making too big a deal out of this, Maci. But if it'll make you feel better, I promise it won't happen again."

"I wish I could believe you, Seymour," she said in a tired voice, "but I can't."

"Sure you can. I'll prove it to you."

Yeah, right. Unwittingly, the thought struck her that leaving Seymour might not be a bad idea. No. Under the circumstances, if anyone went anywhere, it would be him. Telling him to take a hike had never looked more appealing.

Then she thought of Jonah.

Sick at heart, she turned and made her way toward the door.

"Where do you think you're going?"

Maci whirled around and simply looked at him, thinking about how pathetic he was. "Away from you," she said, "before I say or do something we'll both regret."

Fifteen

Buck Collier, a lean and wiry worker, sat in a bar nursing a drink, feeling courageous enough to take on a grizzly bear and win, especially since he'd consumed several beers. While fiddling with his near-empty bottle, he faced the entrance only then to lunge to his feet.

His hand was already extended as his friend strode up to him. "Long time no see, good buddy," he said.

Buck had asked Sid Altman to meet him for a beer at a bar near where Sid worked as an investigator for an attorney. Now, as he gave his friend the once-over, he noted that Sid looked like he always had. Same weight, same heavy-lidded green eyes, same hairstyle.

Oops, wrong there. On closer observation, Sid had lost a considerable amount of his hair. To counteract the loss, he had combed some across from the side over the bald spot, then lacquered it down. Not a pretty sight, Buck thought. But how Sid wore his hair was none of his business.

"Yeah. Too long, in fact," Sid said with ease, taking a seat in the chair across from Buck.

"I really appreciate you taking the time to meet me," Buck said.

"No problem."

"Is beer still your choice of drink?"

"You bet."

Buck signaled the waitress, then pointed to his beer and held up two fingers. "So how are things?" he asked, facing Sid again.

"Can't complain." Sid touched a lacquered spot on his head as if to make sure it was still in place.

Buck withheld a smile. "That's good."

"What's with you? I gather this invitation isn't just for old times' sake."

"You're right," Buck said, his stomach starting to churn, which meant he needed another beer badly.

"Wanna bullshit awhile or get down to the nitty-gritty?"

"Let's enjoy a beer."

Sid shrugged his shoulders. "You're calling the shots."

About that time the waitress arrived with the drinks. Buck watched as Sid downed half of his in one huge gulp. Buck's brows came together in a frown, thinking he wanted Sid sober as a judge to hear what he had to say.

Then he relaxed, remembering that his friend had a high tolerance for liquor and could drink until the cows came home and one would never know it. He envied Sid that ability. A few beers and he was looped. Realizing that he was getting close to that now, Buck took one more sip then pushed his away. He needed to be sharp and in control.

"Is there something wrong?" Sid asked after swiping his hand across his mouth.

"With the beer?"

"Yeah."

Buck grinned. "Nah. It's just that I had a few before you got here."

Sid smiled, then said, "You always were a cheap drunk."

"And I used to want to smack you because you weren't."

"Ah, for those good old days when all we had to do was drink beer and chase women."

Buck chuckled. "That's been so long ago I've forgotten what it was like."

"Hell, I haven't."

"Wish you were still that free and young?"

"And stupid," Sid pointed out, topping off his next sip of beer with a belch.

"Stupid works."

Both men laughed heartily, then Sid sobered. "So what's up with you?"

"Have you read the papers lately?" Buck asked, priming the pump, so to speak.

"About the great Dr. Seymour Ramsey getting arrested? Who hasn't. That rocked this town back on its heels."

"That wasn't what I had in mind," Buck snapped, then made an attempt to temper his next words. "I saw that, of course, but since it had nothing to do with me, I didn't pay it much mind. Anyway, it's no big deal. People like Ramsey aren't held accountable for their wrongs." His tone was bitter but he didn't care.

After Sid gave him a rather strange look, he signaled the waitress himself this time. When she whipped over to their table, he looked back at Buck. "You want an extra for posterity?"

Buck didn't hesitate. "Might as well." So he got drunk. His wife wouldn't care. She was too busy with the kids. Just as long as he didn't wrap his truck around a telephone pole somewhere and end up in jail. That would cost him his job. He couldn't afford that, especially now.

For a moment, they sipped in companionable silence.

"I guess I must've missed the article you're referring to," Sid said at last.

"There was another murder about the same time."

Sid wrinkled his brow as though deep in thought. "Seems like I did see something about a woman who'd taken a tumble down the stairs, though I can't begin to remember any details."

"She wasn't just any woman." Buck cleared his throat.

"Oh?"

"She was my twin sister."

"Damn, Buck, I had no idea."

Buck shrugged. "I know, and that's okay. I didn't expect you to."

"Hell, I'm sorry."

"Me, too," Buck responded, infusing more bitterness into his tone. "She was a good woman."

"I'm sure she was."

Buck could tell that Sid was sympathetic, yet he was also confused and appeared uncomfortable. But so was he. He still couldn't believe Rachel was dead. Discussing it seemed to make it real where before he'd kept telling himself it was a bad nightmare from which he'd soon awaken.

"I wish there was something I could do to help," Sid said.

"Maybe there is."

Sid raised an eyebrow.

"I hope you won't think I'm taking advantage of our friendship..." Buck let his voice trail off, suddenly embarrassed.

"Not at all. So start talking."

Buck took consecutive sips of his beer, needing more courage to continue than he'd imagined, especially since a big lump was lodged in his throat that not even the beer could wash down.

"Are you asking for my help?" Sid pressed. "Is that what this is all about?"

"In the beginning, it was just to pick your brain as an investigator."

"And now?"

"I actually want to hire you."

Sid looked taken aback. "Hire me?"

"That's right." Buck's tone didn't budge.

"As a rule, I don't do outside investigative work. The firm keeps me too busy. In fact, I've been out of town more lately than I've been in. That's another reason why I'm out of the loop."

"I was afraid of that," Buck said, not bothering to hide his disappointment.

Sid was quiet for moment, his eyes narrowed, as though he was warring with his conscience.

Buck could only hope.

"Suppose you tell me what happened."

Buck felt his stomach uncoil. "The kids were gone and Rachel was home alone with her husband. He said he took the dog for a long walk and when he returned she lay dead at the foot of the stairs, like she'd tumbled down the stairs accidentally."

"And pigs fly," Sid muttered.

"My thought exactly."

"What do the cops say?" Sid asked.

"They arrested her husband for murder."

"Sounds pretty cut-and-dried."

"That's what I'm banking on," Buck said, gnawing slightly on the inside of his left cheek.

"Who's the husband?"

"Lucas Tom Sanders."

Sid's eyes widened.

"You know him?"

"Not well, but I do know him. Still, I didn't realize he was married to your sister."

"No reason for you to."

"I could argue the other way and say this town's not that big, that I should've known because we're friends."

Buck waved the air with an impatient hand. "Hell, we all live in our own insulated worlds."

"Still, with my kind of job, I'm usually in better touch with what's going on."

"You know twins are like joined at the hip."

"So I've heard," Sid commented, "which means it's gotta be doubly hard on you having lost her."

"It's making me crazy."

"What's really gnawing at you, Buck?"

"I'm that easy to read, huh?"

"No, like I told you earlier, I figured you weren't interested in friendly chitchat at the neighborhood bar."

"I was serious when I told you I wanted to hire you."

"You may be serious but only because you're drunk."

Buck straightened, slightly offended. "You don't know that."

"Sure I do and so do you. No matter, I'll repeat myself. I don't work independently."

Buck felt his hope fade. "I heard you." However, he wasn't ready to give up.

"And even if I did moonlight, the cops are apparently on top of it. You said Sanders had been arrested, right?"

"Well, I guess he hasn't actually been arrested. Not enough evidence."

"Mmm, that puts a different spin on things."

Buck leaned forward. "I want this to be a slam-dunk case, and it's not."

"I don't know the particulars, of course."

"Neither do I. That's why I want you to do some snooping."

Sid shook his head. "No can do, my friend. You just let the law work."

"I don't trust the law," Buck spat. "If Sanders beats this, I'll kill the bastard myself. I swear I will."

"Hey, hold on a minute." Sid's tone was fiercely adamant. "That kind of talk's no good. It'll land *you* behind bars."

"I've got some money."

"Aw, hell, Buck, I don't want your money."

"Then please, I'm begging you, just see what you can find out. With your expertise, that'll be a no-brainer."

"Who's his lawyer?" Sid asked in a resigned, but glum tone. "I know he's not from our firm."

"I don't remember, but I guess it doesn't matter. I heard that Lucas fired him."

"That's odd, since the case seems to be going his way."

"Well, he's up to something. You can count on it."

"Do you know if he ever abused your sister?"

Buck looked startled. "If he did, Rachel never said anything."

"But since you two are...were so close, you would've known." Another statement of fact.

"Absolutely. We didn't have any secrets from each other." Once he said that, Buck wondered if he was being incredibly naive or just didn't want to face the truth. There were things in his life that he hadn't shared with Rachel but nothing that smacked of anything as serious as abuse.

"Did she work?" Sid asked.

"Damn straight. For a big investment company."

"Mmm, that's interesting." Sid paused and took a swig of his beer, then lightly belched.

"What are you saying?"

"Hey, rein it in," Sid responded. "I'm not saying anything since I haven't read the charges."

"But I can tell you're interested."

"Only because she's your sister."

"I meant it," Buck said. "I'm not above begging."

Sid threw up his hands. "I guess I can check into it for you. I have a friend on the force."

"I'll—"

Sid interrupted. "But there's a condition."

"What?"

"That you won't mention paying me again."

"If that's the way you want it," Buck replied in earnest.

"That's the only way it can be."

"Again, I just gotta make sure the bastard gets what's coming to him," Buck said with heat. "And even though I feel good about the way things are going now, there's no guarantee that tomorrow the pendulum won't swing in Lucas's favor."

"As far as that goes," Sid said in a flippant tone, "tomorrow may never come."

"Shit, you know what I mean." Buck knew he was slurring his words. But did he care? Not in the least. He hadn't tied one on in a long time and it felt good.

"You can't drive home," Sid said in a half-teasing, half-disgusted tone.

"Aw, sure I can. Now that I've got you on my side, I can do anything I damn well please." Buck managed not to slur one word of that sentence.

"I don't know if your besotted brain will soak this up or not, but I may end up chasing my tail."

Buck picked up his beer and drained the bottle. Grinning, he sat it down on the table, then gave Sid a thumbs-up. "That won't happen. You're the best."

Sixteen

Holt knew he should go to the mansion and crash, yet he didn't make a move in that direction. Bushed was too mild a word to describe how he felt. Run over by a Mack truck actually nailed it. He'd gone virtually two nights without sleep. Oh, maybe he'd dozed for an hour or two during that time, though he wouldn't bet anything important on it.

Every time he closed his eyes, his thoughts swirled around in his mind. At this point, his brain was his own worst enemy which made him one miserable son of a bitch.

He should've stayed in a hotel. Wild dogs shouldn't have dragged him back to his old home. And once he'd realized who Maci was he should have left.

Since his mother's suicide, the house gave him the creeps anyway. Again, if he'd used his head, he wouldn't be in this situation. He'd be shacking up on his boat.

Deep down he knew that was exactly why he'd opted not to sail here. It would have been too easy to leave.

The two days since he'd been away from the mansion camping out on the sofa in his office hadn't been all for naught. He'd gotten a lot accomplished. He cleared his files of all the old cases that were pending. As a result of those efforts, he had a stack of billing invoices for Marianne to send out. She'd love that, he thought with more of a smirk than a smile.

Whether or not any money would result from those efforts remained to be seen, but he wasn't worried about that. What he earned from representing Lucas Tom Sanders should fund his next sailing venture and then some.

Besides, he wasn't totally broke. He had the trust fund his mother left him, though he swore he'd never touch it except in a emergency. So far, he'd dodged that sort of emergency. He'd even forgotten how much it was worth and didn't care. The only importance money played in his life right now was as a means of feeding his habit. Maintaining a sailboat was not cheap.

Holt made his way to the tiny kitchen at the rear of his office suite. Once he'd opened the fridge, he hesitated, looking at the bottles of beer there. His hand itched to reach in and grab one, but he refrained. He'd had more booze over the past days than his body could tolerate. Yet he hadn't been able to keep his demons at bay.

He closed the door with a savage thrust only to jerk it back open and reach for a beer. To hell with it. It was nearing dusk. It wasn't as if he was drinking at eight-thirty in the morning. At least not this morning, he reminded himself ruefully.

After downing the beer in record time, Holt paused, then thought to hell with it and reached for another one, nursing it on the way back to his inner sanctum. His gaze went immediately to his desk where he noted with a sense of pride that the only files there were Seymour's and Lucas's. Next to them both was a stack of law books.

No doubt, his work was cut out for him. Both cases were different but equally difficult. It would take every ounce of brain matter and concentration he possessed to try both cases. And win.

He had to keep his mind off Maci.

He felt sick and for a second, the beer actually tasted sour. With disgust, he plopped the bottle down on his desk before plopping himself on the sofa. He bent and cradled his head in his hands.

Holt knew the real reason he hadn't gone back to the mansion was her. Since she had slapped him, he'd been nursing a hard-on for two different reasons—one from fury and one from lust.

When he'd accidentally stumbled upon her that evening, looking graceful, elegant and gorgeous in that slinky cocktail dress, he felt like he'd slammed into a mirror and slashed his gut into a million pieces.

Her dynamite shaped body aside, the vision of her oval face framed by that cap of ebony hair, deep dark eyes, high cheekbones, moist, plump lips and porcelain skin made him think of a saint.

But she was no saint, he reminded himself.

His hand unwittingly touched the jaw she'd slapped. A groan overpowered a curse as he fell back against the cushion and continued to massage that jaw. He had to hand it to her, she was no lightweight, though to look at her, one would never know that.

He suspected boiling fury had given her the power she needed to punch him. When he'd made that inappropriate comment he saw the anger rise in her chest. Her breasts had heaved, ripening her nipples to full potential.

It had been all he could do not to say to hell with the consequences, grab her, pull her dress down, push her onto the hardwood floor and make hard love to her.

That thought brought Holt to his feet with a lunge, and he stomped to the window where he massaged his neck muscles until he felt the kinks give way.

"Man, you look like death warmed over."

At the sound of the unexpected voice, Holt whirled, his gaze locked in a fierce frown.

Vince shrugged. "I saw the light and the door was open. Need I say more?"

"Since you're here, you might as well come on in."

"Thanks for such a warm welcome."

"That's in return for telling me I looked like a walking corpse."

"Do you disagree?" Vince asked, sauntering into the room and sitting down.

"No." The word came out in a snarl.

Vince chuckled. "Got any more beer?"

"You know the answer to that." Holt's tone was sullen.

Vince chuckled again. "I'll help myself. You ready for another one?"

"Not yet."

"Sounds and looks like you could use one in each hand."

Holt merely glared at him.

"Okay, so I'll shut up," Vince said, walking out of the office. Seconds later, he returned with a long-neck bottle.

"What's up?" Holt asked, forcing himself to be civil.

But it was hard. He wasn't fit company for anyone. The thought of making conversation, even if it didn't have to be polite, irked him. Yet Vince's unexpected appearance had at least severed his thoughts of Maci.

"Not anything, really," Vince said, hooking a booted ankle across his knee.

"Thought maybe you had something for me."

Vince shook his head. "Not yet, though it's not from the lack of trying."

"Meaning?"

"Meaning Dr. Ward Chastain, who assisted Seymour, was in surgery when I paid a visit to the hospital."

"What about the nurse and anesthesiologist?"

"I'm getting there. Nurse Dawn Gilbert was and still is on her five days off and doesn't answer her door or her phone. The anesthesiologist, Dr. James Hancock, clearly wasn't interested in talking to me."

"Think he knows something?" Holt asked.

"More than he wants to share, that's for sure."

"Here's hoping that includes the police."

"Oh, I suspect it does."

"Keep at 'em," Holt said. "If there's a crack in their conscience, I want to know it first."

"What about you? You have any better luck?"

Holt made a face.

"Hello?" Vince said, making a face. "With your buddy, the M.E."

Holt walked back to his desk, reached for his beer and took a swig. "I struck out as well. He's on vacation."

"How convenient."

"Don't worry," Holt said. "I'll corner him the second he gets back."

"I noticed you cleaned off your desk," Vince said, changing the subject.

"Tomorrow is D-day for getting back to work."

"Ah, so we have a plan."

"For what it's worth."

Vince gave him a long, hard look. "What's eating at you, really? When I said you looked like death, I meant it. But more than that, you're distracted as hell."

Holt let go of a weary sigh. "It's something I just can't talk about."

"But it has to do with your old man, right?"

"Yes," he said, lying with such ease that it frightened him. Still, the idea of letting Vince or anyone else in on his secret concerning Maci was repugnant.

Vince pushed to feet. "If you don't get some sleep, you won't be worth doodley squat when it comes to getting Seymour out of his jam."

"Seymour's not my only concern."

Vince looked taken aback. "How so?"

"I've agreed to represent a friend on a capital murder charge."

"That friend wouldn't happen to be Lucas Sanders, would it?"

"How'd you know?"

"Just took a wild guess."

"Well, you guessed right."

"Have you lost your mind?"

Holt jammed his hand down into his pockets. "Probably."

"From what I hear, he's as guilty as they come."

"I don't think he is."

Vince's head popped back. "You don't?"

"Nope, but I'm not in the mood to discuss that case right now, not when my head feels like one big cotton ball, and not from too much booze either. It's lack of sleep."

"Hey, you don't have to convince me."

"Then get your fat ass out of here."

"I will, but only if your narrow ass follows."

Holt glared him. "Dammit, I don't need a keeper."

"I think you do." Vince's tone was adamant.

"Go to hell," Holt muttered, joining his friend at the door where he switched off the light. "Satisfied now?"

Vince stood his ground. "Not until you shower, shave and get some sleep."

Holt didn't bother to respond.

One more load and Maci would be finished.

Since Seymour had a meeting at the hospital this evening and wouldn't be home until late, time appeared to be on her side. Still, she wasn't taking any chances.

He'd presented her with a gift she wasn't about to squander.

His absence couldn't have come at a better time, especially since it gave her the perfect opportunity to move out of their suite into another guest room down the hall. The only imperfect factor was that now she was closer to Holt's room than Jonah's. But after she'd caught Seymour high on drugs the other night, she couldn't bear to sleep in the same room with him much less the same bed.

And the thought of him touching her was clearly out of the question until he proved to her that he could be trusted. If his most recent behavior was anything to judge by, her worst fear was fast becoming reality. Seymour would never be drug free. She would probably never trust him again.

The phrase *once hooked always hooked* constantly nagged her.

She was in for a fight. Vacating their suite would infuriate Seymour, but she wouldn't let that stop her. She had to hold on to her sanity because of Jonah. She couldn't fall apart and take care of him. Their baby had given her the strength she needed to make the critical decision to follow through.

Too, she wanted to get Seymour's attention, make him see that he couldn't play with her emotions, that when he made a promise to her, she expected him to keep it.

If not, there would be consequences.

For her, too, she reminded herself, hanging the bundle of clothes in the closet. He could demand that she return to their bedroom or else. While she knew what that "else" would be, she refused to think about it.

With the perilous position he was in, Maci was gambling on him wanting to keep up appearances, portray that everything was okay on the homefront. After all, a loving and sympathetic wife went a long way with a jury. But could she play such a role?

"Mrs. Ramsey, what on earth are you doing?"

Maci paused in her thoughts and stared at the housekeeper, whose eyes were wide with shock. "Exactly what it looks like."

"But—"

When it was apparent that further words had jammed in her throat, Maci gave her what she hoped was a confident smile. "It's going to be all right. There's nothing for you to worry about."

"Why didn't you ask for help?" Annie's tone registered horror.

"Because you have enough to do as it is."

"Oh, but—"

"It's okay, Annie," Maci interrupted. "Just know that what I'm doing is best for now."

"I understand, but I want to help."

"But I don't need your help," Maci said in a firm but kind tone.

"Yes, ma'am."

"And please don't say anything about this to anyone, not that my actions will remain a secret. However, I'd rather it not be discussed out of hand."

"Of course," Annie responded, sounding quite offended that Maci might think otherwise.

"I'll see you at dinner."

Annie merely nodded, then left.

A frown marred Maci's forehead as she returned to the suite for the last load, aware that moving into separate living quarters would cause another stir in the household. Still, she hadn't planned on it being this evening. She had hoped to get moved and settled before anyone was the wiser.

Except her husband, of course.

Now, however, it was too late. She just hoped Annie would heed her words. She wanted Seymour to hear the news from her, not from the help.

Her makeup bag was the last item. Maci grabbed it, and without bothering to look around, scurried out of the room and back down the hall into her new bedroom.

She wanted to put away all her personal as well as professional items. This room, though large, was not anywhere near the size of the master suite or nearly as luxurious.

She would make do. At this juncture, her well-being was more important than comfort.

A noise startled her from behind. Thinking it was Annie again, she whipped around prepared to reprimand her for further intruding. Only it wasn't the housekeeper who had crossed the threshold.

"*You,*" she mouthed, watching as Holt stepped deeper into the room and closed the door behind him.

Seventeen

Holt didn't respond.

Instead he paused in the middle of the room and stared at her through the heavily lashed eyes most women would kill for. She wanted to look away, but she couldn't. His probing gaze held her rooted to the spot. She tried to swallow; she couldn't do that either. Her mouth was too dry.

As always, he looked so good.

Dangerously good.

His rumpled attire heightened the sense of capricious danger he exuded. Although a misshapen blue T-shirt hung on his broad shoulders, nothing could mask the outline of the rippled muscles in his upper torso, and though his slacks were loose fitting, his narrow hips and powerful legs were obvious. The blond strands of his hair were tousled, and his unshaven face looked tired and drawn.

Holt cleared his throat. "Can we talk?"

"About what?"

She saw his eyes scan the room before returning to her. "I think that's obvious."

"Is it?"

She was stalling for time, which was so wrong. What she should be doing was ordering him out of her room. Her instincts told her he wouldn't balk. Holt didn't have to beg for women's favors. A more likely scenario was that he had to beat them off.

Yet she wasn't one of his women, she reminded herself with brutal frankness. So why was he still here?

"Yes, it is," he said breaking the simmering silence. "So why have you moved out of the master suite?"

"That's none of your business." In spite of her efforts her voice faltered.

"You're right, it isn't."

"But you still want to know." Maci's flat statement was barely audible.

"Yes."

"Why?"

His eyes continued to probe. Even deeper. "You know the answer to that."

"You shouldn't be here." Her heart pounded.

"I know that, too."

Her whole body weakened at that admission.

"I don't want to argue with you." Holt's tone was bleak.

"Nor do I."

"Then talk to me." His voice dropped to a husky pitch.

"Holt—" He shouldn't be here, in her room, with the door closed, shutting them off from the world.

"What's this move all about?" he pressed.

Maci wished she could continue to act dumb, but she couldn't. To do so would be wasted effort. He was no idiot. The room was a dead giveaway strewn as it was with clothes everywhere.

She exhaled with a troubled sigh.

"There has to be a reason for this."

"There is."

"So tell me." He paused. "Please."

Again she hesitated.

"Did he hurt you?" The huskiness in his voice was now laced with controlled anger.

"No. At least not physically."

"You caught him high again, didn't you?"

She nodded, her throat suddenly too full to speak.

"Why, that son of a bitch."

"I don't know why I'm telling you this."

"Because I'm his attorney, for one."

"And his son for another."

"Don't remind me," Holt spat harshly.

"He promised me he'd stop."

"Famous last words."

"I wanted to believe him, to trust him again." Maci's tone was filled with an agony she couldn't mask.

"And now you can't—trust him, that is—so you moved out."

"I just thought he needed some incentive to do the right thing."

"Like depriving him of sex?"

Maci sucked in her breath and stared at him.

As if he sensed how fragile she was, he closed the distance between them and stood close enough to touch her. Her eyes landed below his belt to the impressive bulge behind his zipper.

Instantly, she felt her stomach tighten and her nipples

harden. And while that was bad enough, it was the heat that pulsed between her legs that panicked her. She backed up. Dear Lord, it was frightening how much sexual power this man had over her.

"Will you be all right?"

"Yes."

"Are you sure?" he rasped.

"I'll bounce back."

"Was he stoned?"

"I really don't want to talk about this anymore," she said. What she really didn't want was for him to stand so close to her that the male scent of his body, punctuated by the thin sheen of sweat on his face, made her ache to feel his arms around her, holding her, comforting her.

She stepped farther back and swallowed hard.

"I'm not going to touch you."

"I wouldn't let you."

For a second, she thought he might test her. But he didn't. "Again, this is none of your business," she managed to say.

"Wrong. Anything and everything to do with Seymour is my business."

"Not this. This is personal and doesn't concern you."

"Does he know you've moved out?" Holt demanded, ignoring her jab.

"Not yet," she answered before she thought.

Holt expelled a weary sigh. "Seymour will likely be furious."

"I expect he will."

"Are you prepared for the consequences?"

"Meaning am I prepared to lose my gravy train? Isn't that what you're asking?"

"No, dammit, it isn't."

"Oh, I think it is."

His nostrils flared in anger. "You don't know what I think."

"Go away, Holt." Her voice was low and weary. "Out of our lives."

"Seems like we've had this conversation before."

She took a shuddering breath.

"Which means you haven't told Seymour you asked me to leave."

Since she had no suitable comeback or defense, she remained silent.

"Anyway, it's too late," he said in a tormented tone.

"No, it isn't."

"I can't go back on my word."

"Your mother's dead."

His jaw compressed and he glared at her.

"I'm not to blame for what happened between your mother and father," Maci added.

"Dammit, I told you—" She could feel his breathing on her face as he towered over her.

"You don't have the right to tell me anything." She paused. "And furthermore you don't have any right to be in this room."

"Except that you want me here." His voice lowered to almost nothing.

She reeled as if he'd hit her. "That's a lie."

"Prove it," he challenged in a low deep voice, moving towards her again, slowly, deliberately, like a panther stalking its prey.

Fear, anxiety, remorse and excitement all clogged Maci's throat and she couldn't say a word. As if her silence gave him the green light he needed, Holt grabbed her by the arm and yanked her against him.

"This has been too long in coming," he whispered, slanting his mouth across hers.

At first, Maci froze, then the feel of his taut muscles against her, the feel of his lips, brought back the night on the beach with such heat and intense longing that a whimper escaped and she slumped against him.

Taking advantage of her weakness and her moist, parted lips, his kiss was ravishing in its hunger, intensifying until she thought he might pull her very soul from her. When she could no longer stand on her own, she looped her arms around his neck and their bodies almost became one as she felt every plane, every angle of his hard frame.

It was when his hands cupped her buttocks and he began rubbing his throbbing penis against her that her sanity returned. Was she about to have sex with her stepson under his father's roof?

"No," she moaned into his lips, prepared to fight him off if she had to.

She didn't. He let her go so unexpectedly that she almost lost her balance. For more than several beats, speech was impossible for both of them as their breathing was hard and erratic.

"Thanks," he said harshly, "for stopping me from doing something I'd regret."

He turned, walked to the door, then slammed it behind him.

"I wish you'd come clean."

"What did you say?" Holt demanded, anger in his tone.

Vince shrugged. "You heard me."

"You should get in the habit of minding your own business."

Vince chuckled. "Something's gotta be squeezing your balls big time because you've been in a foul mood the last two times I've seen you. And by the way, don't you ever shave anymore?"

"I wouldn't push my luck if I were you."

"'Cause you might fire me?" Vince's chuckle deepened. "Go ahead. I'm only here as a favor to you."

"You're a lying s.o.b., too. You're here for the money."

"You calling my bluff?" Vince tone sobered and his eyes narrowed.

"Ah, hell, Hillyard, sit down and give it a rest."

"I've been trying to," Vince declared, "but it ain't easy, when you're walking around with a hard-on."

Holt turned away so that Vince couldn't read his expression and see just how close he'd come to the truth. Ever since his last verbal skirmish with Maci, his insides had been as tender as raw meat and his nerves shot. As a result, he'd gotten almost zilch done.

All because of his obsession for his father's wife, a woman he could never have.

"Does your hard-on have to do with a woman?" Vince probed, shattering the silence.

"Didn't you hear what I just said?" Holt's tone was terse.

Vince threw up his hands as if in surrender. "Okay, if that's the way you want to play it. But—"

"I know what you're going to say. I need to get my head out of my ass and get to work."

"I couldn't have put it any better myself."

Holt changed the subject. "Before we talk about the Sanders case, is there anything new on Seymour?"

"I finally spoke to Dr. Chastain and Nurse Gilbert."

"And?"

"Like their cohort the anesthesiologist, they weren't forthcoming. But—" Vince paused.

"Something tells me I'm not going to like the rest of this story."

"Probably not, as I'm still convinced the nurse is plum scared and that it's just a matter of time until she cracks."

Holt pulled a face, then muttered sarcastically, "That's encouraging."

"On the other hand, the doctor's a different matter altogether. If he knows anything, he's keeping it close to his chest."

"Well, let's hope they stay mum and unshakable."

"Again, that's not likely," Vince said in a discouraging tone, "especially with Nurse Gilbert."

"Any suggestions as to how we can fix that?"

"Yeah, pray."

Holt rolled his eyes, then changed the subject. "Anything on the Dodson family?"

"Ah, might have struck gold there," Vince said with renewed confidence. "Old man Dodson has a history of medical problems. In fact, one of his favorite pastimes was going to the hospital."

"Meaning he was either one unhealthy bastard or a bona fide hypochondriac?"

"Right."

"If it was the former," Holt said, "then his physical

condition might have been such that he shouldn't have undergone surgery."

"If that's the case, Seymour should've told him, which makes him that much more culpable."

"Not necessarily," Holt exclaimed. "What if Seymour told him the risks and Dodson opted for the surgery anyway?"

"That's certainly food for thought."

"So work that food group for all it's worth," Holt ordered, "starting with Dodson's close friends."

"Will do."

"Meanwhile, I'll get Dodson's medical records from Seymour and Dodson's other doctors."

"Sounds like a plan to me."

Holt rubbed the back of his neck, fighting off the anxiety and fatigue that had plagued him since he arrived back in town. Both threatened to undermine his good sense and his ability to reason.

"So what about Lucas Sanders?" Vince asked.

"What about him?"

"You're still going to defend him?"

"I told you that already," Holt said with impatience.

"I know, but I thought maybe you might have had a change of heart."

Holt remained silent.

"My philosophy is that if you know going in that your head's likely to be under water, then don't jump in."

"In his case, your philosophy sucks."

Vince gave a nonchalant shrug. "Don't say I didn't warn you."

"You want to be paid, don't you?"

Vince gave him a look.

"Then I suggest you don't look a gift horse in the mouth, my friend."

"He plunked down big bucks, huh?"

"My head's not so far up my ass I'd let him get out of here with anything less."

Vince laughed. "I don't agree—about where your head is—but we'll discuss that another time. So what's next on the agenda?"

"Start the ball rolling on the Sanders case. Here's a copy of the police report." Holt handed the manilla folder to Vince. "What they have is circumstantial."

"Which has put many an innocent man away for life."

"All the more reason why you need to find out who really took Rachel Sanders's life."

Vince stood. "That's a tall order."

"That it is."

"So you still think Lucas is innocent?"

Holt's eyes remained steady. "Unlike my father, yes I do."

Eighteen

"Son."

Seymour calling him son more than surprised Holt. But he kept his cool and forced himself to show no reaction. He also forced himself to look at his father who was standing in the doorway to the study dressed in a suit that exuded opulence.

Yet no matter how stylish his clothes, they couldn't hide the fact that he'd had a few tough days and nights. The lines around Seymour's eyes and mouth were more pronounced, and his skin was ashen in color.

Holt bet he knew the main reason his father appeared so worn-out. No man, who apparently still loved his wife, would cotton to having her move out of their bedroom.

He almost smiled. He wished he could have witnessed the confrontation between his father and stepmother. It couldn't have been a pretty scene. Even though he hadn't seen Maci since their confrontation, he had no doubt who had won the first round.

Underneath her grace and elegance was a woman

who was strong-willed and knew her own mind as well as any man. He ought to know. He'd been on the receiving end of her feistiness. His cheek had smarted for hours after she'd slapped him. He was lucky she hadn't hit him again after he'd kissed her.

"Have you got a minute?" Seymour asked.

Holt heard the uncertainty in his father's voice and for a second felt a twinge of sympathy, only to remind himself that Seymour didn't deserve sympathy. His father had brought his troubles on himself by making stupid choices.

"Sure," Holt said with an ease he was far from feeling. He couldn't continue to avoid Seymour, not if he was going to adequately represent him. He also had to discuss the issue of the drugs.

Yet when Holt followed Seymour into the study, he felt like Daniel must have felt when he entered the lion's den.

"Would you care for some breakfast?" Seymour asked, indicating the plate of scones and muffins on a tray. Beside the tray was a carafe of coffee.

"Coffee's all I want." Holt didn't really want that, but it would keep his hands busy and off Seymour's throat. Would there ever come a day when he could let go of that festering hate for the man who'd bred him?

The fact that his father was married to Maci kept knocking the scab off that old wound. Just the thought of her and Seymour sharing a bed filled him with revulsion.

Once he had a cup in hand, Holt stood against the mantel and blew on the hot coffee to cool it.

"I've been suspended," Seymour said, his voice a tad unsteady.

Holt raised his eyebrows. "Are you surprised?"

"Of course," Seymour snapped. "After all I've done for that hospital, that's the thanks I get."

"You're under criminal investigation. Need I remind you of that?"

"No, dammit, you don't." Seymour paused and took a deep breath. "Look, I didn't call you in here to argue with you."

"I'm listening." Holt's tone was hard, determined to cut him no slack.

"I told you I wanted to be kept informed."

He paused and Holt moved in. "And I told you when I had something you needed to know, I'd tell you."

Seymour's lips thinned. "You're enjoying every minute of this aren't you?"

"I thought you didn't want to argue."

"I don't." Seymour's tone suddenly sounded weary. "So are you working on my defense?"

"Yes," Holt admitted with reservation "I have a P.I. checking out several angles."

Seymour's features brightened. "That's a start."

"Were you aware of all Dodson's medical problems?"

"Of course, but I wasn't his primary care physician."

"But as his surgeon," Holt pressed, "you had to know if he was a high risk for surgery."

"That's right and I told him that, too."

"His response?"

Seymour shrugged. "He wanted the surgery anyway."

"Can you prove that?"

Seymour gave him a strange look. "If you mean is that particular statement in writing, no. Where are you going with this, anyway?"

"Maybe nowhere. But I'll need a list of his other doctors."

"That's no problem. Is there anything else I can do?" Seymour asked, reaching for a scone and biting into it.

"Yes. You can lay off the drugs."

All the color receded from Seymour's face and he said in a huffy tone, "I don't know what you're talking about."

"Don't play games with me, or I'll hightail it out of here." Fury shook Holt's voice. "I swear to God, I will."

"You're looking for a reason to do that anyway."

"Did you hear what I said? Lay off the drugs."

"How did you know?"

"I have my ways."

"Maci told you, didn't she?" His tone was tight with resentment. "She had no right."

"Oh, please," Holt rebutted with sarcasm. "She had every right. She's your wife, for god's sake. And I'm your attorney."

"Did she also tell you she'd moved out of our suite?"

Seymour's tone and expression were pointedly harsh. Did his father suspect something? For a second, Holt's gut clenched. Then he relaxed. Nah. His guilty conscience was just coming into play. Still, he let the question slide, realizing he was treading on slippery ground.

Seymour must never guess he and Maci had a past. And not because he wanted to protect her, either. He didn't want any more complications in his own life. It was twisted enough already.

"Holt, I asked you a question."

"No, she didn't," he said in a brusque tone. He hadn't

lied either. He'd caught her in the act, which was not the same. He wasn't about to let Seymour rake him over the coals about his wife or anything else.

"Look, I gotta go."

"Don't, not yet," Seymour responded.

"Why?" Holt asked, poised for flight.

"I have a favor to ask."

Another one, don't you mean? Holt thought as he let go of an impatient breath. "I'm listening."

"I insist on getting this over with."

"Meaning?"

"I want to go to trial as soon as possible."

"That's my call."

Seymour stiffened. "It's my life, my future hanging in the balance. Not yours, which makes it *my* call."

"There are no guarantees, Seymour, certainly not with a speedy trial."

Seymour blew out an unsteady breath. "I see."

"You don't, but that's okay."

A thundering silence fell over the room.

"I wish you'd lighten up," Seymour said. "I—"

"I suggest you don't go there. When we're together, business is all that needs to be discussed."

"Not quite." Seymour's tone was grim.

Holt bristled, but before he could reply Seymour continued, "Back to Maci."

"What about her?" Holt asked, his gut clenching.

"I don't want you hanging around her. I know your reputation with women, and she's off-limits."

Holt snorted. "You gotta be kidding. That gold-digging bitch is the last person I'd want."

This time it was Seymour who bristled. "I suggest

you show more respect when you speak of my wife." His voice was on a tight rein.

"And I suggest we shut this topic of conversation down as well."

Seymour paused as though he wanted to challenge Holt, but he wisely changed the subject. "You will see what you can do about getting a speedy trial?"

"I'll look into it, but don't hold your breath." Holt then walked over to Seymour and got as close to his face as he could stomach. With his teeth bared he spat, "Meanwhile, you stay the hell away from drugs. If not, don't depend on me to keep your unhappy ass out of the slammer." He poked Seymour in the chest. "'Cause it ain't gonna happen."

"Are you serious?"

"Yes, Bobbi, I'm serious."

"But why would you want to rent an office when you have an ideal spot to work at home?"

Maci paused before answering. She was on her way to the mansion following a meeting with a Realtor when Bobbi called her on her cell. Her friend was the first to know about her new plans.

"The why is a long story."

"I've got plenty of time," Bobbi said in an unhurried tone.

Maci sighed. "But I don't. I spent more time with a new client than I meant too. Jonah's not happy when his mommy's late."

"All the more reason why you shouldn't keep that precious darling waiting."

"I try not to, but sometimes it's necessary."

"Boy, you're really setting the woods on fire. How many new clients have you gotten lately?"

"Several, and I'm grateful."

"I am, too, because it keeps your hands and mind busy."

"And off my problems," Maci added with another sigh.

"So back to why you're interested in office space."

"I just think it will make what I do appear more professional." Which was only part of the reason for her sudden change in plans—a very minor part, actually. When she'd moved out of the master suite with its sitting room/office combination she no longer felt comfortable going back there to work when Seymour was gone.

Together with all that had been happening in her life lately, she needed a change. Between Seymour and Holt, her insides felt like they might explode at any time.

And when she thought about that kiss…

"You still there?"

"I'm here."

"You got quiet all of a sudden and with these cell phones, you never know."

"I can't believe you haven't heard from the adoption agency yet."

"Me, either," Bobbi said, sounding perturbed. "I'm getting as nervous as a cat on a hot tin roof."

"Chill. Everything's going along according to plan."

"It's just that I can't wait to have a precious darling of my own."

"I know you can't, dear friend," Maci said around a lump in her throat.

"You must be nearly home, so I'll let you go. But don't forget I want to see the new place."

"It's not a done deal yet. If and when it is, I'll holler."

"Later, then," Bobbi said, hanging up.

Glad to have both hands back on the wheel, Maci headed home with a sense of foreboding she couldn't shake. Then she thought about Jonah and her overburdened heart leaped with joy.

Maci stood at the window and watched as daylight slowly faded into twilight. She had just left Jonah's room after putting him down for the evening. Liz had returned from having the afternoon off, so Jonah was in good hands.

Her gaze wandered toward the bathroom. What she needed to counteract her exhaustion was a soak in a hot tub of bubble bath. But even that seemed too much of an effort. And even after spending those priceless hours with her son, she still hadn't been able to completely shake that sense of foreboding.

She couldn't stop thinking of Holt. And the fact that he had kissed her and she had kissed him back.

Feeling her stomach turn over, she placed a hand across it and squeezed. She wished she could throw up. Maybe that would help her feel cleansed again.

She had done exactly what she'd promised herself she wouldn't. But when Holt had grabbed her, his touch had ignited a flame that only he could put out by making love to her.

Since that hadn't and *wasn't* going to happen, she had come away from the encounter with a hunger for something and someone she couldn't have.

I hate you, Holt Ramsey, she said to herself.

But that wasn't completely true. Part of her did hate him for turning her into something she wasn't—a woman who craved sex for the sake of sex. She didn't love him. Just the thought almost stopped her heart. But she wanted him, wanted her *stepson* with every pulsating nerve in her body. How sick was that?

Even now she wanted to taste him again, to feel his erection against her, *inside her.* Maci's entire body suddenly clenched with another bout of hunger that almost sent her to her knees.

And to think a trial date hadn't even been set, which meant Holt wasn't going anywhere. She stifled her rising panic as she made her way toward the bathroom.

She was halfway there when the phone rang, stopping her midstride. Thinking it was probably Seymour telling her he was on his way home, she didn't bother to check the caller ID.

"Hello," she said without enthusiasm.

"Mrs. Ramsey this is Debbie."

"What's wrong?" It wasn't what her mother's sitter said but rather the tone of her voice that alerted Maci."

"I just called 911. Your mother has had some kind of seizure."

"I'll meet you at the E.R."

Maci grabbed her purse and flew down the stairs, straight into Holt's arms.

"Whoa," he said, clamping his hands around her upper arms and steadying her.

She took several gulping breaths of air before she peered up at him.

"What the hell, Maci?"

"It's…it's my mother," she said breathlessly.

"What about her?"

"I have to meet the ambulance at the hospital."

"Come on, I'll drive you. You're in no shape to drive yourself."

"But—"

"For once, don't argue, dammit," Holt said in a gruff voice.

For once, she didn't.

Nineteen

"Your mother is fine."

Maci wilted with relief, though she had suspected as much.

"Are you okay?" Holt asked.

Without looking at him, she nodded, then concentrated once again on the short, bespectacled doctor who stood in front of her. She had left Debbie in the E.R. cubicle with her mother so she could speak with him alone. Throughout the examination, Holt had remained outside the room, using the wall as a crutch for his big body.

Now, he stood beside her, much too close for comfort, but she didn't say anything. She hadn't wanted him to drive her to the hospital. But he had caught her when she'd been terribly frightened and vulnerable. As a result, her good judgment had been impaired.

"So it wasn't a stroke?" she asked at last.

"No, ma'am," Dr. Phillips said. "It was a petit mal seizure."

Maci released a sigh. "From the way her sitter described what had happened, I figured as much. But you can never be sure because Mother can't tell you."

The doctor shoved his glasses back onto the bridge of his nose. "Does she have those often?"

"No. I can't remember the last time she had one."

"But she has had seizures in the past?" Dr. Phillips probed, his eyes alert.

"Oh, yes," Maci responded. "They started when I was in high school. But the doctors could never come up with a definitive reason why. Anyhow, she's been on medication for years and to date it's worked."

"It either needs adjusting or changing," Dr. Phillips said, rubbing his jaw. "But just to be on the safe side, I'd like to keep her overnight and watch her. Especially since Dr. Chambers is out of town and I can't consult with him."

"So that's why he's not here," Maci commented, having asked the nurses to call her mother's primary care physician shortly after she and Holt had arrived.

"He should be back tomorrow. We'll see what he says."

"Is it really necessary to keep her?" Maci's voice faltered. "It's just that with her disease, she gets so disoriented when she's out of her home and normal routine."

"I understand where you're coming from. Still, I'd like to observe her overnight."

"Fine. I want to do what's best for her."

"The sitter is welcome to stay. In fact, I'd recommend that."

"Oh, I wouldn't dare let Debbie leave her." Maci's tone brooked no argument.

"I have to warn you it will be some time, maybe

even midnight, before we can transfer her to a room." The doctor frowned, denting his unlined forehead. "Actually, we're out of beds right now on all floors."

"Oh, dear." Maci didn't bother to hide her dismay.

"We can't pull any strings?" Holt asked, speaking for the first time.

His voice was so calm, but so deep and authoritative that both Maci and the doctor immediately looked at him. Before the doctor could take offense at Holt's arrogance and interference, Maci spoke up, "It's okay, Doctor. Mother won't know the difference. Please, just see that I'm notified when she's finally assigned a room. I'll tell the sitter that as well."

Dr. Phillips nodded, then gave Holt a look before turning and walking off. A silence followed his departure. Then keeping her eyes averted, Maci said, "I'll be right back."

"No hurry. Take all the time you need."

Without replying, she made her way back into the cubbyhole where her mother lay sleeping. Debbie rose. Maci shook her head. "Don't get up. How is she?"

"Seems to be resting comfortably." The sitter toyed with her lower lip. "Is she going to be all right?"

"Yes," Maci responded, squeezing the sitter on the shoulder while looking at her mother. She felt the sting of tears behind her eyes. It just wasn't fair, she told herself. Her mother didn't deserve this. Then blinking hard, she told Debbie what the doctor had ordered.

"I'll take care of her," Debbie said. "You don't worry."

"I won't. And thanks."

"If anything changes, you'll be the first to know."

Again, Maci felt so blessed to have Debbie who handled things with such calm and self-confidence that it bolstered Maci's spirits.

"I'll see you later, Mother," she whispered, leaning over and kissing the old lady on the cheek.

Hannah's eyes opened and she saw Maci, but with no sign of recognition. Another lump clogged Maci's throat, and she had to swallow several times before it disappeared.

A few moments later, Maci stepped back into the hall, her eyes darting around the waiting area.

"I'm here," Holt said, easing away from the wall and walking toward her.

She took a quivering breath. On the way to the hospital, she'd been too distraught to consider the consequences of Holt driving her.

It crossed her mind to tell him to go on without her, then call Seymour to come after her, only to scratch that thought. Involving her husband at this juncture would be asking for more trouble than she needed.

"What's the verdict?" Holt asked, reaching her side and peering down at her.

Before she thought, she lifted her head and met his gaze. What she saw there rocked her. Gone was the aggressive contempt. In its place was warm compassion. Would she ever understand this man?

"Debbie will stay with her," Maci said, looking away.

"Do you need to stay?"

"No."

"Come on, then, let's get out of here." He gestured for her to precede him.

Once they were in his SUV, Maci felt like a wet blanket had been thrown over her. Even though the interior of the luxurious vehicle was roomy, his big body seemed to instantly reduce the space. The fact that the evening itself was hot and humid didn't help matters. But right now the problem wasn't the outside temperature. It was the temperature inside her own body.

She only had to be near Holt and her insides heated like a furnace.

"I'm sorry about your mother," Holt said, shattering the mounting silence.

"Thanks."

She heard him expel a deep breath. "Have you eaten anything?"

His question caught her so off guard that she responded without thinking, "No, I haven't."

"You need something in your stomach."

Panic filled her. "No, please, I couldn't eat even if I wanted to."

"Look at me, Maci." His voice had dropped to a husky pitch.

She faced him.

"At least drink something. Afterward, I'll swing you back by the hospital. What do you say?"

She knew he was a master manipulator. Yet she'd been a willing participant in that manipulation she reminded herself, just as she'd been on that beach in Jamaica. That was then and this was now. She would like to think she had grown stronger and more in control of herself.

"To go home now would be foolish," Holt added. Although his voice was light, it had a rusty edge to it.

He was right. She could use something to drink. More than that, maybe this was the opportunity she needed to make him understand that she was off-limits to him, except when it came to discussing her husband's legal problems.

"I know the perfect place," he said, taking further advantage of her silence. With that, he shoved the powerful motor in gear and took off.

Silence continued to hover over them until he pulled into an out-of-the-way restaurant, one she'd never been to and one that looked almost deserted. But that didn't matter. She just wanted this night to be over. She wanted her life to be as she'd once known it.

"What can I get you to drink?" he asked, after they were seated at a table in a closed-in atrium room filled with lovely, exotic plants.

Holt gave their order to the waiter, and while they waited for their drinks, Maci kept her eyes on the plants, soaking up their beauty.

"Neat place, huh?" he asked.

She turned to look at him. This time his eyes were unreadable, even innocent in their expression, though Maci knew there was nothing innocent about him.

"That it is," she said quietly. "Somehow I missed it."

"I came on it by accident the other day. Looked like it might have possibilities so…" He let his voice trail off.

"Here we are," she said in a flippant tone, which was the only way she could cope with her growing reservations about having consented to this outing.

"I'm sorry about your mother."

A safe topic. "Thanks. Me, too."

"It's gotta be tough to have your mind slowly but surely deteriorate."

"It's awful."

"Will that seizure set her back?"

"For a few days. She'll be lethargic and tired."

"And sleep a lot?"

"That, too."

The waiter arrived with their beverages and Maci latched onto the stem of her wineglass with a vengeance, then took a deep sip. God, it tasted good. More than that, she knew the drink would unkink her nerves, despite the fact that she was aware of Holt with every breath he took.

"Maci, I've made a decision."

"About what?"

He peered in his beer bottle instead of at her. "I'm leaving."

Twenty

Maci's mouth fell open in astonishment.

"Why are you so shocked? That's what you've been wanting, isn't it?"

Maci forced her jaws together while her heart continued to race out of control.

"Actually, I thought you'd be singing the 'Hallelujah Chorus.'"

Somehow, Maci managed to pull herself back together enough to finally respond. "You're right, I should be." Her voice held a tremor.

An eyebrow cocked as his eyes examined her. "Only you're not?"

He was stunned. He looked like she'd just taken a baseball bat and knocked the stuffing out of him. She couldn't blame him. She couldn't believe her own reaction.

This sudden move on his part shouldn't have been totally unexpected. She had even told him she wanted him out of their lives.

"What's going on, Maci?" he demanded in a gruff but weary voice. "We both know—"

"What will happen to Seymour if you bail now?" She had to cut him off. She couldn't let him wander down that forbidden track, fearing he would drag her with him. She had to stick to the issue at hand. This was about her husband's fate and her future, not about her wild feelings for a man she could never have.

"I'll see that he gets another attorney, like I proposed from the get-go."

Those words jerked her back to reality. "But isn't it too late for that?"

"I hope not."

A sudden spurt of anger forced her to say, "You hope not. What kind of answer is that?" She felt the tenor of her voice rising.

"Hey, take it easy. Yelling at me won't help."

"I wasn't yelling."

"Whatever."

Her eyes flashed. "Look, how do you expect me to act when you just dropped that bombshell in my lap?"

"Oh, come on," he said in that mock drawling voice. "I hardly think it's that, in light of everything that's happened."

She felt color steal into her face and averted her gaze. It was hard to walk the imaginary chalk line she had drawn in her heart. She couldn't pretend she didn't know what he was talking about. The volatile situation between them hovered over every facet of their lives, thicker than the humidity outside.

"Why are you doing this?" Her voice shook big time now.

"You know the answer to that." His features were grim.

"It's to get back at me, isn't it?"

"Dammit, Maci—"

"I'm the reason you want out, not Seymour."

"Unfortunately, honey, you're a package deal."

That remark severed the sexual tension that hung between them. "I'm not your honey," she spat.

He shrugged, swirling the beer around in the bottle. "Just a figure of speech."

Maci shifted her gaze again, feeling her heart continue to pound out of her chest. Then she looked back at him. "No one knows more than I do what a strain it is having you here, but—"

"But what?" he cut in when she hesitated.

"You want out."

"You don't have a clue what I want." His tone was as dark and sullen as his features. Then a glint jumped into his eyes. "On second thought, maybe you do."

The air was suddenly so stymied with tension that it took Maci's breath, remembering how his lips and body felt against her.

A whimper almost escaped her lips, especially after their eyes met and clung for the briefest of moments. God help her, but she felt heat pool between her legs, leaving her wet and wanting.

"Maci," Holt ground out in a tormented tone.

Her stomach bottomed out. "Please, let's don't do this."

"What do you suggest we do? Kiss and make up?"

She flushed, nursing a renewed spurt of anger. "Damn you, Holt."

He muttered a curse at the same time he rubbed the back of his neck. "I'm sorry. That was uncalled for."

"I agree," she countered with a tremor.

"When I'm around you, all I seem to do is fuck up, then apologize."

"Are you apologizing now?"

"Yes."

"Apology accepted," she said, her voice still not back to full strength.

"Are you asking me to stay, Maci?"

"And if I am?"

"Then you'll have to ask."

She didn't so much as flinch. "All right, I'm asking."

Silence followed her words.

He sucked in his breath then blew it out. "Why?"

"I think that's obvious."

"Not to me, it isn't."

"Okay, I'll spell it out."

"Go ahead."

The tension had evaporated somewhat. And while she counted that a godsend, she'd rather have had it than the contempt that had crept back into his voice.

"Maci?"

She shook her head to clear it. "I think you're Seymour's best chance of getting off."

"When did you suddenly develop all this confidence in me?"

She felt the sting in her cheeks but she didn't back down. Instead, she lifted her chin a bit and said, "Despite how you feel about your father and me, you'll do your job."

"And just how do you know that?"

She didn't balk. "Because I sense you don't like to lose."

He seemed to mull that over before rubbing his jaw and drawling, "You'd better watch out."

"I don't know what you mean."

"Sounds like you're real close to paying me a compliment."

Her temper flared again. "Stop toying with me. I've asked you to stay." Her voice broke. "You've extracted your pound of flesh." She paused and took a deep breath. "I can't bear the thought of Seymour going to prison."

"Not even if he's guilty?"

That question caught her so off guard that for a second she couldn't respond. "I…we have a son, Holt. Think of what that would do to Jonah, to have a father in prison." A hand flew to her mouth, feeling her stomach pitch.

"You okay?"

He was much too aware of everything about her, which both disconcerted and excited her. He was a man who never missed a thing.

"All right."

She held her breath a second too long, making her feel dizzy. "All right, you'll stay?"

"I'll stay."

Their eyes met and held. Maci noticed that a dark flush rivaled his tan, and he was breathing hard.

She wasn't faring any better. Her insides felt like they were in a meat grinder. She was risking emotional suicide by blatantly issuing him an invitation to stay.

As if he knew once again what was charging through her mind, he said in a low, gruff voice, "I just hope to hell we both don't regret this."

Additional color stained her cheeks. "Meaning?"

"I think you know the answer to that," he said.

His voice was thick and tinged with bitterness. She opened her mouth to refute his statement, but she never got the chance.

He stood abruptly, causing his chair to scrape unmercifully across the floor. "I just hope to hell I can keep my hands off you."

Gripping the table for support, she also stood.

"Forget I said that," he muttered savagely. "Come on, let's get out of here."

"Hey, Bro, it's been a helluva long time."

"Too long," Holt responded, vigorously shaking the hand of an old school buddy, Pete Ashburn, whom he rarely saw.

"Whose fault is that?" Pete demanded, narrowing his eyes. "Since you stopped practicing law, you've been more scarce than hen's teeth."

"Hey, even when I was practicing, I never saw much of your ugly mug."

Pete grinned. "True."

"And that's a shame, you know," Holt said with quick response.

"Hell, man, life's a treadmill and nobody can seem to find a place to get off, if you get my drift."

"Oh, I get it, all right. But remember, you're talking to a guy who jumped off that treadmill."

"So you did, and I admire the hell out of you. And I'm envious to boot."

"Hey, come on in and have a seat," Holt said. "I didn't mean to keep you standing in the doorway."

"No problem, since you weren't expecting me."

"Oh, but I'm glad to see you."

"Sure I'm not interrupting anything important?"

"Not that important."

Pete's overabundant brows shot up, but he didn't say anything.

Holt watched as the M.E. strode to a chair and sat down. Though Pete was short and rather small-boned, he was nonetheless very much a man. And good-looking, too, with thick brown hair, a perfectly shaped mustache and twinkling blue eyes.

"Coffee?" Holt asked once the medical examiner was seated.

"Got some?"

Holt grinned. "Always."

"Then bring it on."

Once they were both seated and had taken several sips of coffee, Pete looked at Holt, the twinkle no longer visible in his eyes. "You know why I'm here."

"Yep."

"Let me say up front how sorry I am about all this."

"I'm sorry, too, but it doesn't change anything."

"No, you're right about that."

"How did you get the nod to do the autopsy?" Holt asked.

"We take turns. When Dodson came across the board, it was my turn." He paused and took another sip of coffee. "At first, I thought about passing, but then something told me that wouldn't be the thing to do."

"I'm glad you didn't."

Pete set his cup back down. "I came as soon as I got back in town and got your message."

"I appreciate that."

A silence followed as though both men realized they were on slippery ground.

"I understand you're representing your father," Pete said, breaking the silence.

"You heard right."

"I'm surprised you can be that objective."

"Who says I can?" Holt sighed. "Sorry, I didn't mean to sound flippant."

"Hey, sound anyway you want. You've got to feel like you're sitting on a hot griddle."

If only you knew the half of it, Holt mused to himself. Then realizing Pete was waiting for a response, he let go of a sigh and said, "It is. That's why I needed to talk to you."

"You've read my report, right?"

"No, actually, I haven't."

"Why not?" Pete asked bluntly.

"For some reason, a copy wasn't in the charges against Seymour. One of those items that slipped through the cracks. It's no big deal. I pretty much know what it says."

Pete leaned forward, a troubled look marring his features. "It's not in Seymour's favor."

Holt nodded, his features grim.

Pete sat back, the troubled look remaining. "Dodson hemorrhaged to death."

"Because Seymour botched the surgery." Not a question.

"That's what I wrote in my report."

"You can say that without any doubt whatsoever?"

"Are you asking me if there's wiggle room?"

Holt didn't hesitate. "Yes."

Pete was quiet for the longest time before replying, "Nope. Not that I can see."

"Are you aware that his cohorts haven't implicated him?"

"Doesn't surprise me. We both know how tight the medical profession is and how we protect our own."

"What about you, Pete? You're part of that equation."

"I call the shots like I see 'em, which doesn't always make me the most popular guy on the block."

"I'm not asking you to do anything unethical here," Holt said. "I hope you know that."

"As your friend, I hate to be the one who puts the final nail in your father's coffin."

"But you wouldn't hesitate," Holt interrupted, "if you had to."

Pete's gaze didn't waver. "That's right."

Holt swore under his breath.

Twenty-One

Maci hadn't seen Holt in several days, which was a very good thing for her peace of mind. She still couldn't believe she'd done a hundred-and-eighty degree turn when she'd all but begged him to stay and defend Seymour. Thinking back on that conversation now made her knees tremble and heat surge into her face.

But she wasn't sorry. If she had it to do over again, she would do the same thing. Even though Holt's presence would continue to be a thorn in her side, she was convinced he remained Seymour's best chance for staying out of prison.

Now, though, was not the time to give in to her doubts and fears. A show of strength was what she had to display in order to see this ordeal through to the bitter end. And she had to be savvy as well. She wanted to keep abreast of what was going on, but Maci couldn't ask her husband because he was never around to ask. It was now evening and she hadn't heard from him all day. Since she'd moved into a spare bedroom, their relationship had been strained. In fact, she doubted their marriage would ever be the same again.

She hoped it survived.

When Seymour was exonerated, she hoped their marriage would settle back into its routine, minus the physical side. Until Seymour proved beyond a shadow of doubt that he'd conquered his drug problem, she couldn't bear the thought of his touching her.

If only she felt the same about Holt.

Realizing where her thoughts had turned, Maci forced herself upright then went upstairs to take a peek at a sleeping Jonah.

Liz was off this evening, so her son was in her care. After she scrounged up a light dinner for herself, she planned to devote the remainder of the evening to him. She couldn't wait.

Stealing a moment, Maci sat next to his bed and watched him breathe, gratitude flooding through her. Not everyone was lucky enough to have such a treasure, certainly not her friend Bobbi.

Maci's heart suddenly wrenched, thinking of her friend and what had taken place earlier that day. She had gone to Bobbi's to do some more measuring for window treatments. When she'd received no response to the doorbell after ringing it a second time, she had experienced a frisson of alarm.

Later, Maci didn't know what possessed her to try the doorknob, but she did. When it opened, that alarm escalated. Something was wrong. Bobbi never left her door unlocked, always fearing her ex might show up.

That thought alone had sent Maci dashing inside to the living area. No sign of her friend.

"Bobbi!" she cried.

No answer.

With her heart lodged in her throat, Maci took the stairs two at a time until she reached Bobbi's bedroom. That was when she heard the sobs. Expecting the worst, Maci barreled across the threshold, prepared to find her friend beaten again by her husband.

Bobbi was on the floor, curled in a fetal position, her cries as pitiful as they were mournful.

"Oh, honey, what happened?" Maci asked, dropping to her knees and placing her arms around her friend.

Grasping Maci's arm, Bobbi raised a grief-stricken but unblemished face and stammered, "My…my… baby—"

"What about the baby?" Terrible things stampeded through Maci's mind while waiting for Bobbi to tell her what was going on.

"I'm…she's not sure—" Bobbi's voice broke again and she couldn't finish.

She didn't have to. Maci knew the rest of the sentence—the rest of the story, actually. The birth mother was threatening to change her mind and not give up the child for adoption. Since she had been on the board of that particular organization, she had seen that scenario more often than she cared to admit. For the persons who counted on getting the baby, like Bobbi, it was especially heartbreaking.

"Shh," Maci told her, cradling her in her arms like she did Jonah. "You have to stop this or you'll be sick. Besides, I need to know the details if I'm going to help you."

Finally, Bobbi regained some semblance of composure and was able to confirm Maci's fears.

"What am I going to do?" Bobbi wailed. "I wanted that baby so much. I've been living my life for the moment I'd get it."

"For starters, you're not going to give up." Maci's tone was crisp. "Most of the time, the mothers never go through with their last-minute threat."

"Oh, God, Maci, I pray you're right. If I have to start all over—" A sob robbed Bobbi of further speech.

"I know. Look, I'll see what I can do. Meanwhile, you have to promise me to keep your chin up. That's the only way you're going to get through this."

"I'm tired of holding my chin up," Bobbi wailed again.

"Me, too, but that's the way it is sometimes, my friend."

As though Bobbi realized she wasn't the only one experiencing heartache, she sucked in a deep breath and said, "I'm sorry for burdening you with this. You have enough on your plate to digest without me adding to it."

"I don't want to hear that again. I'm your friend through thick and thin. Besides, you've been there for me, letting me cry on your shoulder. Turnabout is fair play."

Maci had disentangled herself and risen to her feet. Bobbi had followed suit. "Come on, I'm going to brew us some tea. That'll make us both feel better."

A sudden noise broke into Maci's thoughts, forcing her back to the moment at hand. Jonah was standing in his crib with his arms outstretched.

Pushing her worries about Bobbi aside for now, she grinned at her son. "Ah, so you're awake." She lifted him, then nuzzled his neck, making him wiggle and giggle that much more. "You're Mommy's big lump of sugar, aren't you?"

"Outside."

"Oh, no you don't. It's too late. Besides Mommy's hungry. You can watch me make dinner."

A while later, she had fed Jonah and herself and was in the process of clearing the table when she had a premonition that she was no longer alone. She spun around and saw Holt standing in the doorway.

Would there ever come a time when he wouldn't upset her equilibrium?

Probably not, especially when he stood lazily in front of her, his body beckoning her like an open invitation. He had on worn jeans and an open-necked cotton shirt. But it was his jeans, bleached in places that should have been forbidden to her gaze, that held her attention, dredging up too many memories.

With that thought burning inside her, Maci shifted her gaze, conscious suddenly of how she must look. When she'd come home from Bobbi's, she'd immediately removed her makeup and showered. Hence, she had on a pair of lounging pajamas that were far too revealing. Since there was nothing she could do about that now, she wasn't going to behave like an outraged virgin.

After all, he'd seen her naked flesh. She let go of a breath she'd scarcely been aware of holding.

"Sorry, didn't mean to frighten you," he said as though he could read her mind.

"Well, you did," she muttered rudely, hoping to burst the sexual bubble that encapsulated them.

After tossing her an unreadable look, he strode to Jonah who was staring at him with avid curiosity, though a grin covered his tiny features.

"Hey, fellow, what's happening?"

Jonah held out his arms to Holt. "Down."

Holt grinned. Maci's heart suddenly melted.

"Is it all right if I hold him?" he asked in a husky tone.

"Ah, he's not very clean."

"Do you think I care about that?"

"Go ahead, then," Maci said with veiled reluctance.

Holt lifted Jonah out of the high chair.

"Hey, you're quite a chunk of change, kiddo."

"Down," Jonah said again, once he was in Holt's arms.

Holt chuckled, turning to Maci. She couldn't help but return that smile. Her composure took another dive.

"Want me to let him have his way?"

Although his voice was calm, it was a tad thicker than before, his way of letting her know he was as affected as much as she was.

"Sure. I'll just have to take every step he does."

"That'll work." Then to Jonah, "Down you go, chunk."

Before he lowered the child to the floor, he pitched him high in the air. Jonah laughed so hard Maci feared he might lose his breath. But it was a joyous sight to watch until fear of another kind jabbed her heart.

She couldn't let Holt worm his way into her heart through her child or otherwise. It was too dangerous. He was off-limits to her except as her stepson. When Seymour was vindicated, Holt would walk away from their lives, probably never to appear again.

"Man, he's swift afoot."

At the sound of Holt's voice, Maci hurriedly joined them in the living room where Jonah was toddling over to a box of toys. After grabbing two or three, he sat on the floor and began playing. Maci eased down on the edge of the ottoman close to Jonah while Holt remained standing.

For a moment the only sounds in the room were from Jonah's jabbering.

"Mind if I sit with you?"

Maci cut Holt a glance. "You don't have to ask that."

"Sure I do."

She continued to stare at him.

"I wasn't sure I'd be welcome."

In spite of herself, Maci felt a flush sting her cheeks. "Would you like something to drink?"

"If I do, I'll get it. You don't have to wait on me."

"You're right, I don't."

His jaw tightened before asking, "Where's Seymour?"

"I have no idea."

A frown drew his brows together. "What does that mean?"

"Exactly what I said. He left early and hasn't come home yet."

She watched Holt's eyes narrow at the same time he rubbed his sandpapery cheek. "Are you worried?"

"Yes, I am."

"Are you thinking what I'm thinking?" Holt asked, his voice harsh.

"Yes," she whispered.

"Dammit, Maci, you shouldn't have to put up with this kind of crap."

She gave him a startled look. "What do you suggest I do?"

"Leave his ass."

She lunged to her feet and glared at him. "So when he's down, I should kick him, right?"

"We both know that's not the reason you won't leave him." Holt's tone had turned sour.

Maci's eyes flashed. "You bastard."

Holt's features tensed. "Look, forget I said that. I didn't mean to start another argument."

"I don't want to argue either," she responded in a terse tone. And she didn't. Her nerves were already on edge from trying her best to ignore the sexual haze that hung between them, clouding everything they said, every word they spoke. She didn't suspect that would change. As long as he was here, she would always be aware of him as a man.

A man she couldn't have.

"Do you think he's off somewhere on a binge?"

"Yes," she said with a tremor, "I do, though I have no proof."

"If he gets caught, I don't have to tell you the consequences."

"I know, but he won't listen to me."

"Apparently moving out of his bed didn't do the trick."

Another beat of silence more provocative than before settled over the room.

"Forget I said that, too," he said savagely.

"Has anything new developed on the case?" Maci forced herself to ask in as calm a voice as she could muster. She wished her insides would do the same.

He told her about his visit with Pete Ashburn.

"Oh, God, Holt, he's not going to beat this, is he?"

Holt didn't so much as flinch. "I'm giving his case my best shot. That's all I can promise."

She nodded, drawing her lip between her lower teeth.

"Maci—"

The tone of his voice forced her to look at him. For another beat of silence, the air seemed to have left the room.

"Mommy!"

They both jumped like they had been shot. Maci was the first to recover, turning to her son who had tossed his toys to one side and was scrambling to his feet.

"Where are you going, squirt?" she asked on a breathless note.

"Outside."

"Boy, does he ever have a one-track mind," Holt commented with a trace of humor in his voice.

"Doesn't he, though?" Maci watched as Jonah toddled off far in advance of her. "Whoa, wait up, pal. Mommy's coming."

Jonah's chubby legs churned that much faster.

"Ah, so you think this is a game?" Maci said, laughing.

Then in the blink of an eye, Jonah hit the floor, grazing his head on the corner of the coffee table.

His screams rent the air.

For what seemed like an eternity but was actually only seconds, Maci couldn't move. Fear paralyzed her. Then she ran to him, screaming, "Jonah! Oh, my God. Oh, my God."

Holt reached the baby first and gently turned him over.

Blood covered his tiny face.

Twenty-Two

"I told you he was going to be okay."

"You didn't know that for sure," Maci replied fiercely, her lovely features still drawn and strained from the effects of pain and fear. And her eyes were red and smudged from a bombardment of tears. Despite the scare she had just survived, there was a spark of the old fire in her as she glared at him.

But Holt didn't take offense. He was glad to see some life return to her face.

They were in Jonah's room following their return from the hospital. It was past midnight and since the crisis had passed, Holt should've already gone to his room.

Yet he hadn't been able to bring himself to leave either her or the baby. He suspected Maci would spend the night in Jonah's room on the daybed, even though Jonah had been put through the works in the emergency room and pronounced none the worse for the fall he'd taken.

They had brought him home with only a butterfly Band-Aid on his forehead.

Although Holt hadn't let it show, when the kid had taken that tumble, it had shaken *him* to the core, especially after he'd turned Jonah over in his arms and had seen all that blood. His heart had almost stopped beating, and he, like Maci, had thought the worst.

But only for a short time. After he had handed the screaming baby to Maci, he'd dashed into the powder room where he'd grabbed a towel, wet it, then dashed back to Maci.

"We have to get him to the hospital," she cried.

"Not without a towel."

"He's…he's going to die, isn't he?" she whispered, trying to place the rag on Jonah's face.

Her voice was barely audible and Holt feared she was close to slipping into shock. That couldn't happen.

"Of course, he's not going to die," he assured her roughly, steadying her hand so that she could clean the wound enough to see the damage.

However, Jonah had other ideas.

"Oh, please, honey," she begged her son, "be still and let Mommy see your hurt."

Jonah couldn't be consoled. He continued to squirm and scream.

"Come on, let's get him to the E.R.," Holt said in a calm but firm tone.

Thirty minutes later the doctor returned to the cubicle where they anxiously waited, all the while hovering over Jonah's bed. But Jonah was totally unaware of what was going on as he was sleeping soundly, his pale little face finally free of blood.

"He's going to be as good as new," Dr. Paul Baker said, a bright-eyed young man whose complexion looked like it had never been exposed to a ray of sunlight.

"Is...is anything broken?" Maci stammered.

"No," he said. "No concussion either. Scalp wounds are notorious for bleeding, and that's all your baby suffered."

"Thank God," Maci said, her voice sounding so frail that for a moment Holt thought she might pass out. If so, he figured she was in the right place.

"He should sleep the remainder of the night," Dr. Baker added. "If there's a problem, your pediatrician wants you to call him."

"So you spoke to Dr. Vickers?" Maci asked.

Holt heard the relief in Maci's voice which in turn relieved him. The thought of her passing out didn't bear thinking about, especially when he felt responsible for both her and the child's welfare. That was a ridiculous fact, he knew, but one he couldn't ignore nonetheless.

Hell, Seymour should be the one here with her and Jonah. But for a reason he hated to admit to himself, Holt was damn glad he wasn't.

"I just spoke to Dr. Vickers a few moments ago," Dr. Baker was saying. "He asked that you give him a call for sure in the morning and let him know how the little fellow is."

Maci nodded, her gaze straying back to Jonah. "May we take him home now?"

"Anytime you'd like."

"If you're sure he's out of danger." Her eyes and voice were anxious.

"I assure you, he's fine."

Holt looked on as the doctor reached into the crib and lifted the sleeping child into Maci's arms. He could only see her profile but that was enough to make his breath catch. Her night-black hair was swept away from her face allowing him to see the perfection of her profile. No matter how hard he tried, he couldn't look away, not when she appeared so broken, so vulnerable.

So needy.

Ignoring the tightening in his gut and the lump in his throat, Holt made his way to their side and said in an abrupt tone, "I'll bring the car around."

Maci nodded, keeping her eyes focused on the sleeping child.

After murmuring a brusque thank you to the doctor, Holt strode out. Only after he reached his vehicle did he take his first easy breath. Maci joined him a few minutes later and was quiet until they were back inside the mansion.

Then in a tremulous voice, she said, "All that blood."

Maci's softly spoken words made him turn to her. That was when he noticed the fresh tears pooling in her eyes and the slight tremor to her lips. He felt his heart wrench again because he felt sorry for her, an emotion he didn't want but couldn't help.

He didn't want to feel anything for her.

Lust was one thing. He could handle that emotion as he knew it was only temporary. But this other emotion churning in his gut bore no resemblance to lust and that scared him.

When this fiasco with Seymour was over, he wanted to walk out of this life and back into his other, unscathed. But whether he liked it or not, this woman and her child had put a hex on him, a hex that threatened to change him.

No way could he let that happen.

"How could he lose all that blood and still be all right?"

He knew she was second-guessing the doctor and herself, which was understandable as a mother.

"Please, don't," he muttered hoarsely, still a safe distance from her, though he couldn't swear how long that was going to last. He itched to close the distance and pull her against him.

Maci sniffed back the tears. "I'm sorry. I just can't seem to pull myself back together. I feel like such a failure as a mother."

"That's nonsense."

"How can you say that?" She lashed back. "Jonah fell, didn't he? Right in front of my eyes."

"Yes, he did, but accidents happen. He's a boy, for heaven's sake. This won't be the first or the last good tumble he'll take."

"Don't tell me that," she said on a wailing note.

His gaze softened on her. "Hey, you didn't do anything wrong here and the only reason you think that is because you're exhausted."

For some strange reason, her mouth relaxed into a bitter-sweet smile that sent his blood pressure skyrocketing. He could count the times on one hand that he'd seen that smile. But when it happened, it was a traffic-stopping event.

"You find that funny, huh?" he asked, hearing the light humor in his own voice.

Maci crossed her hands over her body as if to ward off a chill. "Not so much funny as truthful. Even my bones are tired."

"At least you don't have to worry about Jonah anymore. He'll be going full-speed ahead in the morning."

"Let us pray."

Her voice caught and he knew she was having difficulty speaking through threatening tears. If she didn't get control soon or he didn't get out of there, it was going to be too late. He couldn't take much more before he added another screwup to an already long list.

"I keep telling myself that," she continued in that same agonized whisper. "But again when I think of all that blood on my baby—" Her voice broke on a fresh sob.

His control snapped and he shot across the room. He pulled her against his chest, feeling her breasts flatten against him. Then with a smothered expletive, he pushed her back so that his mouth could reach hers. Once it did, he kissed her.

Hard.

And deep.

And long.

He hadn't really known what to expect. Perhaps a struggle to break loose, followed by another slap in the face. Both were more than possibilities. It was as if he waited in suspended animation for her weapon of choice.

What he hadn't expected was that her mouth would turn wet and pliable under his or that her lips would part and admit his tongue. Heat pounded through his body, settling in his groin. He knew he was taking advantage of her vulnerability, but he couldn't stop himself, not when she clung to him as though she'd never let him go.

Then, as if it was the most natural thing to happen, he lowered his hands to her buttocks, kneading them before moulding her lower half to his. The way she was splayed against the length of him left no doubt as to his arousal, all the while his tongue filled her mouth, teasing and tormenting.

Only after he pulled away to drag more air into his lungs before going back for another dose did he realize his face was wet from her tears.

He froze, sick to his stomach with sudden shame for using her weakness for his own sexual gratification. Still, he found letting her go was next to impossible. Every muscle, every nerve in his body screamed to take this to fruition, to come away satisfied.

That was why it took every ounce of strength he possessed to thrust her away, then cross to the door where he paused and whispered, "I'll see you in the morning."

The next morning Maci told herself she couldn't be alone with him again. At least not in the condition she'd been in last evening.

She could conjure up all kinds of reasons why she'd let him hold her until their passions had ignited out of control. None of them, however, held merit. The truth of the matter was, she had no willpower when it came to him.

Her body had betrayed her.

She should thank God for *Holt's* restraint. Color so hot surged into her face, making her feel like she had a high fever. She certainly hadn't been the one to back off.

How could she continue to behave in such a wanton manner? Where was her pride? Was she that sex-starved she would have actually let him make love to her?

Maci cringed, the memory of how she had aligned her body with his caused a pain too acute to ignore.

She couldn't blame him entirely. Any hot-blooded man would react as he had in that situation. And any hot-blooded woman would have reacted as she had when she felt a man's raging erection pressed against her.

Her life was careening out of control right in front of her eyes.

Where was it going to end? Her son had come close to getting seriously hurt while her husband still hadn't come home.

The weather didn't help her mood. It was raining outside, which exacerbated her depression. But she wouldn't bow to that futile emotion. Despite her despicable actions, she had so much to be thankful for. Jonah was well and, making her way into his room, she saw he was still sound asleep. She stared at him for the longest time, counting her blessings.

Blinking back the threat of tears, Maci went downstairs to the breakfast room. Her coffee and the morning paper were waiting for her. The only break in her routine was the absence of her husband.

She picked up the paper and scanned the front page.

At first, she didn't believe she'd read the article right. Fury boiled inside her. Pitching down the paper, she charged out of the room and up the stairs. She didn't stop until she reached Holt's door and knocked on it.

"It's open," he called out.

Without hesitation, she flung open the door.

He was standing in the middle of the room, barechested and barefooted. He was wearing a pair of jeans though they rode far too low on his slender hips.

For a moment, his gaze held hers while the air seemed to vanish from the room.

He was the first to recover. "Is something wrong?"

"What were you thinking about?" she demanded, her voice shaking.

His eyes narrowed. "What are you talking about?"

"Have you seen the paper?"

"Yes, as a matter of fact I have." He paused. "So what?"

"So what?" she cried, clenching and unclenching her fists.

"Yeah, that's what I said."

"Then it's true." Her voice shook with suppressed emotion.

"That I've taken on another case. Yes, it's true. Why the hell do you care?"

"I don't want your loyalties divided, that's why."

"Well, that's too bad," he drawled in a mocking tone. "At the moment, I don't really care what you want."

"Go to hell," she cried before slamming the door and leaning against it, feeling as though she had the weight of the world on her slender shoulders.

Twenty-Three

"Can I get you some coffee?"

Holt turned from his stance by the window and shook his head at Marianne. "I'll pass, thanks."

"Are you sure?"

He gave her a smile of sorts. "Are you telling me I look like I need some?"

"Yes, I am," she said bluntly.

"What I need is something a whole helluva lot stronger than coffee."

"Bad night, huh?"

Holt had to think about that for a moment. "More like a bad start to the morning."

"Well, this rain doesn't help. It tends to make me feel a little down, though everyone says we need the rain."

"On second thought, maybe I will take that cup of coffee."

"I can take a hint. I'll get it for you, then get busy."

"You don't have to wait on me, you know."

She smiled. "I know, but I don't mind."

"Thanks," Holt muttered, then faced the window once again, though he couldn't see anything. The rain was peppering down too quickly. Thunder boomed and lightning danced in one of those summer storms that moved through the area fast and furiously. By noon the sun would probably be parboiling everyone.

A sigh filtered through him as his thoughts turned away from this stormy day. How he longed to be away from here, out to sea, feeling the warm breeze caress his face as his sailboat skimmed through the blue waters.

But he was tied to land, and he couldn't blame anyone but himself. If only he'd known what lay in store for him, he would have never in a million years made a silent vow to his mother or a verbal commitment to his father.

Thoughts of Seymour suddenly soured his stomach. Where the hell was he? Off on a binge, as Maci suspected? If Seymour got picked up by the police, then his case was all but ruined. That meant Holt could wrap up the Sanders murder case and haul ass. If that were to happen, he'd be one happy bastard.

But what about Maci?

He swore. He didn't want to be concerned about her. She wasn't his responsibility. Never had been. Never would be. *So why did he feel otherwise?*

Despite the hot fiery kisses they had exchanged, Maci was off-limits. Now all he had to do was convince his body of that.

On the one hand, he was so hot for her, thinking he couldn't go another moment without taking her into his arms and making love to her. On the other, he felt nothing but contempt for her, convinced she was out to get what she could for herself.

Was he screwed up, or what?

Thoroughly disgusted with his thoughts, Holt swung around and noticed that Marianne had placed the coffee on his desk. He'd been so lost in his jumbled-up thoughts that he hadn't even heard her.

He reached for the cup and took a sip only to make a face. Colder than a mother-in-law's heart.

"Yo."

He looked up as Vince strolled into his office.

"You looked surprised, good buddy. Did you forget you summoned me to the inner sanctum this morning?"

"Actually, I did," Holt admitted with a smile. "Too much on my mind."

"Care to dump some of it?"

"On you?"

Vince grinned. "I've been told I'm a good listener."

"What you are is full of it."

"Been told that, too," Vince said, walking over to the coffeepot and helping himself. "Are you ready for a refill?"

"Nah. I still have a full cup."

Vince nodded before easing down into his favorite chair and shoving back his Stetson. "So how's it going?"

"That's what I'm supposed to ask you."

"True, but you've got that look on your face."

"And just what kind of look is that?" Holt asked, humoring his friend.

"Like you got something wedged up your butt."

Holt scowled. "Remind me to tell you sometime how I really feel about you."

Vince laughed.

Ignoring that, Holt zapped his coffee in the microwave. When he returned to his desk, he eased down in his chair and asked, "You got anything for me on the Sanders case?"

"Ah, speaking of Sanders, I saw the article this morning."

"Yeah, me too."

"You don't seem too happy about it."

"I hate publicity of any kind."

"I wonder how the paper got hold of the story."

"Don't know. Don't really care." Holt paused. "Maci climbed my ass about it this morning."

"Really."

"She thinks my loyalties will be divided."

"That's interesting."

"That's baloney. Besides, it's none of her business."

"Why are you so bent out of shape? You should've expected that kind of reaction. After all, she's looking out for her own skin as well as her husband's."

"She doesn't call the shots. I do."

"So you two are mixing it up real good." Vince made a flat statement of fact.

Holt clamped his jaws together. If Vince only knew the rest of the story. But Vince didn't and Holt wasn't about to enlighten him. "You could say that," Holt muttered darkly.

Vince gave him a strange look, but didn't say anything for which Holt was grateful. But his friend was sharp in more ways than one.

"How's Seymour?"

"He's AWOL."

Vince's jaw dropped. "What?"

"He never came home yesterday or last night." Disgust colored Holt's voice.

"Well, I'll be damned."

Holt told Vince what happened with Jonah, but not with Maci.

"Oh, man, that's terrible. So Seymour knows nothing about his kid's accident?"

"Not unless he's found his way back home." Sarcasm took the place of disgust. "When I left at eight-thirty this morning, he wasn't there."

"If he's on a binge—"

Holt held up his hand, nipping Vince's sentence off. "Then the bastard deserves what he gets."

"This may all be over before the fat lady has a chance to sing."

"It might be."

"Want me to see what I can find out?"

Holt nodded, rage making it impossible to talk. Only after he cleared his throat was he able to speak. "But be discreet."

"That goes without saying."

Silence fell between them. Then Vince said, "Keep me posted on Seymour. When you get ready, I'll take another run at the doc and nurse just to make sure they're still keeping mum."

"Let's hold off awhile longer there. I might want a shot at them myself."

"You're the boss."

"So back to why you're here," Holt said. "The Sanders case."

"I've been busy as hell, but I can't say I've accomplished a whole lot."

"Meaning?"

"Meaning we have our work cut out in defense of

Lucas," Vince said. "I've canvassed the area. The entire subdivision to be more exact, and no one saw him with or without a dog."

"Okay, so that's against us." Holt rubbed his jaw. "What else?"

"Nothing positive, I'm afraid."

"Swell."

Vince shrugged.

"Positive or not, let's hear it."

"I checked on their finances and sure enough, both are insured big time."

"But Lucas is worth several million. Why would he off his wife for money when he doesn't need it?"

"You've got a point. So don't pursue that?"

"Not now."

"I spoke to their closest friends but no one was really forthcoming," Vince added. "You could tell they felt sorry for him but hey, they couldn't get involved."

"That doesn't surprise me," Holt said, his shoulders slumping. "When push comes to shove, most people are scumbuckets."

"Man, are you ever cynical."

"You disagree?"

"Nope, can't say that I do. People are flat scared to take a stand against anything or for anybody. But you'd think one son of a bitch would come to Lucas's rescue, if he could help, that is."

"Keep going back to the well. Maybe it'll eventually yield some water."

"Another thing I did was talk to the woman he had an affair with, which ended up being another dead end."

Holt made another face. "She confirmed what Lucas had said about the affair being over."

"That's right. The woman's name is Cynthia Newsome, a divorcée with two kids. Anyhow, she told me Sanders wanted out and she let him."

"Sounds too good to be true."

"That's what I thought." Vince removed his Stetson, rubbed his balding head, then put it back on. "But when I checked into her past, she has no history of anything close to violence. In fact, she's never even had a speeding ticket."

"Miss Goody Two-shoes, huh?"

Vince's mouth took a dip. "Like I said, it seems that way. But if you want, I'll deepen the hunt, though my gut tells me it's unlikely she had anything to do with smoking the wife."

"I trust your gut, so we'll let her be for now."

"There is something I didn't check on."

"What?" Holt asked, his hope renewed.

"Her finances."

"Let her be. You're right, we're barking up the wrong tree."

"So what's Plan B?"

"Don't have a Plan B, but I'll think on it."

Vince stood, reached for his cup and downed the remainder of his coffee. "If there's nothing else, I'll get back on Seymour."

Holt's features darkened. "Find him and bring him home."

"I'll be in touch."

Once Holt was alone, he swivelled in his chair while his mind backtracked through his and Vince's conversation. Neither investigation was going his way, which led him to believe that he'd lost his touch. A better assessment was that he was distracted.

By a lovely dark-haired woman who was married to his father.

He got up and began pacing the floor, his thoughts turning to Maci. When he heard the phone ring he paused waiting for Marianne to interrupt. She soon stuck her heard through the crack in the door. "You have a call on line one."

"Who is it?"

"She didn't say."

She? Could it be Maci? He reached for the receiver in record time.

Twenty-Four

If Seymour didn't show up this evening or call, she would have to do something. Maci cringed at the thought of notifying the police. But Seymour's absence could no longer be ignored.

She had thought about getting in touch with the doctors he worked with, but she deduced from what Seymour had said that he wasn't the most popular guy on the block right now, though none of his cronies had turned on him. At least not in an incriminating way. At this point, his cohorts were merely giving him the cold shoulder until the verdict came in.

She knew all doctors feared this same thing happening to them. That was why their code of silence was so strict and so unbreakable. And in all fairness, she figured none of his associates knew where Seymour was.

The only person she had felt comfortable calling was Keefe Ryan.

She had hated to disturb him during the predinner

hour when she figured he'd be sharing cocktails with his family. But she decided to call because pacing the floor in the living room wouldn't accomplish anything.

When she identified herself, Keefe immediately asked, "What's wrong?"

She was slightly taken aback by his bluntness, only to decide to be equally as blunt. "I hope nothing, but I'm worried."

"About Seymour?"

His tone told her he knew the answer before he asked the question. "Yes. Have you seen or spoken to him within the last two days?"

"No, I haven't." There was a pause. "Are you telling me you haven't?"

He sounded shocked. And well he should. Maci suddenly felt mortified and embarrassed herself. Then fury overrode both of those emotions. How dare Seymour put her in such an undesirable position? Damn him. She had known he could be selfish, but this behavior went beyond common decency.

"Yes, Keefe, that's exactly what I'm telling you."

"Good heavens, Maci. You have no idea where he is?"

"No, I don't." Anger caused her voice to tremble.

"Has he ever just disappeared like this?"

"Of course not."

"What does Holt have to say about it?"

She was afraid that would be his response. She had wanted to leave Holt out of the equation, permanently if possible. "Holt knows Seymour hasn't been around, but we really haven't discussed it."

"Well, then, I suggest you do."

Maci felt color creep into her face, color that she was

glad he couldn't see. "I thought I'd try you first," she said lamely.

"Are you and Seymour having marital problems?"

Maci knew Keefe's diplomatic question was his way of asking if perhaps Seymour's disappearance involved another woman. His voice was filled with concern.

"I hope you won't take offense at that question," he said into the silence.

"Not at all. I'll admit things are touch and go with us right now, but it never entered my mind there could be another woman."

"But now you're not so sure?"

"I'm not sure about anything."

"How's his drug problem?" Keefe asked.

"That's what I've been working around to saying but just didn't quite know how to get there."

"So it's not another woman but drugs."

"That's my guess."

"You're probably right." Keefe's tone held concern.

"So do I call the police?"

He was quiet for a moment, then said, "Look, I'll be glad to see what I can do, but you really ought to discuss this with Holt, especially since he's now Seymour's attorney of record."

Maci blew out a breath. "You're right, of course."

"But if I can do anything, I'm here." He paused. "If you want, I'll be glad to come over now."

"Oh, no, that's not necessary. I'll keep you posted."

"I'll check with you later this evening."

"Call anytime," Maci said. "And thanks."

"I didn't do anything. Listen, you hang in there. This

is all going to go away soon and your life will settle back in place."

"You have that much confidence in Holt?"

"Don't you?"

"I'm not sure," she said with caution.

"I think I know why, but suppose you tell me."

"You saw the headlines." Maci's tone was short.

"I saw them." He paused again. "Does Holt know how you feel?"

"Oh, yes," she said with bitterness.

"And?"

"He told me to mind my own business."

"He's a top-notch attorney, Maci. He can juggle both cases and represent each with ease."

"That's not the point. He shouldn't want to. He should want to just concentrate on Seymour."

"I agree. But unfortunately, that's not our call."

"You're right. It isn't." She heard the bitterness creep back into her tone.

"Look, I'll be in touch, okay?"

After she had hung up, Maci knew she'd wasted her time calling Keefe. Still, she remained reluctant to call Holt. But her options were running out. As Keefe had said, Holt was the most logical person to look into Seymour's disappearance. Perhaps he had and just hadn't informed her.

She could understand why he would keep quiet, especially after what had happened last night. It seemed they couldn't interact normally. They were either arguing or kissing.

That all-consuming kiss had caused further havoc on her already unstable body and mind. Until Holt had come back into her life, she had never looked at another man, never thought about another man. Cheating on her spouse was something she would never do.

Yet when Holt walked into the room and looked at her, she took on another personality, became another person, one whom she didn't know and whom she didn't like.

If only…

"Maci."

At the sound of her husband's voice, she swung around. She knew her features must have registered her shock and disgust as the smile on his face quickly disappeared.

"You don't appear glad to see me," he commented in his deep voice.

He acted as though nothing out of the ordinary had happened, which made her fume. He didn't look like he'd been on a drug binge, or if he had, he'd certainly pulled himself together. He was dressed as impeccably as ever and walked with a spring in his step.

Maybe Keefe had called it right. Maybe he'd been with another woman. Either scenario made her stomach queasy.

"Where have you been?" she demanded without preamble.

Without answering, Seymour walked up to her, reached out and caressed her face.

She flinched and turned away.

"I didn't mean to upset you," he said with a slight gruffness in his tone.

She whipped her head back around. "Oh, really? You couldn't prove that by me."

"Look, I'm sorry. Okay?"

"No, it's not okay."

"I just had to get away and think things through. Call it self-preservation."

"You could have told me, Seymour."

"You're right. I realize now I made a mistake, that I shouldn't have worried you for no reason. Will you forgive me?"

No way in hell was her initial thought. But she didn't voice that nasty comment, knowing that it would only make matters worse. He was back, unharmed, and that was all that counted, at least for the moment.

Right now, she was too emotionally fragile to get into a full-blown argument with him.

"Aren't you going to ask where I was?"

"If I did, would you tell me the truth?" she flared back.

His lips thinned. "What's happened to us, Maci? Ever since Holt—"

Her heart sank. Had he noticed the sizzling chemistry between them, a chemistry she had tried so hard to keep under wraps? No, she told herself. That wasn't possible. He was just looking for a scapegoat, and she wasn't about to let him get away with that.

"Don't you dare blame Holt or anyone else for your dependency on drugs."

"I'm not dependent on drugs," he countered sharply.

"I wish I could believe that, Seymour, if for no other reason than our son's sake." Even she heard the weary note in her voice.

"I'll make you believe it."

There was a desperate note in his voice that didn't escape Maci, but it did nothing to soften her heart or change her mind. Seymour needed professional help and until he got it, then proved he was drug-free, she would never trust him again.

"That remains to be seen," she replied in that same weary tone.

"So you're unwilling to forgive me?"

"It's not that simple." Maci breathed a troubled sigh. "Our son had an accident while you were off doing whatever you were doing."

Seymour looked taken aback. "Is he all right?"

"Yes, but no thanks to you."

"What happened?"

She told him.

"So Holt came to the rescue, huh?"

"Yes, and thank God, he did." Her tone dared him to take umbrage.

Seymour turned and walked over to the bar where he mixed himself a drink, then drained the glass.

It was all Maci could do not to lash out at him, to beg him to get control of himself. Mixing alcohol and drugs would only make matters worse. But he wouldn't listen to her. He was going to do what he was going to do no matter what she said. His disappearing act had already proved that.

He swung back around and pinned her with his eyes. "We'll be a family again soon. I promise."

"Oh, Seymour, you just don't get it, do you?" Her voice was filled with grief and regret.

His features darkened. "You're making more out of this than is necessary, Maci. While we're at it, I want you to move back into our bedroom."

"That's not going to happen, Seymour."

"Not ever?"

"I didn't say that. Just not right now."

"I won't—" Seymour broke off midsentence and faced the door.

Maci followed suit, only to have her hand involuntarily rise to cover her heart. *Holt.* He couldn't have appeared at a more inopportune moment.

"Where the hell have you been?" he demanded, glaring at Seymour.

Seymour flushed a deep red. "How dare you talk to me in that tone?"

"Answer my question, dammit."

Seymour opened his mouth, only to slam it shut.

Smart move, Maci thought, realizing that Holt was furious and wasn't prepared to listen to his father. For once, she was on her stepson's side. Seymour needed to be taken down a peg, and Holt seemed to be the only one who had the power to do that.

"That's immaterial," Seymour said. "I'm back now and that's all that counts."

"The hell it is," Holt countered. "Were you off on a drug binge?"

"I don't owe you an explanation. You're my lawyer, not my conscience."

"Wrong," Holt spat. "If you don't want me to walk out of this house and not come back, you'll do exactly as I tell you. And I'm telling you not to ever pull a stunt like this again."

Seymour's red face suddenly lost all its color. "I won't have you talking to me like that."

Holt hammered on as though Seymour hadn't spoken. "If you get stopped while under the influence, your ass will be under the jail instead of in it."

Maci's eyes sought her husband's. "He's right, Seymour. You'd better listen to him."

Seymour's features turned from dark to nasty. "Stop it. Both of you. I have no intention of letting you gang up against me."

"I don't see that you have any choice," Holt lashed back.

"We'll see about that." Pivoting on his heel, Seymour turned and walked out of the room.

Following his abrupt departure, a heavy silence hung in the air.

Twenty-Five

The smell of cigarette smoke clouded the air. Buck scarcely noticed, however, which was unusual. Too much smoke always messed up his sinuses, clogging his nostrils. But not this evening. Maybe that was because he felt numb all over, with the exception of his gut. And it burned like hell from sheer anger.

"You look like you're about to blow a gasket," Sid said, squinting his heavy-lidded eyes at him.

"I am," he said, fury traveling into his voice.

Sid guzzled down some more beer. After sitting the near-empty bottle down, he shook his head. "I saw the article about Ramsey defending your brother-in-law."

"I told you Lucas was up to something."

"Yeah, you did."

"And I was right, damn him." Bitterness now superseded Buck's anger.

Sid crossed his arms over the table and leaned in closer to Buck. "I don't want you to have a stroke over this."

"Are you telling me I don't have reason to be upset?"

"You know better than that." Sid leaned back again. "But you have your family and your sister's kids to think about. What would they do without you?"

Buck knew his friend was right. If he went off the deep end, then who indeed would take care of his own? Equally as important, who would be around to make sure his sister's murderer was punished?

"So what do you have for me?" Buck finally asked.

"Not much, I'm afraid."

Buck clenched his fist, aching to slam it against the table. "Lucas is going to walk, isn't he?"

"With Holt Ramsey now representing him, that's a real possibility. I have to be honest."

"That can't happen, Sid."

"Hey, like I just said, get a grip." Sid nodded toward Buck's beer. "Finish that off and I'll get us another round. It'll help take the edge off."

"I'm pretty well smashed as it is."

"So?"

"So I don't want you to have to haul my ass home like you did last time we met."

"Not a problem," Sid replied in an easy tone. "That's what old buddies are for."

Buck downed the rest of his beer, then fixed a hard gaze on his friend. "Tell me about this Ramsey guy."

"He's got a reputation for being a mean son of a bitch in and out of the courtroom."

"That's not what I wanted to hear," Buck muttered on a soured note.

"You want the truth, don't you?"

"Hell, yes. Otherwise I won't know what I'm up against."

Sid patted his plastered-down hair, then lowered his hand. "Even though Ramsey's been out of the thick of things for a couple of years, he's still someone I wouldn't want to tangle with."

"So even with the evidence stacked against Lucas, you think Ramsey has the smarts to get him off?"

"Yes, I do."

Buck muttered an expletive.

"I had that friend of mine on the force do some checking," Sid went on as though Buck hadn't said a word. "All he could come up with was that Ramsey has put an investigator on the case who's snooping into Lucas and your sister's affairs."

"That bastard better lay off Rachel. If he tries to dig up any smut on her—" Anger choked off his voice.

Sid leaned in again. "Speaking from experience, that's exactly what Ramsey's going to do."

"Put my sister on trial, is that what you're saying?"

"You got it."

"That's not going to happen." Buck's tone shook with renewed fury.

"I hope you're right."

"Because I'm going to stop him."

"Stop who?" Sid asked, his body coming to full attention.

"Lucas." Buck paused and swallowed the contents of the bottle.

"Like I told you a few minutes ago, you'd best not go off half-cocked."

"He's not going to get away with my sister's murder." Buck's features twisted and his eyes narrowed to dark slits. "I'll do whatever it takes to make sure Lucas pays."

* * *

Maci pulled into Bobbi's driveway but stayed in her car. She needed a moment to compose herself before she saw Bobbi, though she was eager to visit with her friend. The last time they had been together hadn't been a pretty scene. Now, though, Bobbi was flying high. The birth mother had changed her mind as Maci had predicted and was going to give up her baby after all.

But because of the upheaval in her life, Maci hadn't had a chance to celebrate with Bobbi. Even with the engine running, Maci knew she couldn't remain in the vehicle too long. It was just too hot, especially with the sun's rays beating down on her. She peered out the window and noticed there wasn't a cloud in the sky.

Maci wished that were so with her heart.

She had just come from her mother's house. Although she couldn't wait to see Hannah and make sure her every need was being met, the visits were getting harder and harder to bear. She came away feeling so down.

Today she had even taken Jonah, hoping Hannah would react to her grandson. Her ploy hadn't worked. Her mother had no clue that Jonah was even in the room much less who he was.

Bless his tiny little heart, Maci thought with another pang, still picturing Jonah trying to get a response. He had toddled up to his grandmother, whose frail body was propped upright in a chair, and pointed at her with a grin.

"Tell Gram hi, Jonah," Maci had coaxed, blinking back tears.

"Hi, Gram," he repeated as plain as day, looking up at Hannah.

Maci's heart turned over at the poignant scene.

Her mother, of course, did nothing. She didn't even bother to lower her eyes to the child. She simply sat there like a zombie, staring straight ahead. That was when Jonah turned and toddled back to her, flinging himself in her arms.

"It's okay, darling. Gram's not feeling good today. Maybe next time."

Only there wouldn't be a next time. She had to accept the reality of her mother's condition. Hanging on to hope was breaking her heart.

"I know this is hard on you," Debbie said, reaching over and squeezing Maci's hand.

"It's just not fair." Maci felt swamped with despair.

"You're right. It's not."

"But then, who ever said life was fair." Maci, appalled at the bitterness she heard in her voice, forced a smile. "I'm just glad I have you to take care of Mother."

"Well, you do. As long as there's a need, I'm here."

"No sign of her having had any more seizures, minor or major?" Maci asked around Jonah's wiggling body.

"Not at all. The only difference is that she's more lethargic than before. But as you know, the doctor still hasn't gotten her medicine completely regulated."

"After one of those seizures, it takes time. Meanwhile, I have such difficulty watching her suffer."

"I know." Debbie's tone held sympathy.

"Mommy, go," Jonah cried, struggling to get out of her lap.

That was when she had kissed her mother goodbye and taken Jonah home to Liz. Now, prepared to see

Bobbi, Maci peered in the visor mirror to make sure her makeup was in place. She didn't want Bobbi to know she'd been weeping because she didn't want to put a damper on her friend's spirit.

The first thing Maci noticed when the door flung open was Bobbi's glowing face.

"Get your buns in here, girlfriend." Bobbi grabbed her, jerked her over the threshold, then gave her a bear hug. "The coffee's ready and waiting."

"What a difference a day makes," Maci commented with a warm smile as she followed Bobbi into the kitchen where a wonderful scent filled the air. "Mmm, that smells delicious."

"Know what it is?"

Maci wrinkled her nose. "Can't say that I do."

"Me either." Bobbi smiled. "Actually it's several flavors blended, but it's yummy."

"I can't wait to try it."

"Want to sit in here or the living room?" Bobbi asked, filling their cups.

"Here's fine." Maci plopped down in the breakfast room chair and watched her friend while she sat a tray of goodies on the table as well as their cups.

Bobbi sat down, then pointed at the tray. "Dig in."

Maci shook her head. "Thanks, but no thanks. It's too late for me to be eating that kind of stuff."

"Wouldn't hurt you to put some meat on those bones," Bobbi said with a snort.

Maci merely grinned. "You're beating a dead horse, my friend."

"Don't I know it," Bobbi said, rolling her eyes.

They both chuckled, then sipped on their coffee.

"So when is the big day?" Maci asked in an upbeat tone.

"I'm not for sure about that, but the birth mother did sign the papers."

"Are you going to be there for the birth?"

"Absolutely."

"Oh, Bobbi, I'm so thrilled for you."

"Me, too." She grinned. "If you can't have a baby yourself, this is the next best thing."

"You're going to be a great mom." Maci paused. "And dad," she added with a smile.

"We'll see. Only time will tell."

They talked about the baby for a while longer, then Bobbi switched the subject around to Maci. "So tell me the latest with Seymour's case."

Maci hesitated.

"If you'd rather not open that can of worms, I'll understand."

"It's not that."

"Then what is it?" Bobbi probed, not pulling any punches.

"I moved out of our suite."

Bobbi whistled at the same time her eyes widened. "Meaning you're no longer sharing a bed."

"It's awful, but I just couldn't stand the thought—" Maci's voice faltered, unsure of how much she wanted to take Bobbi into her confidence. This topic of conversation was so personal. Yet Maci realized she needed a listening ear, feeling that might somehow assuage some of her doubts and fears.

"Did he go on another binge?"

"Yes, he did. And simply disappeared while indulging."

"You did the right thing, honey."

"Maybe and maybe not, but it was the only way I could...can...handle the situation."

"I know you were really never passionately in love with Seymour, but I had hopes that your marriage would be all you wanted it to be."

"Me, too, but it never happened, and I know it never will now. I don't intend to desert him like a rat on a sinking ship, but our relationship will never be the same. His actions have killed something inside me that can never be revived."

"He should've thought about that before he got himself hooked."

"To make matters worse, he's not at all remorseful. He still doesn't think he's done anything wrong."

"You can't help people like that," Bobbi pointed out. "You're just wasting good breath after bad."

"I know." Maci pressed her lips together to hold them steady. "But when I think of Jonah—" Her voice faltered again.

Bobbi reached over and covered Maci's hand. For a moment, she clung to it, feeling her friend's love and concern warm her chilled blood.

"What is Holt's take on his father's latest shenanigans?" Bobbi asked, withdrawing her hand and taking a sip of coffee.

"He's livid, of course."

"Does he show signs of bailing out?"

"That threat never goes away."

"Great," Bobbi said drolly. "Holt's desertion would be the worst-case scenario."

Actually, it wouldn't. But she couldn't say that because it would open up a subject she wasn't prepared to discuss. Just the mention of Holt's name sent her heart racing.

"So did the two of them tangle?"

"Seymour just wandered in off the streets like nothing had happened and I was trying to get him to talk to me when Holt walked in. The conversation headed downhill from that moment on."

"How did it end?"

"With Seymour going on the attack."

"As in how?" Bobbi sounded incredulous.

"He warned us against ganging up on him."

"Oh, my," Bobbi said, leaving no doubt that she was stunned. "I can just imagine Holt's reaction."

"He told me not to worry, that he'd take care of his father."

"Did that make you feel better?"

"I'm not afraid of Seymour." Maci paused on a troubled sigh. "Actually that thought never occurred to me, until lately, that is."

"You're wising up, thank God," Bobbi said with punch. "If Seymour is still using, then you can't trust anything he says or does."

"I'm beginning to see that."

"Look, promise me you'll stick close to Holt."

"Oh, Bobbi, I can't—"

"Promise me," Bobbi cut in, her tone frantic.

"I promise."

The moment she said it, Maci knew it was a promise she couldn't keep.

Twenty-Six

"I'm expecting them any minute."

Holt gave Vince a hard look. "You're sure about that?"

"Hell, no," Vince responded, standing in front of Holt's desk. "I'm not sure about anything except death and taxes."

"Spare me, okay?"

Vince shrugged. "All I can go by is their word."

"And that might not be worth squat."

"I don't remember you being such a cynic."

Holt grinned but with no real warmth. "Sure you do. That was always part of my charm."

Vince scowled.

This time Holt grinned for real. "Sit down. You're driving me nuts hanging over my desk."

"Want some coffee?"

"Good idea."

Once they were sipping on the fresh brew, Vince plopped down in his usual chair and stared out the window. He had asked Vince to call the nurse and doctor who were in the O.R. with Seymour and see if they'd be willing to meet with him. He'd expected an emphatic no from both, but to his surprise that hadn't happened.

"What's got you so deep in thought?"

He focused on the P.I. "I'm just curious why they agreed to this meeting."

"Dunno. Maybe they're scared."

"All the more reason not to be trapped in a room with an attorney and a P.I."

"Beats the hell out of me. But I guess we're about to find out, if they show, that is."

"Well, Marianne's armed and waiting."

Vince chuckled. "Man, she's a piece of work. Does she ever shut her mouth?"

"Not often."

"If I was around her much, I'd have to get a set of earplugs just to survive."

"Been there, done that," Holt responded with a near-smile. "But you have to keep in mind, good help is hard to find."

"Especially when your ass is gone most of the time, and she's call-on-demand."

"I can't argue with that."

Vince worried with his Stetson for a second, then said, "I guess the first order of the day before our guests arrive—" a sardonic smile rearranged his lips "—is to bring you up to speed on Seymour."

"He's back, by the way."

"I'm surprised."

Holt remained quiet.

"When did he show?" Vince asked.

"Last night."

"I bet he didn't enlighten you on his whereabouts."

"What do you think?"

Vince snorted. "No way, since he was definitely off on a binge. And I got the goods to prove it.'

"That son of a bitch," Holt muttered, lunging to his feet. "I won't ask how you tracked him."

"No need. That's what you pay me for."

"He just doesn't get it, dammit."

"Most addicts don't, which means you're wasting your time trying to reason with him."

"I'm finding that out." Holt cut Vince a sharp glance. "He even had the balls to threaten Maci and me."

"That's not surprising either. You can expect a lot more bloodletting before this baby is put to bed, especially after he made the threat."

"Ah, he's just spouting off, blowing a lot of hot air, actually. He knows better than to pull any stupid stunt like that, but still I'd be worried about Maci."

Holt felt his gut clench, remembering the look of shock and fear that had flicked across Maci's face following the threat. It had been all he could do not to rip his father's head off. But he'd refrained because of Maci.

Despite his mixed feelings for her, she shouldn't have to take any crap from Seymour for something that wasn't her fault. And if Seymour even looked like he wanted to lay an unfriendly hand on her, he'd opt for jail any day over the wrath he, Holt, would bring on him.

"I can see the wheels turning in your mind," Vince said. "Surely you're not concerned he'd hurt Maci. I figured he was crazy about her since she's his prize trophy."

Holt didn't want to admit why that last statement

made him see red, but it did. "I don't know anything about their personal relationship," he snapped.

Vince raised his eyebrows. "Didn't mean to step on a nerve."

"You didn't."

The door opened suddenly and Marianne crossed the threshold. When the door closed behind her, she leaned against it. "Your guests are here." Her tone was low and conspiratorial.

"Why are you whispering?" Holt asked with a sliver of amusement.

"I don't know, except they appear as nervous as cats on a hot tin roof, if you'll pardon the cliché."

"Send them in."

Moments later, both men stood as the doctor and nurse entered the room.

Doctor Ward Chastain was tall and lanky with an abundance of red hair, some of which draped across his forehead, hiding his eyes. Nurse Dawn Gilbert, on the other hand, was short and squat with dark hair slicked back in a ponytail and deep-set gray eyes.

Once the greetings and pleasantries were over and they were seated, Holt went back behind his desk and sat down.

"First off, I want to thank you both for coming."

"Why did you want to see us?" Nurse Gilbert asked without preamble, though her anxiety was evident in the unsteadiness of her voice.

"Yeah, that's what I'd like to know," Dr. Chastain added, his tone edged with that same anxiety.

"Just to make sure you're still in our corner," Holt said, smiling at both of them, hoping to put them at ease.

Dr. Chastain shoved back a strand of his unruly hair only to have it swoop right back down. "We've already talked to the police and to the district attorney."

"And to Vince, here, which I appreciate," Holt said, his smile warming up.

Nurse Gilbert frowned. "Has something else developed?"

"Like what?" Holt asked.

She squirmed in her seat before flinging Dr. Chastain another look. "I don't know. That's why I'm asking."

"Okay, I'll give it to you straight," Holt said. "After Vince here talked to you, he seemed to think you were holding something back, that you weren't totally forthcoming."

Nurse Gilbert visibly sucked in her breath, her eyes widening.

"I suppose you're about to accuse me of the same thing," Dr. Chastain declared in a harsh tone.

"Do I have a reason, Doctor?" Holt asked him point blank.

The doctor's face suddenly matched the color of his hair. "No. I told you all I know, and I'm sticking to my story."

Holt nodded. "That's exactly what I wanted to hear."

The doctor relaxed.

"We're not your enemies, guys," Vince added into the charged silence.

"Then why do I get the opposite impression?" Nurse Gilbert asked, her eyes darting between Holt and Vince.

Holt stood, deciding he'd procrastinated long enough. It was time to play hardball. "You're both smart, so it goes without saying that you know what perjury is and the penalty it carries."

Nurse Gilbert gasped while Dr. Chastain gulped.

Holt went on as though neither had reacted. "Now mind you, I'm not saying either of you is guilty of that. But if you're not telling the truth, it *will* come out. When the D.A. gets you on the stand, he's going to show you no mercy."

"That's right," Vince added in a drawl.

"But we haven't done anything wrong," Nurse Gilbert responded in a raised voice.

"But someone has, because a man's dead." Holt paused deliberately in order for his words to have an impact. "And the D.A. isn't going to shut up or give up until he's pinned one of you."

"One of us?" Anger flared in Dr. Chastain's eyes. "Why, that's insane. Seymour has been indicted and charged in the death. Why would anyone else be implicated? They have their man."

"Not according to you two."

Color receded from both the doctor's and the nurse's face. Ah, so he had finally gotten their attention, Holt told himself with relief, intending to keep the pressure on by firing questions at them. If they were going to crack, now was the time. And not on the stand.

"I don't understand what you mean by that," Nurse Gilbert cried, a hint of tears in her voice.

Holt ignored her input and her growing agitation, concentrating on the doctor. "What about it, Doc? Didn't you tell the cops and the D.A. that my father did nothing wrong?"

Dr. Chastain shifted in his seat as though the chair was on fire. "I didn't say those exact words, no."

"Then suppose you tell me exactly what you did say."

"First off, they asked me if I thought Dr. Ramsey performed surgery while under the influence of drugs."

Holt's eyes drilled him. "Your response was?"

"That I didn't know, that I couldn't tell."

"But they also asked if you thought Seymour had botched the surgery and was at fault, right?"

Chastain hesitated as though scrambling for something to say that would get him off the hot seat, which told Holt all he wanted to know. The good doctor was indeed hiding behind his oath and with very little finesse. Hence, the D.A. would hammer him until he cracked like a stale nut.

"Answer my question, Doctor." Holt purposely kept his voice even and without rancor as both witnesses were getting more agitated and hostile by the second. If they chose to get up and walk out, he couldn't do one thing about it.

"Yes, they did," Chastain answered with a sullen reluctance.

"So we're back to square one." Holt took a deep breath. "The guy's dead and the D.A. is determined to hold someone responsible. Is that someone going to be you, Doctor?"

Chastain shot out of his chair, his nostrils flared. "I'm not about to hang for Seymour. I didn't do anything but close the patient up. Nurse Gilbert will testify to that."

"Is that correct, Nurse?"

She also stood, but was slow in doing so. Holt could actually see her legs tremble under her long skirt. For a moment, he felt sorry for her, but however distasteful this job was, he had no choice but to continue. He'd promised Maci he wouldn't jump ship, and he intended to honor that promise.

"Nurse?" Vince pressed into the now loaded silence. "I think you'd best answer the question."

Suddenly, Dawn Gilbert seemed to crumble from the inside out. She opened her mouth but nothing came out. She opened it again. Again nothing came out.

For a second Holt thought she was going to faint. Vince must've thought the same thing for he made a beeline to her side and grasped her arm. "How 'bout you sit back down."

"No, please," she said, her breath coming in short, gaspy spurts.

"Dawn, are you okay?" Dr. Chastain asked, also crossing to her side, his brows furrowed in a deep frown.

"I'm...I'm fine," she stammered.

"I'm guessing you have something to say, after all, Nurse Gilbert. Am I right?"

She stared at him through a haze of tears.

"I'm in no hurry," Holt said, his tone softening. "Take your time."

She reached in her purse for a tissue. After dabbing at her eyes, she faced Holt. "Dr. Ramsey was in the recreation room before surgery."

"Go on," Holt urged when she paused again. He figured if she had time to think anymore, she might get cold feet and keep her mouth shut. He didn't know what she was going to say, but whatever it was, it didn't bode well for his father.

"You don't have to do this," Dr. Chastain injected, placing a hand on her shoulder.

She peered up at him. "Yes, I do."

"No, you don't," he argued fiercely. "It's not—"

"I promise you, if you know something, you're doing the right thing in talking about it."

"Holt is right, young lady," Vince interjected. "It's best to get it off your chest, then you won't have to worry about what you say, especially on the stand."

"Dawn, I'm warning you," Chastain put in again.

The nurse held up her hand, then said, "I saw Dr. Ramsey swallow some pills thirty minutes before he went into the O.R."

Holt fought off the urge to vomit.

Twenty-Seven

"I need to see you."

Realizing how abrupt that statement sounded, Holt made an effort to modify his tone before he spoke again. "If it's convenient, that is."

"Where are you?" she asked in an unruffled tone.

"I'm at my office. Would you be able to come here?"

She didn't say anything for a long moment. "What about you coming here?"

"Where's here?" He had called her on her cell, thinking that since it was midmorning she had probably left the mansion to do whatever she did during the day.

"At my office."

He was shocked. "Your office? I didn't know you had one."

"Well, I don't, at least not officially. I'm trying out a small three-room complex to see if it fits my needs."

"Way to go."

"Think so?" He heard the hesitancy in her voice and for some crazy reason, he wanted to reassure her she was doing the right thing. Only he didn't know if that was true or not. Hell, he didn't know anything about her except that he wanted her in his bed as much as he wanted his next breath.

Furious that his mind had suddenly betrayed him, he spoke with that same abrupt edge of a moment ago. "Tell me where you are."

"What's this about?"

Ah, so it finally dawned on her that he wanted to see her and now she was having seconds thoughts. He didn't blame her for that either. "I'd rather not go into it on the phone. I promise I won't take up much of your time."

Still, she hesitated, then said, "If you're sure it's important."

"It is." He didn't know why, but he felt he should talk to her first about Nurse Gilbert before going to his father. Then she would be prepared for exactly what was about to happen and why. He couldn't depend on Seymour to level with her.

"Holt?"

"Uh, sorry. Look, just trust me, okay?"

"Has Seymour—"

"Hey, slow down. As far as I know Seymour's at his office. At least that's where he told me he was going when I saw him this morning."

He heard her release of breath. "That's what he told me, too, but I've learned—"

"That we can't always believe what he says," Holt cut in.

"I'll be expecting you," she said.

"Give me the address."

She told him, and five minutes later, he stood awkwardly in the foyer of a suite that fronted a busy street, his eyes perusing his surroundings. "Nice."

"You think so?"

Maci sounded uncertain, as if she needed confirmation. "Hey, I think it's great," he said with real enthusiasm. "Working at home has got to be the pits."

"I have no complaints, actually. It's just that my business has grown so much that I need more space. And I want to handle a line of fabric and decorative items that I obviously can't do at the house."

He stared at her for a long moment. She looked lovely in a short, crimson, V-necked dress that hinted at rather than flaunted her curves, which to him was a definite turn-on. Maybe it was because he'd once touched every nook and cranny of her curvy flesh…

"Stop it, Holt."

It was her husky cry that jolted him back to reality. He didn't pretend to misunderstand. She'd caught him salivating and called his hand. Deservedly so, under the circumstances.

"Sorry," he muttered.

"Would you like to see the rest of the place?"

Her offer took him aback. "Do you realize that we're actually conversing like two civilized humans?" Now why the hell had he said that? He just couldn't keep his big foot out of his mouth.

"Don't push your luck." This time Maci's voice had a sharp edge to it.

"Thanks for reminding me." He tried to trap her gaze. Unsuccessfully. "Sure, if you've got the time."

"I know I'm just prolonging the bad news," she said on a troubled sigh.

"It's not going anywhere."

He heard the bleakness in his tone and knew that she had, too, for she bit down on her lower lip. For a moment, he couldn't take his gaze off the dewy sheen her teeth and tongue had left behind.

God, if he didn't watch it, she would see his loss of control south of his belt. But since she had her back to him, he was saved. Five minutes later, he had toured the two remaining rooms that were painted in warm hues and carpeted with plush broadloom. They ended up in the small kitchenette where a window overlooked a park across the street. Bright sunshine filled the room along with a heavy silence.

"If I knew the particulars of what you do," Holt said, expelling a breath, "I'd probably say this place is just what you need."

She gave him a fleeting smile. But it was a smile, nonetheless. "I've made up my mind to take it."

"I don't think you'll be sorry."

"Me either."

"Does Seymour know about it?" *Of course, he does, you idiot. After all, he would foot the bill.*

"No, he doesn't."

"Bully for you."

She almost smiled again. "It fits."

"What?"

"Your approval of independent women."

"Is that what you are?"

As though she'd picked up on the challenge in his voice, she lifted her chin a notch. "When it pertains to my work, I am."

But not other areas, he wanted to add but didn't. The

thought of her depending on Seymour for anything turned his stomach, especially now. But then their *marriage* turned his stomach. And while this temporary and fragile truce was nice, it didn't change his opinion of her. As long as he kept telling himself that, the better off he'd be.

"Too bad I can't offer you anything to drink."

"No problem."

She played with her lower lip again which continued to drive him crazy. But there was more. A smudge of something—makeup, ink—was on her cheekbone. It was all he could do to keep his itchy fingers from wiping it off, so he mentally savored the feel of her soft, succulent skin against the callousness of his.

Following a shuddering breath, she said, "You might as well get it over with. The bad news, I mean."

His eyes darkened. "I'm in no hurry."

"That's obvious," she said in an unsteady voice, turning her body toward the window.

His gaze dropped to that dusky hollow between her breasts. He tried to swallow, but his mouth was as dry as a well in the desert.

Sex.

That was all it was. He was horny. It was that simple. After all, he hadn't been with a woman in a helluva long time. Until he'd seen Maci, his celibacy hadn't bothered him. On the contrary, he'd welcomed it.

Not anymore. She'd done a number on him. His body remained in perpetual motion, begging for fulfillment in a marathon of hot, heavy sex.

"I…you shouldn't be here."

Maci paused as if carefully weighing her next word,

then finished lamely, "It's too—" Her voice faltered, and she looked away.

"Dangerous. Is that what you were going to say?" Holt's voice had dropped to a husky pitch, but he couldn't help it.

She shook her head. "No."

"Liar," he said in a low, drawling tone.

Maci visibly swallowed before crossing to the counter and leaning against it. When she looked back at him her dark eyes were unreadable. What was obvious from her stance was that she had her body under rigid control.

"I don't know any other way to tell you this but to just say it."

The color drained from her face. "You can't get Seymour off."

Since it wasn't a question, he didn't treat it as such. "It's looking doubtful."

"What happened?"

Holt had to admire her spunk. She might be crumbling on the inside, but outwardly, she was putting on a damn good show. But then, maybe she'd been expecting the other shoe to drop. After all, he only knew this woman's body, not her mind. These past few minutes were the only time they had spoken without slinging verbal insults.

"The nurse in the O.R. saw him swallow some pills shortly before cutting Dodson open. That, combined with the medical examiner's report pretty much nails Seymour's hide to the wall."

"Oh, my God," Maci whispered, her eyes widening with shock.

He hated to see the first crack in the veneer. He liked her when she was strong because it made him strong. It was when she was vulnerable that he couldn't keep his distance.

"So does that mean you're giving up?"

The chill in her voice spurred his anger. But he tamped it down, knowing she was hurting. "I'm not a miracle worker, Maci."

"But you're his attorney who's not supposed to throw in the towel after the first real setback."

Holt let go of a savage expletive, her words stinging.

"Feel better?"

The chill had turned to ice. Holding back his own anger, Holt said through clenched teeth, "This is more than a setback. It's a crucifixion. Even if the nurse was prepared to commit perjury for whatever reason, she wouldn't get by with it. She's too easy to see through. Any D.A. worth his salt would hammer her until she sang like a canary."

"You just can't quit."

"I'm going to the D.A. tomorrow to get a feel of his pulse."

"I expect you to get him off, Holt."

Holt leveled a hard gaze on her. "That's not likely to happen."

"Make it happen." She wrapped her arms across her chest. "For Jonah." Her voice broke.

Dammit, but she was one hardheaded woman. Or maybe she just couldn't face the truth no matter how much he stressed it. Either way, the situation was not good.

If he didn't get the hell out of there right now, he'd have something more to add to his list of regrets.

* * *

She dreaded this encounter with every fiber of her being. Yet she had no choice. She had to be there, especially since she didn't know what would be said.

Holt had told Seymour he wanted to meet with the two of them this evening in the parlor. Apparently Seymour didn't suspect anything amiss or he wouldn't have been in such an upbeat mood.

Damn him, Maci thought again. Damn him for bringing shame and disgrace down on his family.

Damn her for wanting Holt.

She was married to one man but wanted another. There, she'd admitted it. But with that admission, nothing really changed. When this was all over, Holt would walk out without a backward glance.

Yet that didn't temper the unfulfilled ache inside her that she'd further aggravated by inviting Holt to her new office.

She had to pull herself together. Despite the nurse's claim, she had to believe Holt could still pull a rabbit out of the hat and right Seymour's wrong, make this nightmare from hell go away.

That happened everyday, didn't it? The streets were full of people who had murdered in cold blood and gotten off scot-free. Even though she no longer loved Seymour—didn't even like him right now—she knew he wasn't a murderer, that he hadn't meant to take his patient's life. What he needed was professional help, not prison.

She also knew that when he'd swallowed those pills, he'd thought that he was untouchable.

That insidious arrogance had been his downfall.

"Are you ready to go downstairs?"

She hadn't realized Seymour had entered her room until she heard his voice. The fact that he hadn't knocked infuriated her, but she didn't say that. Right now was not the time to get petty or incite another confrontation.

"As ready as I'll ever be."

Seymour raised his silver eyebrows but refrained from answering. When they entered the study, Holt stood by the fireplace, his features drawn tight. Maci's heart skipped a beat, but she refused to show that her nerves were frayed.

"What's this high-level meeting all about?" Seymour asked in a light tone, crossing to the bar and making himself a generous drink of scotch and water.

Maci noticed Holt refrained from looking at her. Instead, his somber gaze tracked Seymour. She could read the disapproval in his eyes when Seymour downed a goodly portion of the drink.

"I spoke to the D.A., Hal Hubbard, today."

"Why would you do that?" Seymour asked, his tone sharp.

"Because Nurse Gilbert caught you red-handed."

Seymour shrugged. "So I took a couple of pills? So what?"

Ignoring his question, Holt went on, "I asked Hubbard if my client were to decide to plead guilty, would he talk plea bargain?"

Seymour let go of a string of curses, then said, "I'm not interested in a plea bargain."

"Yes, you are," Holt said with steel.

"The hell I am," Seymour counted. "I want to walk. Oh, maybe pay a fine and do some hours of community service, but that's all. While we're at it, I want my medical license left intact."

"People in hell want ice water, too, but they don't get it."

Seymour flushed a deep red and he snapped, "Just where are you going with this?"

"The D.A.'s willing to cut you a deal."

"Oh, I'm sure he is," Seymour said, followed by a round of empty laughter.

Then to Maci, "Did you know about this?"

"No," she said, feeling like her heart was going to cave in. So much for the power of positive thinking. Things looked like they were going downhill at a rapid clip.

"Five years."

"*Five years,*" Seymour screeched, his face looking like it was ready to explode. "I'm not about to serve five years behind bars."

"How 'bout twenty-five? That's what you'll get if you're convicted."

Maci sucked in her breath while the room spun.

"Are you all right?"

At first Maci didn't realize Holt was talking to her until Seymour said, "Forget about her. It's me we're talking about, dammit."

Holt's features turned savage. "Get a grip, Seymour."

"No, you get a grip," Seymour countered, closing the distance between him and Holt. "And while you're at it, tell that D.A. I said go to hell."

"That's your call, but you're making a big mistake. You *will* go to the pen."

"I'll see you in hell first." Seymour punched Holt in the mouth, knocking him to the floor.

"For god's sake, Seymour," Maci cried in horror.

"Now get the fuck up and out of my sight," Seymour added, his breathing heavy.

Without taking his eyes off his father, Holt got to his feet and strode to the door. After placing his hand on the doorknob, he swung around. "I'm leaving before I give you the ass kicking you so richly deserve."

Twenty-Eight

Maci felt numb to the core. Yet she functioned like she always had. Jonah and her work had been the panacea that kept her from completely falling apart. Still, it was like she was on the outside looking in at her life, like someone else was living in her skin.

Seymour was in prison.

She still couldn't believe that he had been hauled away three weeks ago, to serve a five-year sentence behind bars. How could that be? How could that have happened?

Holt.

He was supposed to have prevented the one thing that she had feared most, the breakup of her family, the loss of her husband and Jonah's father. Yet Holt hadn't lived up to his end of the bargain. But was he remorseful? On the contrary, he thought he'd done Seymour a huge favor by getting his sentence reduced.

The morning after Seymour had hit Holt, Seymour had come to her room, looking his years for the first time since she'd known him.

For a second, her heart had softened, but just as quickly, it hardened again. He deserved no sympathy. He had brought his fate down on himself and his family. For that she would never forgive him.

"Can we talk?" Seymour asked in a tone that was almost repentant.

"What is there to talk about?"

"Don't shut me out, Maci."

"Give me one good reason why I shouldn't."

"Because I'm your husband. And the father of your child."

He knew how to jerk her chain. "I'm listening."

He crossed to the chaise and sat down while she remained standing, belting her robe tighter.

"You know I have to take the deal. Holt's right. If I chance a jury trial and I don't win, I could go away for much, much longer."

Maci willed back unwanted tears at the same time her throat threatened to lock up on her. "I know."

"And I'd rather die than do that."

"I know that, too," she whispered.

"You and Jonah will be all right," Seymour went on awkwardly.

She could only nod, her throat completely closing.

"I shouldn't be going down for this. I didn't do anything wrong."

Some of the old defiance and arrogance had returned to his voice. It made her sick. "I'm sorry you feel that way, Seymour, that a person's life is that cheap to you. I'm not saying you deserve prison, but you need some serious help."

His eyes narrowed on her. "Have I made you hate me?"

Did she hate him? No. She didn't feel anything for him anymore which was actually worse. Maybe if she did hate him, she could heal faster. The emptiness inside her was much harder to deal with.

"Maci, I asked you a question."

"No, I don't hate you, but—"

"But what?"

"Never mind. It doesn't matter how I feel. It's too late for that. You chose drugs over Jonah and me. That was a choice, and as we all know, choices have consequences."

"And prison is my consequence." Seymour's tone was bitter.

She didn't bother to answer.

"When I get out, I'll make this up to you and Jonah. I promise you that."

"Don't make promises you can't keep."

"Like I make a habit of that." He was on the defensive.

"What about getting help for your drug problem? That was an unkept promise."

"That's different."

She might as well be talking to a brick wall. He didn't get it, would *never* get it. As before, she was wasting her efforts and his time.

"Once I'm home—"

"I don't…can't talk about the future right now, Seymour. The wound's too fresh and painful."

He stood, his shoulders sagging. "I'm going to the D.A. with Holt today and seal the deal."

Tears spilled down Maci's face, but she couldn't bring herself to reach out and touch him. Even when Seymour had walked out of the house the following day in handcuffs on his way to prison, she hadn't been able to touch him.

Still, as a dutiful wife, she'd gone to see him at the allowed visitation times, which had been one of the hardest things she'd ever done. If someone had told her she'd be visiting anyone behind bars, much less her husband, she would've told them they were nuts.

In spite of the humiliation and pain that dogged her like the most dedicated of stalkers, life went on. The fact that Bobbi had gotten her baby had helped buoy her spirits somewhat. As a new mother, her friend had needed Maci's guidance and assistance, and she had been glad to give it.

While one part of her life had changed, another had not. Holt's presence and his volatile effect on her remained the same even though they had had little contact since Seymour's departure. She had gone to great lengths to avoid him and he her.

Right now, just thinking about Holt struck a nerve. That was why she needed to get up from the breakfast room table and go to her office. Later in the day, she planned to take Jonah to the zoo, providing the mercury didn't reach ninety-five. After last night's rain, she was keeping her fingers crossed that the outing would come about.

Spending time with her son kept her sane.

"Good morning."

She swung around and stared at Holt who was striding toward her, a muffin and cup of coffee in hand.

"Good morning," she managed to say around her hammering heart. He was the last person she wanted to see. And she damn sure didn't want to make idle conversation with him.

As always, his presence seemed to dominate the premises, forcing her to concentrate on just him. He wore a pair of slacks and blue cotton shirt that accentuated his blue eyes. It was obvious he'd just gotten out of the shower; his hair was damp and unruly. Suddenly she felt the urge to run her fingers through it, to…

How could she have those kind of thoughts about a man for whom she held nothing but contempt and who returned the favor? Waves of self-loathing washed over her as she watched Holt sit in the chair in front of her. That was when she noticed the dark circles under his eyes and the tightness of his face.

"I know you'd rather I get lost."

"How did you know?"

A cynical smile eased across his lips. "Body language. The minute you saw me, you turned into a wooden statue."

"That's absurd."

"Whatever."

"Look, I was just leaving."

She picked up her empty cup and was about to make good on her words when a hand shot out and grabbed her around the wrist. The feel of his flesh against hers electrified all her senses.

He muttered a curse, then released her. But she knew he had experienced the same reaction for the blood completely drained from his face.

"Don't go," he said in a thick-toned voice. "Please."

She didn't know why she consented to his husky plea, but fool that she was, she did, knowing that she would surely regret that momentary weakness.

"We can't keep going on like this."

"Like what?"

He muttered a curse. "You're being deliberately obtuse."

"Oh, really. And just how should I be?" she demanded, feeling the need to make him suffer. "I don't even know who I am anymore."

"Dammit, Maci, don't you think I know that?"

"Forget it," she responded in a wooden voice. Somehow getting even was no longer palatable. "It doesn't matter."

"It matters to me, especially when I know you blame me."

"Yes, I do," she admitted with glaring honesty.

"I can handle that. I did what I had to do and it was in Seymour's best interest."

"Says you."

"You're damn right. I made the call and it was the right one."

She stood and moved away from the table. "What do you want from me, Holt?" The instant she voiced that question, she realized she'd made a grave error.

Stark desire darkened his eyes as they trapped hers. "I think you know that."

"Damn you," she said through gritted teeth.

In two strides he was in front of her, looming over her. "I don't know why I give a damn. You are what you are and I know that. But—"

Rage took over. Before she could stop herself, she raised her hand, determined to slap him again.

"Oh, no you don't," he said in a tight voice.

Then in a lightning-quick move, he shoved her against the wall, pinned her hands back and ground his lips into hers. The sweet-savage assault was so abrupt and so fierce that it literally took Maci's breath, making it impossible to respond. Finally, though, his lips softened and coaxed hers apart. The invasion of his tongue, mating with hers, was her undoing.

Clinging to him, she drowned in pure pleasure. His hand reached under her blouse and covered a breast.

He shouldn't be touching you like this, she told herself, though the voice of conscience was weak and far away, leaving her like putty to make and mold as he saw fit.

Lifting his mouth from hers, he rasped, "You're driving me crazy."

"Holt," she whimpered, feeling him press her harder against the wall with his erection. Dear God, this was madness.

"I can't get you out of my head," he rasped again, his glazed eyes holding her captive while she continued to crave the feel of his hardness grinding against her.

"We—"

He unsnapped the front closure of her bra and his rough hands touched her bare flesh. The combination of his arousal and hands on her breasts melted away all her resistance. She felt herself about to climax.

No, she had to stop this insanity.

"Shh, don't fight it," he said in a low, rough voice as though he had read her mind. "Let it happen."

"Please—"

The rest of her sentence jammed as an orgasm pounded her body with such an intensity that a cry slipped from her lips, a cry that was quickly smothered by another hot, raw kiss.

Even after it was over and she was limp, Holt still

didn't let her go. He only took his lips off hers long enough to take a breath. It was as if he couldn't control his greediness, his mouth closing over hers once again.

At first Maci wasn't sure what the noise was that invaded her semiconscious mind. But after the noise didn't let up, she realized it was the door chimes ringing.

Someone was at the front door. Oh, God. Holt must've reached the same conclusion because he thrust her away, but not before saying, "Don't for one second expect me to apologize."

Feeling as though her face and body were on fire, Maci did her best to put herself back together. But her hands were shaking so badly, she found that even straightening her blouse was next to impossible.

"Mrs. Ramsey."

She lifted her head. "Yes, Annie, what it is?"

"I'm sorry to disturb you."

Thank God you did.

"There are gentlemen waiting in the foyer to talk to you."

Without looking at Holt, she made her way to the front of the house, albeit on unsteady legs. When she reached the two men, she sensed that Holt had followed her.

"I'm Maci Ramsey."

The taller of the two stepped forward. "I'm afraid we have some bad news. Your husband has had a heart attack."

Twenty-Nine

Holt killed the engine in the emergency room parking lot, then looked at Maci, waiting for her to act. She made no effort to move. Instead she sat staring straight ahead, her perfect profile looking like it was carved out of stone.

But again, he had to hand it to her. When push came to shove, she was no shrinking violet. He guessed she was trying to mentally prepare herself for what she might encounter when she went through those double doors.

After the officials had informed her that Seymour was in the hospital in critical condition, Holt had moved as close to Maci's side as possible, fearing she might faint. Hell, the unexpected news had thrown him for a loop.

A small cry had escaped her lips and her face had turned whiter than parchment.

"Come on, let's go see what the hell happened."

She hadn't argued with that either. It was then that he realized that she was in shock. Or at least close to it. With this latest tragedy, her nerves were stretched to the breaking point.

Taking charge, he had told Liz what had happened then hustled Maci out the door.

On the way to the prison hospital, silence had reigned supreme. She had sat very much the same as she sat now, facing the front, her body rigid. He'd wanted to know what she was thinking, but he hadn't dared ask. After the stunt he'd pulled in the breakfast room, he knew he'd pushed his luck about as far as he could.

God, he couldn't believe his control had snapped in a blink of an eye and that he'd taken advantage of her. Again. Only this time he had no doubt that she hated him. No more than he hated himself, he thought savagely.

Yet if the opportunity were to present itself, he would go back for seconds. When his lips had meshed with hers and he'd touched her flesh, he'd felt his control slipping. And when he realized he was about to bring her to orgasm, he was convinced he'd knocked on heaven's door.

But to have entered the pearly gates, he would've had to carry her upstairs, lay her on the bed, remove every stitch of her clothing, spread her legs, then bury himself inside her over and over until they were both crying for relief.

Just thinking about how soft her skin was, how tantalizing she smelled, how good she tasted activated his groin until the pain was more physical than mental.

He might not like her, but he damn sure wanted her.

"Holt."

The sound of her fragile voice jerked him back from heaven's gates to the reality of a cruel world. "Are you ready?" he asked.

"As ready as I'll ever be for something like this." Her voice shook.

"Want me to go in first? Alone?"

"No." That tiny word was barely audible.

"It's your call."

He ached to reach out to her, to reassure her that everything would be all right. But he couldn't make a promise he couldn't keep. If his father didn't make it, then…

Shutting that thought down, Holt leapt out of his side of the SUV and bounded around to hers. Too late. She was already out and headed for the E.R. entrance. He caught up with her, and they fell in step together.

In a minute they found Seymour's cubical. A doctor swept around the curtain and paused midstride, narrowing his gaze on them.

If the look on the doctor's face was a barometer by which to judge Seymour's condition, it wasn't good, Holt told himself. The physician's thin face wore a solemn and pained expression.

"My husband—" Maci's voice cracked.

"I'm sorry, Mrs. Ramsey, but your husband didn't make it."

She shook her head and wavered. Holt clasped her arm tightly.

"You…you mean he's dead?" she cried.

The doctor's features became even more pained. "Yes, that's what I mean. And I'm not sure of the cause yet."

Maci simply stood there and stared at the doctor, her features twisting in pain and horror. And while Holt was grappling himself to come to grips with the blow, he rebounded enough to asked, "What the hell does that mean, Doctor?"

"Prior to his heart attack, he took a fall in the exercise yard that may or may not have been accidental."

"You mean—" Again Maci's voice cracked then faded into nothing.

"Yes, ma'am. He may have been murdered."

Holt caught her as she fainted.

"You poor baby. What else is going to happen to you?"

"I'm afraid to even go there," Maci said to Bobbi in the living room of her home. Bobbi's baby, Emma, was sleeping in the crib nearby. Every so often Maci's sad eyes would seek out the child and smile. Jonah had the same effect on her. She could barely bring herself to be apart from him. The children tempered her sadness.

These past few days she had loved and hugged her son more than she ever had.

"When are you going to get a definitive answer?"

Maci shuddered, knowing that Bobbi was referring to the much-anticipated autopsy report. "According to Holt, anytime now."

"Hold that thought," Bobbi responded, uncurling her legs and getting up from the sofa. "I'll be right back. I'm going to get us something to eat and coffee."

"Nothing for me, please."

"I'm not taking no for an answer. You look like you're about to dry up and blow away."

Maci didn't have the wherewithal to argue. Instead, she remained silent and stared out the window with unseeing eyes. Every bone in her body ached, yet she couldn't seem to slow down.

She no longer had a husband.

Since Seymour's death three days ago, the only time she had stopped had been when friends came by to pay their respects and give their condolences.

Sleep had become a thing of the past. Though exhausted mentally and physically, her body wouldn't relax.

When the medical examiner released the body for burial and the funeral was over, she suspected Holt would hightail it out of town. What made her so angry with herself was that the thought of him leaving both depressed her and relieved her.

But she didn't want to think about Holt, especially when she hadn't even buried her husband. And not after what had transpired between them the morning Seymour had had his heart attack.

She still couldn't believe he had made her come with so little effort. Maci lifted her hand to her scalded cheeks while her stomach turned over. Only after taking several deep breaths did she feel her muscles uncoil.

This afternoon here at Bobbi's was the most relaxed she'd been. But then Bobbi had that effect on her. Her friend had insisted she come see her in order to get away from the press and friends who were just snooping, hoping to get more fodder for the gossip mill.

"Here we go," Bobbi said, interrupting her morbid thoughts.

Maci returned to her spot on the sofa and eyed the tray Bobbi plopped down with a frown.

"Stop it," Bobbi ordered. "You're going to eat. You hear me?"

Maci forced a smile. "Yes, ma'am."

"Good." Bobbi grinned. "I love it when you do like you're told."

Maci reached for a cucumber sandwich and munched on it, though it tasted like she was eating a piece of cardboard. When she couldn't take any more, she reached for the cup of flavored coffee and washed it down.

Bobbi's eyes drilled her. "Eat another one."

"I can't, not right now. Give me a few minutes."

"All right, but I'm not letting you off the hook."

"You have no idea how hard it is for me to eat," Maci admitted with reluctance.

"Oh, yes, I do. Remember, I've been down that road only in different shoes."

"You're right. We've both been to hell and back and lived to tell about it."

"I can't believe they haven't released the body yet," Bobbi said around the food in her mouth.

Maci placed her cup back down and noticed her hand shook. "Me either."

"When the reason for a death is suspect," Bobbi said, "the state has to do their thing."

"That's what Holt told me."

"By the way, how's he holding up?"

"Who knows," Maci responded, trying to keep her voice neutral. "We don't have much to say to each other lately. And it was no secret how he felt about his father."

Bobbi merely shook her head. "I can't believe all this is happening. First, Seymour gets hooked on drugs, then is accused of taking a man's life. If that's not bad enough, he goes to the pen, falls, then dies from a heart attack." She paused and stared pointedly at Maci. "Or maybe not."

"It's the *not* that has me crazy," Maci said in shaky voice. "It's hard for me to believe that someone could have deliberately hurt Seymour."

A wave of despair suddenly washed over Maci,

bringing tears to her eyes. While she no longer loved Seymour, she would still miss him. After all, he had been her husband and her child's father. And now that he was gone, what did the future hold for her? She had Hannah and Jonah to think about.

And Holt.

A sob broke loose.

"Oh, honey, I'm so sorry about all this," Bobbi said in a soothing tone, scooting over and putting her arms around Maci. "This too shall pass, I promise."

Maci clung to her and let the cleansing tears flow.

"Two beers, please.

Once Holt had ordered and the waitress left their table in a café close to the county medical facilities, Holt perused his friend Pete, who looked a bit different from the last time they'd met. A pair of wire-rimmed glasses now covered his blue eyes, significantly dimming their twinkle.

"Thanks for meeting me," Pete said, his lips looking a tad pinched.

Holt didn't know what his friend had to say, but he knew it wasn't going to be good or Pete wouldn't be sitting in front of him with a hang-dog look on his face.

"I know what I'm doing is not according to the book," Peter said in an uneasy tone. "I should be having this conversation with Mrs. Ramsey."

"No, you shouldn't. I am…was Seymour's attorney."

"True, but—" Again Pete hesitated, grabbing on to his beer that just arrived. After swigging down some, he still didn't look at Holt.

"What's going on, man?" Holt asked, a knife twisting in his gut.

"Another blow."

"Just what Maci needs."

"What about you?"

Holt stared into his beer bottle, then looked up. "I'm okay."

"You sure? He was your father, after all."

"Yeah, he was," Holt said with bitterness.

"Look, I'm sorry he's gone and I'm even sorrier for all the grief associated with his death."

"Thanks," Holt muttered, taking a gulp of the brew. He was sorry, too, but he couldn't talk about it. Granted, he and his father had never seen eye to eye on anything, especially where his mother was concerned. Yet, Seymour's untimely death had been a shock.

He had never envisioned them patching up their differences, but now that option had been jerked out of his hand, and he didn't like that.

"Maybe we should call your stepmother after all."

"Spit it out, Pete," Holt said with authority. "I'll handle Maci."

"Suit yourself."

Another short silence.

"Dr. Ramsey didn't die of a heart attack."

Holt was taken aback and knew it showed.

"I know what you're thinking," Pete said, "that a heart attack's a good thing."

"Not really, because I know there's another verse to the song you're singing."

"Unfortunately, you're right," Pete responded, toying with his bottle.

"So did the fall that precipitated his attack kill him?"

"No," Pete said bluntly.

Holt frowned "I don't get it."

"He got ahold of a shitload of bad drugs."

Holt swore.

"Man, I'm sorry. I hated to tell you that."

"I'm sorry, too, but not for the same reason." Holt didn't bother to hide his disgust. "But for Maci's sake, I'm glad he wasn't murdered."

"That's the bright side of dark," Pete responded. "Apparently he was hooked—line and sinker."

"That's no surprise," Holt said. "Since prisons in general are a hotbed for drugs."

"You're right on target there."

Holt chewed on his lower lip. While the news wasn't what he'd wanted to hear, an overdose was better than murder.

Pete cut Holt's brooding short by asking, "How will Maci take the news?"

"How would you think?"

"Not good," Pete said, down-in-the-mouth. "So how do you get along with your young, good-looking stepmother?

It's none of your damn business, Holt was tempted to say, but he refrained. Pete had done him a favor by calling him first. Hence, he didn't think it would be a smart move to insult him. Still, his question was out of line and the answer off-limits.

"You know how gossip paints her," Pete added, "as the consummate gold digger. Is that really true?"

For a reason he didn't want to explore, blind fury rose inside Holt. Nothing would've satisfied him more than to jerk Pete off his seat and punch him.

Holt no longer wanted to see Maci in that kind of bad light. But he didn't know exactly what that meant in terms of his feelings. And the idea of exploring such a thought made his stomach heave. Still, he felt the need to defend her reputation by keeping his mouth shut.

"That's not something I'm comfortable talking about."

Pete shrugged. "No problem. Just thought I'd ask."

"Look, thanks for calling me. I owe you one."

"Aw, heck, you don't owe me anything. That's what old friends are for."

"Again, I appreciate it."

They both stood, then shook hands.

After Pete had disappeared, Holt downed the remainder of his beer, thinking about how he would tell Maci the latest bad news. Minutes later he walked out into the heat, dread dogging his every step.

Thirty

Thank God it was over.

Maci had survived the funeral with strength and decorum.

At the burial site she hadn't known which was worse, the heat or the humidity. It hadn't mattered; the combination made for a lot of misery, though nothing could surpass the wretchedness of simply existing. Although the funeral had been a private ceremony with only family and the closest of friends in attendance, getting through the day had been one of the hardest things she'd done in her life.

Throughout both services, she had been flanked by Bobbi on one side and a grim-faced Holt on the other. And though he hadn't touched her, he hadn't budged from her side either. She had forced herself to keep her composure; she'd never cracked for a second. But it was comforting to know that if she had passed out, Holt would have caught her.

What a waste of life, she had thought, listening to the

preacher. Seymour could have had many good years left. But for some reason she still couldn't fathom, he had squandered them. The drugs he'd used to heal so many people had ended his own life.

Even now, back in her room alone at the mansion, following the catered luncheon for friends and distant family members, Maci's head continued to spin. It just didn't seem possible that she had buried her husband, that her life as wife to Dr. Seymour Ramsey had come to an abrupt end.

It wasn't a neat and tidy end either, but rather a sick and bizarre one.

Feeling her stomach churn, Maci sank onto the chaise longue and closed her eyes. She didn't want to throw up, but she knew she might, although she didn't have anything in her stomach to lose.

Three days ago following Holt's revelation of exactly how Seymour had died, she'd had the dry heaves.

A shudder went through her as she recalled her conversation with Holt. She'd been hanging pictures in her new office when she'd heard someone come in behind her.

"Mornin'," he'd said casually just as she swung around to see who it was.

Embarrassed at being caught with her rear extended, Maci had stepped off the short ladder and faced him. "Did it ever occur to you to call first?" Her voice sounded quarrelsome, but she didn't care.

"Not in this case," he countered with a nonchalant shrug, though his voice was devoid of rancor.

"You seem to have a habit of sneaking up on people. Or at least on me."

His smile took her breath for a second.

"Guilty as charged."

Maci was taken aback by his ready admittance, leaving her momentarily disconcerted. "That's hard to believe."

She watched as he walked deeper into the room, his features once again sober and a bit pinched. Her instinct told her he'd come with bad news, news that she didn't want to hear. Prolonging it as long as she could, she asked, "What do you think?"

"About what?"

She made a face.

"Okay, the room looks great."

"Thank you, even though I had to pull the compliment out of you."

"With you, I never know."

"What does that mean?" she asked in a huff.

"I never know how you'll react. It's walk up turkey get your heard chopped off."

His words incensed her. "That's not true."

"Yes, it is. You just proved my point."

Though his words were serious, his eyes glinted and his mouth twitched. It dawned on her that he was teasing. She felt her lips spread into a smile. That was when their eyes met and held.

With her heart beating out of sync, she heard him say, "I have bad news." Gone was any hint of teasing in his voice. His features now looked carved out of stone.

"I knew that, but—" Her voice faltered.

"I just met with the medical examiner."

"Oh, God," she whispered, placing her hand over her mouth. "Seymour was murdered after all, wasn't he?"

"No."

He told her then about the bad drugs and how his fall had been the result of a long binge.

"Well, at least he died doing what he liked best," she finally responded, unable to hide the bitterness in her voice.

"Yeah, I guess the bastard did do that."

She lifted her chin. "Thanks for telling me."

He nodded.

"I know this has to be hard for you, too, even though you and Seymour had major issues between you."

"I'm not glad he's dead, that's for sure." His tone was as brooding as his gaze. "I'd much rather see him punished for all the hell he put everyone through, mainly you."

Color stung her face. "I'll survive."

"I'm sure you will."

Maci ignored the hint of sarcasm in his tone. "If there's nothing else, I have a funeral to take care of."

He hadn't argued with that or with any of her plans that had followed. Deep inside, she had wondered if Holt would even attend the funeral. When he showed up a few minutes before the service, she'd felt a sense of relief.

Trying to shut out the day and her thoughts of Holt, Maci opened her eyes to find herself staring through tears.

Suddenly an intense feeling of loneliness and despair swept over her. She had suffered too much pain and sorrow in her life and she wouldn't start whining now. She would simply glue the pieces of her life back together one more time and look forward, not backward.

She had a son for whom she was responsible. Nothing must stand in the way of helping Jonah become an honest, caring and decent man who felt good about himself despite what his father had done.

While Maci's mind grasped what lay ahead, her heart didn't. Even though Seymour had killed whatever feelings she'd had for him, his absence and her subsequent loneliness would not be easy to handle.

It would get even worse when Holt left.

Unwilling to dwell on him again, Maci decided that a glass of wine might help her settle down and fall asleep. Bobbi had offered to bring her baby and spend the night with her, but Maci had told her that wasn't necessary, that she would be fine. And she would. It was just going to take time to adjust to her new life.

Feeling slightly better, Maci made her way downstairs only to find Holt in the living room. Drinking.

She remained still while her heart raced out of control. How long had he been home? Long enough to get drunk? Drowning her troubles in booze was suddenly somewhat appealing, though not the answer. Not her answer, anyway.

"I didn't expect to see you," she said for lack of anything better to say, thinking he suddenly looked like the stranger he actually was.

Even though he was now dressed casually in a pair of cutoffs, washed-out T-shirt and tennis shoes he seemed sullen and unapproachable. He looked like he was heading for the water.

Perhaps he was.

Holt's brooding eyes pinned her. "Just where did you think I'd be?"

"Gone."

"Gone?"

"Back to your boat."

"As appealing as that is, I'm still on the Sanders case, remember?"

She shrugged. "I figured that wouldn't matter."

"I'm glad your opinion of me hasn't changed. I'd be disappointed."

"You asked for that." He hadn't and they both knew it. But he could get under her skin and loosen her tongue quicker than anyone she'd ever known.

Holt cursed before draining his glass. "I'm not in the mood to argue with you tonight."

"Nor me with you," she said in a tired voice.

"In fact, it's been a rather shitty day all the way around."

"I couldn't agree more."

They stared at each other while the tension climbed to a high pitch.

"Care to join me?"

His voice had dropped to a husky pitch, which she chose to ignore. Still her heart raced faster. "Actually, I would," she finally muttered, though she had no intention of indulging in more than one glass of wine. Her limit was two. She saw no reason to change that, especially in the company of Holt. She needed all her wits about her.

"Ah, we finally agree on something."

She crossed to the bar and poured herself a glass of white wine, all the while feeling his heated gaze follow her. She was treading on dangerous ground and she knew it. If she were smart, she'd take her wine and head back upstairs away from him.

But when it came to Holt, when had she ever been smart?

"What shall we drink to?" There was a leer in his voice. "To my dearly departed father and your dearly departed husband. Will that work?"

Disgust filled her. "You're drunk."

"I'm working on it, honey, but I'm not there yet."

She took a sip of her wine then edged toward the door.

"You're not running off, are you?"

"I'm going back to my room, if that's what you mean."

That glint remained in his eyes. "I wish you'd reconsider."

"I don't think that's wise."

"You can't keep running away from me, you know."

She swallowed hard. "I don't have to worry about that."

"How so?"

"Surely you won't stay here. In this house, I mean. Now that Seymour—" She let the sentence go, but he got the message.

He gave a nonchalant shrug. "Hadn't really thought that much about it."

"Don't you think it's time you did?"

"Okay. So I thought about it."

"And?"

"I think I'll stick around until dear old Dad's last will and testament is read."

That declaration shouldn't have shocked her, but it did. How many times had he told her he didn't want any of Seymour's money? Why was the reading of the will important to him, unless he had lied to her all along and he did want something?

She decided not to react to his comment. If he expected to get a rise out of her, he would be disappointed. Seymour had the right to do as he pleased with his estate. If he chose to include Holt, then so be it. She wouldn't cause any trouble.

"Does that upset you?"

She shook her head. "No. Why should it?"

"Then why do you look like you just bit into something distasteful?"

"If you're staying, then I think it's best you check into a hotel."

"Not a chance," he said flatly. "I'm staying right here."

Suddenly the temperature inside the room rivaled that on the outside.

"But why?" she asked, clutching the stem of her glass so hard she feared she might break it.

"Why not?"

"This isn't a game, Holt."

"Didn't think it was."

"What if I told you I don't want you here?" The truth of the matter was, she wanted him to remain in the mansion because she didn't want to be alone. But she also knew that he should go, that it wasn't safe for him to stay.

She was simply too vulnerable. And weak. Another truth, even more disturbing, was that if he tried to take her in his arms, she would go. Though she was ashamed to admit it, she could no longer ignore that unvarnished truth about herself.

"I don't care what you want."

She shook her head, anger getting the better of her. "Just exactly what do you care about?"

The room got quiet for a long moment.

"Are you sure you really want to know?"

Heat surged through her. "Forget I asked that."

"Smart move."

She gathered all her dignity about her and said, “Good night.”

A smirk reshaped Holt’s lips at the same time he lifted his glass in a mocking salute.

Thirty-One

"I'm sorry about your old man." Vince paused. "For more reasons than one, I might add. All of which you know without me listing them."

"I know," Holt muttered absently. "And thanks."

"You going to be okay?"

"I'm fine." Holt's tone was abrupt.

"Got any coffee?"

"No. I haven't made any, and Marianne hasn't come in yet."

"You sit tight and I'll do the honors. I've got to have some to jump-start my day. I didn't sleep worth a damn last night, and my head feels like a bowling ball sitting on my shoulders."

Holt nodded toward the coffeepot. "Knock yourself out."

Several days had passed since his latest altercation with Maci. Holt wasn't proud that he'd purposely riled her again. Although it was hell to admit, he couldn't deny his change of heart concerning Maci.

He had no idea when that change had come about. Maybe his mellowing first took root in admiration.

He'd watched her endure the pain, humiliation and heartache and she had never indulged in self-pity. Not once had he heard her whine or ask why me. Instead she'd taken her licks on the chin and kept on going.

Most women he knew would've buckled under the pressure, but Maci was the most determined woman he'd ever met. It made him see her in a different light, and acknowledge that he'd been wrong, that maybe she hadn't married Seymour just for his money, that maybe she had actually cared for the selfish bastard.

Even though that thought didn't sit well with him, it was to her credit.

He was now completely smitten with Maci and wanted to get to know the real woman, not just the hot-blooded vixen he'd slept with on the island, especially now that she was free.

God, where had that thought come from? Cursing silently, Holt drew a calming breath and rejected that idea before it took a life of its own, knowing it would only get him into trouble. After all, she had all but told him to get lost.

That was what had made him see red. He'd hoped that she would want him to hang around in case she might need him. Wrong, he told himself brutally.

He didn't want to leave her. That was the crux of the matter. While he ached for his freedom, he ached for her more.

"My, but you're quiet this morning." Vince placed a cup of coffee on Holt's desk. "Maybe this will start your engine."

"Got a lot on my mind," Holt mumbled.

"You can dump on me anytime," Vince said, sitting down.

"I know."

"That's what I'm here for. Your beck and call."

Holt gave him a sour look. "Since when?"

Vince chuckled. "I knew if I kept on, I'd get you out of that funk."

"Who says I'm in a funk?"

"Me. But then you're entitled. After all, you just buried your old man."

Holt didn't respond.

"So how's the widow holding up?"

"Fine."

"She may be all the things people are saying about her, but in my book, she's a real lady."

"That she is," Holt muttered.

Vince looked taken aback. "Ah, so you've come off your high horse where she's concerned, huh?"

"I wasn't ever on a high horse."

Vince chuckled again, then sipped on his coffee. "Whatever."

"She wants me out of the house." The second Holt uttered those words, he regretted it. That issue was between him and Maci so they would have to work it out. No third party was needed.

"So are you going to a hotel?"

"Nope."

Vince's eyebrows rose, but he didn't say anything, for which Holt was grateful.

"The will's going to be read this afternoon."

"Oh, great," Vince said with sarcasm.

"That's what I think, too. I'd just as soon skip that sideshow."

"Then why don't you?"

Holt shrugged. "Keefe Ryan is insisting I be there, says it will bring closure."

"He's entitled to his line of bullshit, I guess."

Holt sipped on his now tepid coffee, then changed the subject. "I know this may sound paranoid, but I'm going to lay it on you anyway."

"Shoot."

"I could swear I was followed on my way to the office."

"Followed?" Vince looked astounded. "You gotta be kidding."

Holt gave Vince another sour look. "Now why the hell would I kid about something like that?"

"You wouldn't. It was just a knee-jerk reaction."

"Now that I think back, there've been other incidents where I got that same feeling."

"Man, that's weird."

"It's bugging the hell out of me, is what it is."

"Would me, too."

"Thing is, I don't have a clue as to who or why."

"Or if it's just your imagination," Vince qualified with raised eyebrows.

"Let's pretend it isn't my imagination and take the necessary steps."

Vince stood. "If someone's on your ass, I'll nail him. You can rest assured on that."

"Meanwhile, I'll keep a closer watch myself."

"That'll work."

Holt came from behind his desk. "Speaking of work,

I...we still don't have the missing pieces to the Sanders puzzle."

"Trust me, I'm digging."

"Apparently not deep enough."

Vince responded by saying, "I'll keep you posted."

"I'm counting on it," Holt said to Vince's back as he walked to the door then out of it.

Fifteen minutes later, Holt was on his way back to the mansion with the hairs standing up on the back of his neck. Dammit, he couldn't shake the feeling that he was indeed being followed, though he'd peered in the rearview mirror countless times and seen nothing.

Still, his gut instinct had never let him down. If and when he found out who was tailing him, he'd take pleasure in making his life miserable.

Until then, maybe he should move out of the mansion. The thought of putting Maci and Jonah in danger didn't bear thinking about. Yet the thought of leaving them didn't bear thinking about either.

Meanwhile, he'd just have to adjust to having his balls feel as if they were perpetually in the meat grinder.

Maci had dreaded this moment all day.

Now that the time had actually come, her trepidation had increased instead of decreased. Keefe Ryan was in the study and she'd served him a drink while they waited for Holt.

He was already fifteen minutes late.

"I told Holt to be here," Keefe said in an agitated tone.

Maci almost laughed at his naïveté. "That doesn't mean anything."

"Are you saying he just might not show up?" The attorney sounded most undone.

"I don't have a clue, Keefe." Maci heard the agitation in her own voice and made no apologies for it. "I'm sure you know him better than I do."

Keefe rubbed his bald head. "Not really. Seymour never talked much about his son. And he's certainly not easy to get to know."

"Maybe by the time we finish our drinks, he'll be here." Although she had poured herself a glass of wine, it had been out of courtesy more than anything else. She had no intention of finishing it. She knew she had to be in control when in Holt's company. She had learned that the hard way. And the reading of the will would require her full and undivided attention.

"You haven't even asked about the contents of Seymour's will," Keefe said, breaking into her train of thought.

"You sound surprised."

"I am. I'm not used to civility among families when it comes to property and money."

"Then I guess I'm different."

"You aren't the least bit curious?"

"Would it do me any good?" Maci asked, turning the question back on him.

Color rushed into his pale, nondescript face. "No. To discuss the will out-of-hand would be unethical."

"I know and respect that."

"And I respect you, Maci, and would be proud if you'd continue to let me represent you."

She clearly didn't know what to say as she didn't see the need for an attorney. But then, maybe he knew something she didn't.

As if sensing he'd spoken out of turn, Keefe added, "Sorry, I didn't mean to be pushy."

"You weren't, and should I need an attorney of your caliber, I'd certainly consider you."

Keefe nodded, then peered at his watch, his features crunched in a frown. "Where is he?"

"Right here," Holt said, barreling into the room and not stopping until he reached the bar.

Maci wished she could ignore him, ignore the scent of his cologne, ignore the way he look disheveled but sexy as hell, ignore the way her body went into meltdown when he was anywhere near.

Mortal shame filled her. She still wanted him with an intensity that frightened her. He had to get out of this house. Maybe this reading would make that a reality.

With drink in hand, Holt turned around. "Sorry I'm late."

Maci knew he wasn't sorry in the least, but she kept her mouth shut. This meeting was going to be hard enough without them taking verbal shots at each other.

"If you're ready," Keefe said, his tone stiff, registering his disapproval, "we'll get down to business."

Maci watched Holt smirk at Keefe who positioned himself in a chair close to the two-seat leather sofa. When Holt remained standing, she poised on the edge of the chair adjacent to Keefe. If Holt decided to sit, she didn't want to be near him.

Keefe cleared his throat. "Let me begin by saying to both of you how sorry I am about Seymour. He was a good friend and a good client."

When Holt held his silence, Maci said in a soft voice, "I appreciate that, Keefe." Now get on with it, she wanted to scream. Her nerves were frayed and stretching this latest ordeal out was cruel and unusual punishment, especially with Holt's brooding presence weighing on her.

She just wished she could tell him to go to hell and mean it.

Keefe cleared his throat again which reclaimed her attention. "The contents of the will are actually very simple. Cut-and-dried, really."

"Why don't you just cut to the chase, Keefe?" Holt demanded in an abrupt tone.

Keefe's lips tightened and a flush highlighted his face. Maci knew he wanted to make a suitable comeback, but his good breeding and manners kept him in check. Not so with her. While she didn't say anything, she gave Holt a scathing look.

He merely raised his hands in a mocking gesture. It was all Maci could do not to get up, walk over and slap him. As if he could read her mind, his smirk burgeoned into a smile. He was actually enjoying himself, but why she didn't know.

"The bulk of Seymour's estate, Maci, goes to Jonah."

Maci shook her head, hearing her heart pound in her ear. "It does?" she said, her gaze swinging to Holt, wondering what he must be feeling.

"That doesn't include the house," Keefe continued. "It goes to you with the funds to keep it up." He paused and took a breath. "Since you have the lifetime trust that was set up before you married, Seymour felt he'd done his due by you."

"That he did," Maci acknowledged, all but squirming in her seat, wishing Keefe had kept his mouth shut about the trust in front of Holt.

"Now to you, Holt," Keefe said in an almost jubilant tone.

Holt got the jump on him. "I get zip, right?"

Keefe shifted in his chair, but his chin was raised in defiance. "That's right."

"Do you think that bothers me?" Holt asked, finishing off his whiskey.

"It would bother me," Keefe said in a tight voice.

"But then you're not me, are you, Keefe old boy?" He walked over to the bar and poured himself another generous shot of whiskey. "Just so you'll know, I never wanted any of Seymour's money and wouldn't have taken it had it been offered." He downed his whiskey, then made his way to Keefe where he bent over him and poked him in the chest.

Keefe's eyes widened with fear.

"Next time you feel the urge to jerk my chain, I suggest you reconsider." Holt patted Keefe on the cheek, straightened, then made his way to the door. "Y'all have a nice evening."

Thirty-Two

"I hope I'm not calling too late."

"Of course not," Bobbi said.

Maci felt somewhat less guilty when she noticed her friend didn't sound as if she'd been awakened from a sound sleep. But now that she had Bobbi on the line, she regretted the impulse to call her. "Why don't we talk in the morning?"

"Hey, don't you dare hang up on me. You called me for a reason, so let's have it."

"I was just restless and couldn't sleep," Maci volunteered in a lame voice.

"That's only part of the story, right?"

"Right. How come I can't fool you?"

"Because we're friends, and friends know when things are not okay."

"They're far from okay." Maci was close to tears and she hated that. She'd had too much to drink, though she wasn't anywhere near drunk. She was, however, feeling sorry for herself, something she didn't often give in to. But tonight was different.

She was alone in the house with Holt. A shudder went through her.

"It's not Jonah, is it?" Bobbi asked.

"Oh, no. Actually, he's not here. Liz took him to her sister's for her niece's birthday party. I almost didn't let him go, but decided it would be good for him and for me."

"Good girl."

"I don't know about that. I miss him terribly. This is the first time I've been away from him for a night."

"He'll be fine and so will you." Bobbi paused. "So what has you spooked?"

"The will was read this afternoon."

"And how did that play out?"

Maci told her, and she whistled. "You mean he cut Holt completely out? Didn't leave him a red cent?"

"That's exactly what he did."

"Did the shit hit the fan?"

"Not visibly, but with Holt you never know. He holds his cards close." She paused.

"Go on."

"When my trust fund was mentioned, he threw me one of his looks."

"Is that what has you upset?"

"Sort of. No one likes to be thought of as a gold digger." Maci paused again. "More than that, Holt doesn't want to move out of the house."

"Why is that a problem?"

"I just don't think it looks good." Maci realized by taking Bobbi into her confidence that she'd opened that can of worms she'd worked so hard to keep closed.

"Since when have you cared how things look? More to the point, what *will* people think?"

Bobbi was too quick, but then Maci knew she would be. She should have kept her mouth shut. "Never mind. It'll work out."

"Never mind, hell," Bobbi countered. "Is there something going on between you two?"

Maci sucked in her breath and held it.

"Ah, so he does still have the hots for you. And now that his old man has—" Bobbi broke off. "Sorry, didn't mean any disrespect to the dead or to you, my friend."

"It's not like that, Bobbi," Maci said in a weary voice, kicking herself again for opening her big mouth. "With Holt, I mean." She hated lying, but she couldn't bring herself to admit that he'd almost made love to her even before Seymour died. She did care what her friends, especially Bobbi, thought. She didn't want to lose Bobbi's respect.

"Then what's it like?"

Maci paused, struggling to chose the right words.

"You might as well fess up because it's eating a hole in your gut. I can tell that."

"I'll admit the attraction is still there."

"Is that a bad thing, Maci?"

"Yes, it is. First, it's too soon after Seymour's death. And second, Holt feels nothing but contempt for me."

"Then he doesn't deserve you."

"That's not even in the cards."

"So what is in the cards for you two?"

"No future, that's for sure." Maci paused and pulled in a deep, shaky breath. "I never broke my wedding vows, Bobbi."

"Look, that's your business. I'm not sitting in judgment of you or anyone else. I'm your friend, and I'm going to support you no matter what. Just like you supported me."

"Thanks," Maci muttered.

"And you don't have to thank me."

"All I know is I don't want him in the house now that Seymour's gone." For her sake, she added silently. She was simply too vulnerable, too needy, for him to remain even though she suspected she'd be safe as far as he was concerned. The look of contempt he'd tossed her was proof of that.

"Then tell him that and don't mince words."

Maci chewed on her lower lip. "That doesn't mean he'll do it."

"Well, you won't know 'til you try. If he doesn't, then you can go to plan B."

"And just what would that be?"

"We'll figure that out when the time comes."

If her stomach hadn't been tied in knots, Maci would've smiled. But there was no room for laughter in her right now, only extreme sadness and discontent.

"Do you want me to come over?"

Maci was appalled. "Absolutely not."

"You know I would. In a heartbeat."

"I know and I love you for offering. But I'm a grown woman who should be able to handle a crisis on her own."

"Don't be too hard on yourself. You've had more crises lately than most people have in a lifetime."

"I am walking on thin ice, I'll admit."

"You sure you're all right?"

"Now I am. You've made me feel better, given me the courage I needed."

"Good. I'll talk to you tomorrow."

After Maci placed the receiver back in its cradle, she wasted no time in pouring herself another half glass of wine. She took two sips, then eased down on the chaise longue and leaned her head back, feeling the courage of a moment ago slowly seep out of her. Maybe she should scrap the idea of approaching Holt this evening.

The morning would do just fine, she told herself. It had been a long and difficult day. The last thing she needed was more confrontation. She knew if she approached Holt that was exactly what would happen.

Maybe she didn't care. She scrambled off the chaise and when she did, the room reeled. Bracing herself, she remained still until the room righted itself. Was she drunk? Of course, she wasn't. Exhaustion was the culprit.

Instead of wine, she should be drinking a glass of hot milk. That would settle her jangled nerves and help her sleep. And sleep would block out the fact that Holt was just down the hall.

The thought propelled Maci out of the room and into the hall. She was about to pass his door when she realized it was open. Don't stop, she told herself. Keep right on walking.

But she couldn't take another step nor could she stop her head from spinning. He was standing in front of the fireplace in his room.

As if realizing he was no longer alone, he whipped his head up and their eyes locked. Her heart seemed to lurch in her throat. A strangled sound left his as he closed the distance between them.

Maci felt her lips part, but she couldn't say a word. She stood as though paralyzed and waited.

* * *

"Going somewhere?"

"No…yes."

"That makes perfect sense."

Standing within touching distance of her, only not touching her, forced Holt into a rigid stance. He didn't know what kind of perfume she had on, but she smelled like heaven. However, it was what she was *not* wearing, that sent the heat thundering into his groin. Her flimsy pink pair of lounging pajamas didn't cling to but hinted at her luscious curves.

Except for her breasts.

Her nipples were rock-hard and visible where they dented the fabric, leaving no doubt as to her arousal. He groaned inwardly, aching to jerk her in his arms, push her to the floor and take her there. But pride and anger kept his libido in check. For the moment, anyway.

"I just bet you were coming to see me," he said in a leering voice.

She flushed and her chin rose. "Why would you think that?"

"Guilt."

Her eyes widened with unvarnished surprise. "Guilt?

"Yeah. I'd about decided I was wrong about you, that you married my father because you actually cared about him, only to find out it was the money all along."

Anger flared in those widened eyes. "You go to hell."

"I may just do that, but I bet I'll have company."

Tears welled up in Maci's eyes. For a second, he felt like a heel for adding to her pain. But dammit, when Keefe had mentioned the trust Seymour had set up for her, he felt he'd been duped again.

He'd been furious with her for letting him down and furious with himself for trusting her. Yet he still wanted her with an intensity that was physically painful.

"You're despicable," she spat. "Besides that, you don't know anything about me."

"Suppose you enlighten me."

"I'm not going to argue with you." She turned away.

"Dammit, Maci," he said, unable to bury his agony. "Don't walk away from me."

She looked straight at him. "Get out of my way and out of my house."

"And if I don't?"

Her lower lip quivered. "Please, don't do this."

"Do what?" he rasped, his gaze homing in on her lovely mouth, now parted and moist. He barely stifled another groan. He knew exactly what she was talking about. He was deliberately trying to make her as miserable as he was, make her pay for his inability to get her out of his mind. Wanting her and not being able to have her had nearly driven him over the edge.

"Don't make things any worse," she added on another whisper.

He reached out suddenly and touched her face.

She sucked in her breath, but she didn't flinch.

He wondered if she had any idea what she was doing to him, how incredibly sensual and delicious she looked with color staining her cheeks and the tiny tip of that pink tongue sensuously lining her lower lip.

His arousal could not be more complete.

"Holt—"

"You don't understand," he ground out. "I can't go."

"Can't or won't?"

Though barely audible, her voice held a weary note that raised his protective instincts. Suddenly, he felt an acute urgent sense of responsibility. He wanted to take care of her, to right all the wrongs in her life.

"Let me by," she whispered.

He hadn't realized that he had maneuvered his body in front of her, blocking her way, until she said something. Yet he didn't move. He couldn't. He couldn't let her walk away from him.

"Please." She reached out then and placed her hand on his bare chest as if to push him away.

He covered her hand with his. The contact was electric, extinguishing their next breaths. Capturing her eyes with his, he felt a new surge of heat rush into his groin. Placing both hands around her upper arms, he jerked her against him. Caught off balance, she leaned more heavily into him, which caused them to tumble backward into his room.

With one foot, he kicked the door shut, then braced her against it.

No way could he turn her loose. The feel of her soft, pliable body made his head spin. Charged with another emotion, he cupped her under the buttocks and moved her against his erection.

"Holt—" she cried breathlessly.

"Holt what?"

"I—"

"For God's sake, don't tell me to stop."

"We…can't."

"The hell we can't," he muttered against a patch of velvet skin near her ear while his hands frantically unbuttoned her top, peeled it off her shoulders and let it drop to the floor. Her breasts filled his gaze.

Before tasting those sweet morsels, he felt an overwhelming need to explore her tempting lips. Cupping the sides of her face, he lowered his mouth onto hers and drank from the richest of nectar, feeling their tongues mate, then tangle in a war as old as time itself.

He pushed his fingers through the silky stands of her hair and deeply inhaled the scent of her like he would the rarest and most exotic of perfumes.

When he lifted his lips, she stared at him out of glazed eyes and cried, "This is madness."

"A madness I can't control." He molded her body even closer, leaving no doubt as to the extent of his arousal. "Nor can you."

"Holt."

The broken, husky use of his name gave him the confidence he needed to hold her face steady in his hands and gaze into her eyes, feasting on her loveliness.

"I—" Her voice collapsed when her hand connected with his bare chest again.

A strangled sound erupted from deep within her, completely obliterating any resistance he had left. He couldn't wait another second to touch, to taste her more intimately. Returning to her mouth, he rejoiced in the heated parting of her lips and the dizzy mating of their tongues.

He couldn't say which threatened to explode first—his head or his manhood. Both throbbed with the thrust of a jackhammer against them.

Following a muted groan, he dropped to his knees, then reached up and yanked down her pajamas, exposing her entire body.

The hard beat of her heart drew his eyes back to hers. They looked like black holes of passion. Lowering his gaze once again, his eyes landed on the creamy white skin of her stomach and the tiny indent that was her navel. But it was the thatch of black curls at the apex of her thighs, joined by long, shapely legs, that held him transfixed.

It was when he buried his face in those curls that she buried her hands in his hair and cried his name.

Thirty-Three

That moment provided all the encouragement he needed to continue his mission of reuniting their bodies. Holt already knew how it felt to be a part of her, to suckle those nipples until they felt like they would burst, to have access to the moist cavity of her mouth. The memories of that night had never left him; they remained irresistibly haunting.

He wanted to enter her, wanted to feel her softness consume and accommodate his hardness. He wanted to feel that furnacelike heat surround him, drive him to the brink of no return. He wanted to bring her to that same point and test her endurance before that final sweet assault.

But first he wanted to tease her for as long as possible, or as long as his control lasted. With his mouth still on her, he nibbled the succulent skin through the curls before gently nudging her legs apart.

When the tip of his tongue slid up and down, tasting her, he felt her legs quiver at the same time a sob left her mouth. She dug her fingers deeper into his scalp. He felt no pain, just the throbbing of his manhood.

She was already wet.

He inhaled the essence of her, sinking his tongue higher in the hot, melting sweetness while his hands caressed the cheeks of her buttocks, running a finger through that rear delectable valley. That was when Maci gasped out loud and her body convulsed. To increase her pleasure, he stabbed her countless times with his tongue, holding her tightly, until she came.

Continuing to cup her womanhood with a hand, he rose to his feet. Maci's head was against the wall, her eyes closed. When he fingered a nipple, her eyes flew open. "You're beautiful," he rasped.

"We...we—"

"Shh, it's okay. You want this as much as me."

"Yes," she finally breathed, wrapping her hands around his neck.

Giving in to his overwhelming need for her, he sank his mouth onto hers, knowing she tasted herself on his lips, which only heightened the pleasure. With their lips still joined, their tongues entwined, he guided her to his bed, feeling relief when she fell back gracefully.

By the time he had removed his clothes, she was propped up on her elbows, her eyes glazed with desire. Bending over he sucked one nipple until it was ripe, then went to the other. His hand reached down and he again inserted his finger inside her.

Maci bucked then she squeezed her thighs together. He knew she was close to climaxing again. He added another finger.

She cried against the heat of his lips that had claimed hers.

Unable to resist any longer, he straddled her body with his and peered into her eyes. They looked intoxicated with passion. "I didn't think this moment would ever come." His voice sounded thick.

"I want you inside me," she whispered, sinking her fingers into his shoulders.

"And I aim to please."

His breath caught when her fingers circled him and she began to caress him. "Whoa, slow down," he muttered in a low, growling voice. "I can't take much of that."

She paid him no heed. Continuing to massage his penis, she pulled his head down until she meshed her lips with his, kissing him hotly and deeply.

When breathing became impossible, she let him go.

"No more," he ground out thickly, spreading her legs with his hand. Then in a bold, sure move he thrust into her, feeling that wet softness envelop him like a glove. Oh, but she was tight, much like she'd been on the beach that night so long ago. Then he'd felt like he was making love to a virgin. Now, he had that same feeling which ignited his passion that much more.

"Please," Maci gasped wide-eyed.

"I know, baby, I feel the same way. It's been too long."

"Yes, yes."

He pushed higher and harder.

She gasped, clutching at him.

He stopped midaction. "Am I hurting you?"

"No," she exclaimed. "Please, don't stop."

With a moan of intense pleasure, he thrust again and was rewarded. He felt her expand to accommodate him, just as he'd imagined so many times. Yet he hesitated, yearning to prolong this moment of intense pleasure. But his body had a mind of its own. Soon it would betray him, especially when he sensed she was also losing control.

"Maci, Maci," he cried when he felt his own orgasm close. As if she sensed his need, she bucked beneath him, her nails digging into his buttocks, holding him as close as possible.

It couldn't get any better than this, he told himself when he felt her pulsing body and heard her muted cries.

All resistance and reasoning left him, especially when he realized she was going to climax with him. He felt his seed spill into her.

"Holt, yes," she cried when he collapsed on top of her.

He lay still for the longest time, his body too spent to move, but not his mind. He had tasted the forbidden fruit. He had made love to his father's wife. Then it hit him that Seymour was dead, that he had done nothing wrong.

Why didn't that absolve his conscience?

There should have been regrets, but there were none. He could no more have stopped making love to her if someone had held a gun to his head and threatened to pull the trigger. He would have told them to go ahead and shoot.

So what did that mean?

He didn't know. The only thing he did know was he would have a hell of a time walking away from her. But he knew that day would come.

The thought sent chills darting through him.

With a look or a touch, she could ignite his soul. He would readily admit that. How could that be when he wasn't interested in home and hearth? Did he want her at all costs? Wouldn't it keep his life simple if he just thought of her as his father's wife and walked away?

Too tired to pursue the answer to those questions, Holt shuddered, and rolled off her. Peering at Maci, he saw that she was asleep. He sighed, drew her close, and closed his eyes.

Had she lost her mind?

Yes. But did she care? No. When she had passed by Holt's door and saw him standing there, half-naked, the decision had been made for her on the spot. She had consciously stopped and said to hell with the consequences.

Right or wrong, she had stepped across the line and there was no turning back. Only there was, Maci corrected herself mentally, easing her head to one side and perusing his lean features that were now dark with a day's growth of beard.

She could get up and sneak out of his room and tell him that she never wanted him to touch her again. No matter how much he might object to that, he would honor her request. While Holt might be a bastard in many ways, he would never force himself on her.

So why didn't she act on her thoughts? Why didn't she nudge him awake and tell him to get out of her house, that she never wanted to see him again?

Because she loved him.

There. She had admitted what she had been denying and hiding in her heart since Holt had waltzed back into her life. Maybe she had been denying it from the onset of their relationship.

She almost cried aloud, but she managed to bite

down on her lower lip just in time. He must never know. She must guard that secret with as much fervor as she had guarded that first forbidden encounter with him.

When he wrapped up his other case, he would sail out of her life, literally, and she would never see him again. Surely that was the best thing for her and Jonah. She could never justify falling in love with her stepson.

But she knew she would love him for as long as she lived.

While that truth cut her to the core, she had to face it and accept it before she could become functional again. She'd had too many severe blows at one time. Knowing how quickly disaster and unhappiness could strike, she also knew she had to make the most of the time she had left with Holt. With that uppermost in her mind, she scrambled onto her knees, bent over him, and stroked him with her fingertips.

His penis burgeoned instantly, filling her hand.

Then she heard him groan at the same time his eyes shot open. "Maci?"

Her name came out sounding like a croak.

"Don't say anything," she whispered. "Just feel."

"Oh, God," he gasped.

Her lips surrounded the velvet tip as her eyes remained locked on his.

"Are you sure?" he asked thickly, his eyes dark and glazed with desire.

"I'm sure." She heard the tremor in her voice, but it wasn't the result of uncertainty. It was her own insatiable desire. Touching him with her tongue had made her wet and needy again.

"You're killing me."

She ignored him and continued to suck on the tip, then took all of his engorged flesh into her until she felt him grasp her by the hair and pull her up.

"I don't want to come in your mouth," he said hoarsely, lifting her up and on him.

She gasped when she sank onto his spearlike hardness and he began to move her hips against him, all the while watching her.

Only after their cries rent the air at the same time did she collapse on top of him.

A short time later his erection again disturbed her slumber.

"I can't get enough of you," he whispered, his breath hot against her ear.

A shiver went through her as he reached around and surrounded a breast.

"Nor me of you," she whispered in turn, feeling his hand nudge her legs apart.

Moments later, he entered her. She gasped when he began to thrust, not stopping until he had emptied his seed into her once more.

Groaning she turned over and met his hot, seeking mouth, losing herself in the smell, feel, and taste of him.

Thirty-Four

She was gone when he awakened.

He was disappointed, but not surprised. He hadn't been ready to let her go, and he feared he'd be packing by the afternoon and headed to a hotel. Though his stomach twisted at the thought, he would go.

Reaching over, Holt turned off the hot water and instantly felt the cold pelt his skin.

He had better get used to cold showers, he reminded himself, at least when it came to Maci. While she had been everything he'd hoped for and more sexually, he expected her to have deep remorse and regrets this morning.

But he sure as hell didn't. In fact, he'd like a steady diet of having her in his bed every night. Holt suddenly stood deadly still in the shower wondering if that novel thought meant he was in love. Hell, he didn't believe in that nonsense, he told himself quickly.

Love hurt.

He had seen what his mother went through in the name of love. But he cared about Maci; he had no problem admitting that. And that caring went deeper than just screwing her every chance he got, though he wasn't opposed to that either.

Swallowing a curse, Holt stepped out of the shower, dried off, dressed, grabbed his briefcase and headed downstairs. He paused at the bottom of the stairs, feeling his pulse shoot up. Maci had either passed through or was still around. He inhaled again, filling his nostrils with her perfume. For a minute he felt dizzy and blood rushed to his groin.

He clutched the leather handle tighter. His gut told him to let it be. *Let her be.* It was too soon to seek her out. She would need time to come to grips with what had happened between them. Even so, if there was a chance he could see her, he wasn't going to pass it up, regardless of the consequences.

Dropping his briefcase, he made his way into the kitchen. It was empty. No sign of the housekeeper. Holt helped himself to a cup of coffee, then took a chance on the terrace. His hunch paid off. She was sitting at the table, sipping on a cup of coffee, looking lovely in a pair of black slacks and a cream-colored sleeveless sweater that molded the same breasts he'd suckled and kneaded until they were wet from his mouth.

He felt a pinch behind his zipper and winced.

That was when she turned around. He watched as a flush stole up her cheeks, adding to her beauty. She didn't turn away, though he saw her swallow, which told him she was not as calm as she appeared.

Hell, neither was he. His palms and upper body felt

clammy. At any time, he could break out into a full-blown sweat. He couldn't chalk that feeling up to the high humidity. Not this time.

"Good morning," he said in a strained voice.

Maci's flush deepened, but again she rose to the occasion. He'd give anything to know what was going through her mind about now.

"You're up early," she said, her voice sounding equally as strained.

"So are you."

"I...I couldn't sleep."

Silence.

"Neither could I."

Maci expelled a breath, but held his gaze. "Holt—"

"If you expect me to apologize—"

"I don't," she cut in, averting her gaze.

He studied her profile and noticed her pulse beating in her neck.

Holt struggled to get his next breath. It was all he could do to hang on to his control. He wanted to close the distance between them, grab her and rain fiery kisses over her face and mouth.

Hell, if he had his way, he'd bend her over the wrought iron table and take her right there. He must have made a guttural sound because she whipped her gaze back around.

"I should go," she said with obvious difficulty.

"Me, too."

Neither moved.

"If you want me out of here, I won't fight you on that." There, he'd said it. He'd placed his head in the noose, fully expecting to get it chopped off, and deservedly so. After all, he'd homed in on her vulnerability. He'd known how fragile she was, what she'd been through. He should have left her alone, dammit. But he couldn't then and didn't want to now.

"That's up to you," she said.

Holt heard the tremor in her voice, and another shaft of remorse hit him. The last thing he wanted was to bring her more pain.

"Do you mean that?" he asked in a hoarse tone.

Maci nodded, biting down on her lower lip.

He wished she wouldn't do that. It should be him biting on that lip, suckling it until he made her wet. Suddenly, her eyes darkened as if she could read his mind.

He cleared his throat just so he could speak. "So are we calling a truce?"

"Of sorts, I guess."

This time he nodded while another silence fell between them.

"That doesn't mean—" Maci's voice faltered.

"That I'm welcome in your bed."

Her breath caught and her eyes widened.

"Don't worry. If I make love to you again, it will be like last night—because we both want it."

"That's fair enough," she whispered.

He stared at her for a long moment, aching to reach out and touch her, to ease the pain he saw mirrored in those lovely stark eyes. But he didn't move, realizing the ball was no longer in his court. It was in hers. "If you need me, I'm always reachable by cell."

When she didn't respond, he went on in a rough voice, "It's not my intention to hurt you, Maci. For what it's worth, I want you to know that."

* * *

Maci smiled at her newest client, then said, "I'm so looking forward to working with you, Mrs. Galloway."

"Oh, honey, drop that Mrs. stuff. Call me Lois, for heaven's sake."

Maci's smile widened. "Lois it is."

"I may be old, but I'll be damned if I'm going to act or look it."

"Well, you've certainly met your goal."

"Oh," she said again in the same dismissive manner, "you're too kind."

Lois, who Maci suspected was in her mid-sixties, was a piece of work. Maci had figured that out the minute she'd arrived at the Galloway's new, upscale home in the suburbs. She was a people person who never met a stranger.

She was short and more than slightly overweight which accounted for her smooth baby textured skin. She had not one wrinkle on her dimpled cheeks, Maci noticed with a jolt of envy. If it hadn't been for Lois's eyes that looked like they were on stalks, she would've been a real beauty. But those bugged eyes were a distraction as well as a detraction.

Even so, Maci knew she and Lois would work well together and she was excited about sinking her teeth into a new project that would give her a new lease on life.

And help take her mind off Holt.

She quickly turned her head for fear Lois would pick up on the color Maci felt surge into her face. So far, she hadn't let herself replay the events of last night. She simply hadn't been emotionally equipped to do so, especially after admitting to herself that she was in love with him.

That unvarnished fact still had her shell-shocked.

"I hope you're hungry," her client was saying.

They were in the kitchen and Maci looked on as Lois filled a tray with tea and scones.

"These are homemade, mind you," Lois said, lifting the tray and motioning for Maci to go ahead of her back to the living room.

"Oh, my," Maci said. "I'm impressed."

"You should be," Lois countered airily. "I'm glad I made them now, considering you're poor as a snake and could eat five and never know it."

Maci laughed out loud. "Poor as a snake. That's a new one on me."

"It's the truth, if you don't mind me being so frank."

"Frank is good."

"Have you always been so thin?"

"Pretty much, though I've lost some weight lately."

Lois made a face. "Of course. I hope you don't think I'm being insensitive. I should've told you up front how sorry I am about your loss."

"Thank you," Maci replied lightly. "It's been rough."

"I'm sure." Lois's face brightened. "But you have your son, and I know that helps soak up some of the pain."

"That he does. He's a bundle of toddler delight."

Maci wasn't surprised about Lois's condolences. Even though she hadn't said a word about having lost her husband, everyone knew about it. Even if the Ramsey name hadn't been up there with royalty in this town, Seymour's downfall and subsequent death had been headlines in the paper.

Pulling herself out of her reverie, Maci sat down and immediately eyed the goodies with relish. Perhaps that was because she was hungry following her marathon night of lovemaking. Feeling her face suffuse with color again, she made a big deal of serving herself, then munching on the scone.

"This is delicious," Maci said when her mouth was no longer full.

"It is, if I say so myself."

"Tom must adore you for more reasons than one."

Lois seemed girlishly pleased by that comment. "He doesn't even mind that I'm fat."

"You're not fat," Maci said, appalled.

"Yes, I am, but that's okay. I'm comfortable with who I am and how I am."

"Bully for you."

"You seem like that sort of person to me," Lois commented, after taking a sip of her tea. "Comfortable with yourself, I mean."

"Most of the time I am," Maci admitted with caution. "Lately, though I've had some doubts."

"Under the circumstances, that's to be expected. If I lost Tom—" She broke off with an apology, "Sorry, I didn't mean that like it sounded. If I lost my husband, I'd do just what you're doing—get through it and go on with my life."

A moment of silence followed while they both enjoyed the food and drink. Once Maci pushed her plate away, she spoke, "I want you to know how excited I am at the prospect of refurbishing your home. It's lovely already."

Lois flapped a hand loaded with diamond rings. "But it's not me. I can't wait to get rid of that butt-ugly wallpaper in the dining room."

Maci chuckled. "I'm with you."

"So shall we get started? I'm devoting the entire day to you."

"It's going to take that and more."

Several hours later, she had just gotten in her car when her cell phone rang. Recognizing the number, her heart lurched. Jonah was at a private church day care because Liz's mother was in the hospital and she was with her.

"Is Jonah all right?" she asked without preamble.

"He's fine, Mrs. Ramsey." The worker paused. "Jonah is the only one left and I was just wondering when you were going to pick him up."

"Shortly," Maci said in a puzzled tone.

"Uh, there's been an emergency in my family, and I really need to leave."

Frustration colored Maci's tone. "I'll get there as soon as I can."

"Thanks."

It was after she'd placed her cell back on the seat that Maci realized the traffic had stalled. She was too far behind the cars to see what the problem was, but she knew she wasn't going anywhere for a spell.

"Damn," she muttered, reaching for her cell to call the church and tell the worker she was late. Then her hand paused at the same time her heartbeat accelerated.

She'd probably regret this, but she was going to do it anyway. She punched in another number and waited.

Holt faced Vince across his desk. "Got anything for me?"

"About you or Sanders?"

"Both, but let's start with Sanders," Holt said, having just arrived at the office the same time as Vince.

Vince rubbed his jaw. "I've got something, all right, but again, I'm not sure it's anything we can use."

"Let's hear it."

"I checked into Bradford Investments where Sanders's wife worked."

"And?" Holt prodded when Vince paused.

"Seems the company's in financial difficulties, though no one was willing to enlighten me as to why."

"Figures."

"Anyhow, I talked with several of Rachel Sanders's cohorts, and they told me she'd been in a real tizzy for several months, that something had been bothering her. But she wouldn't confide in them."

"You think that something was work related?"

"Yep, I sure do."

"Did you talk to her boss?"

"I tried." Vince made a face. "His name is Dane Melton, and he was about as forthcoming as a mute."

"Think he's hiding something?"

"I'd like to think so simply because he rubbed me the wrong way."

Holt was quiet for a moment. "That aside, what does your gut tell you?"

"That Melton's up to his neck in alligators and that Rachel knew it."

"Let's just say you're right and she had the goods on him. That would give him motive to give her unneeded assistance down the stairs."

"Works for me," Vince exclaimed.

"Well, we know there was no forced entry into the house. So if she had a visitor, he was definitely no stranger."

"Right on."

"What we...you need to do is find out if that someone was Dane Melton."

"I'll give it my best shot."

"So what about me?" Holt rubbed the back of his neck. "Is someone tailing my ass or am I losing it?"

"I'm thinking you're losing it," Vince said with a grin.

Holt scowled at him. "Telling me that made your day, didn't it?"

"You asked, good buddy."

Before Holt could make a suitable comeback, his cell rang. "Yeah," he said, not recognizing the number, only to then feel the bottom drop out of his stomach when he realized it was Maci.

"What can I do for you?" He listened then responded, "Sure. It'll only take me a few minutes to get the extra car seat and go get him."

When he rang off a few seconds later, his head was still spinning. Maci calling him and asking a favor was unbelievable. He refused to admit why a simple request made him so happy.

"What was that all about?" Vince asked with blatant curiosity.

"I have to get Jonah for Maci. She's tied up in a traffic jam."

Vince stood. "I'll call you as soon as I know something."

Less than fifteen minutes later, Holt had a laughing Jonah buckled in the back seat. "It's just you and me, fellow. What do you say we go get an ice-cream cone? Think Mommy would mind?"

Jonah merely laughed and kicked his feet.

"That's good enough for me."

It was when he neared the intersection that it happened. Holt put his foot on the brake only to realize he had no brakes.

God no, he cried silently. This couldn't be happening, not with Maci's baby with him.

Thirty-Five

The lights from the ambulance and two police cars on the scene were as glaring as they were unnecessary. Jonah hadn't been hurt in the crash nor had he. Still, Holt was grateful that a passerby had seen him swerve off the road and called for help. Thank God, he hadn't been going fast or their fate might have been much different.

A shudder went through him.

If anything had happened to Jonah under his watch, he would never have forgiven himself. It would have ruined the rest of his life. He peered at his watch, anxious for Maci to arrive. He'd had no choice but to call her on her cell and tell her there had been an accident.

A cry had erupted from her lips before he could reassure her that Jonah was fine, that he was laughing and playing with the female paramedic. When he finally got that across to her, she'd told him in a shaky but controlled voice, "The traffic is moving, I'll be there shortly." She paused and took a heavy breath. "Meanwhile, take care of my baby, Holt." Her voice had broken on that last sentence and his heart had wrenched.

"Trust me, Jonah is fine," he'd stressed.

"What about you?"

The fact that she cared enough to ask, melted his bones. "I'm fine, too," he said thickly.

Now, as he waited for Maci, an intense anger dogged his every step. She didn't deserve this latest mishap in her life, especially when she was an innocent party. He didn't know what had caused his brakes to fail, but he wouldn't rest until he found out. If it was anything other than an accident, then whoever was responsible had better beware. When he got his hands on him, he would tear him limb from limb.

"If there's nothing else, we're gone," one of the policeman said, jerking Holt out of his thoughts. "The wrecker should be here momentarily."

"Thanks for everything."

"No problem," the officer said, walking off.

It dawned on him that the ambulance would probably want to leave as well since they weren't needed. Frowning, Holt peered at his watch, his anxiety growing because Maci hadn't arrived. He'd also called Vince and told him what had happened and that he wanted him to meet him at his office.

"Mr. Ramsey?"

Holt whipped around and saw the young paramedic making her way toward him, packing Jonah on one small hip. When the baby saw him, he held out his arms.

Again, Holt felt his heart melt as he reached for the child who was beginning to fret. "Mommy, Mommy," he said over and over.

He took Jonah in his arms and kissed him on the cheek, something he'd never done in his life. But then, he didn't recall ever holding a baby. "Mommy's coming soon."

Then around the child's head, he spoke to the young lady. "Thank you so much for caring for him."

"I'll be glad to stay and watch him longer, if you need me to."

"Thanks." Holt forced a smile. "We're fine. I appreciate all your help."

She smiled at him and the baby then went back to the ambulance that was cranked and ready to go. Once Holt was alone, he released a deep sigh, smiling down at Jonah who was pulling on the neck of his T-shirt.

"Hey, buddy, how 'bout we get out of this boiling sun?"

"Mommy," he whimpered, his lower lip protruding.

Oh, brother, Holt thought. What if he started howling? What would he do then? Surely there was something in his car that would distract Jonah, something that he could play with. The ignition keys. He didn't know where that thought originated, but somewhere in the back of his mind, he recalled having seen kids put those in their mouth, which of course was unacceptable. Keys weren't made for a child's mouth, especially not Jonah's.

By the time they made it back to the vehicle, Jonah's frets had increased. "Down," he said, kicking his legs against Holt's thighs.

"Okay, buddy, I'll put you down, but you have to hold my hand."

"Down," Jonah said. "Keep my hand."

"Oh, no," Holt countered. "That's not the deal, buddy."

"Deal," Jonah repeated with a grin.

Ah, so far so good. At least that word had distracted the child for a moment and stopped his fretting.

Holt looked around and spotted a tree close to the embankment that housed the hood of the SUV. He was halfway there when a honking horn behind him stopped him midstride. He swung around as Maci jumped out of the car and ran toward them.

"Mommy, Mommy," Jonah cried, reaching out his arms.

Holt clenched the child tighter so he couldn't lunge out of his arms in his determination to get to his mother.

"Oh, baby, baby," Maci cried in turn, reaching for him.

Once Jonah was in her arms, Holt looked on as she buried her face in his neck and grasped him like she would never let him go. God, Holt couldn't believe it, but he actually felt the sting of tears behind his eyes. He twisted his head abruptly so Maci wouldn't see his vulnerability, only to realize she wasn't paying any attention to him. Her whole self was wrapped up in hugging her child and making sure he was all right.

"He's fine, Maci," Holt assured her again when he felt her tear-filled eyes on him.

"I can see that he is."

"I'm sorry about this," Holt said in a rough voice. "I'd give anything if it hadn't happened."

"What exactly did happen?"

"The brakes failed, suddenly and without warning."

A frown creased her brow. "Has that ever happened before?"

"Hell, no."

"Then—" Her words faded.

"Why now?" he finished the sentence for her. "That's what I'd like to know and what I'm going to find out."

She gave him an incredulous look. "You think it could've been something other than a mechanical failure?"

Holt wasn't willing to confide in her about his suspicions. She was traumatized enough without him adding to it. Besides, he had no proof at this point that it hadn't been a simple malfunction.

"I don't have an opinion one way or the other, except to get to the bottom of what happened."

Before she could reply, the wrecker service arrived. "You and Jonah wait in your car. I won't be long."

Ten minutes later, he climbed in the passenger side of her vehicle and both watched while the tow truck drove off with his vehicle.

"Where do you want me to take you?" Maci asked in a hesitant voice.

He didn't answer right off. His senses were too swamped with the smell of that perfume so uniquely her. He couldn't pinpoint the fragrance exactly, but it didn't matter. It wrapped around him, making him more conscious than ever of how close she was to him, how *touchable* she was.

Only he couldn't touch her.

But dear Lord, he wanted to, feeling that old familiar tightening in his groin. Would he ever get enough of this woman?

"Holt?"

"Take me to the office, if you don't mind."

By the time she pulled up in front of the building, he'd clenched his knuckles until they were white.

"I'm not blaming you for what happened."

Her soft voice was like a caress. He swallowed hard before turning and facing her in the close confines of the car. "Thanks for telling me that, though I feel responsible."

She reached out and placed a hand on his bare arm. Her touch hit him like an electric shock to his groin. If she glanced south at all, she would see the results. She didn't. She kept her gaze on him and for another long moment, they looked deeply into each other's eyes.

"Uh, I guess I'd better go," he said, sounding thick-tongued even to himself.

She didn't say anything.

He had to get out before he did something he'd most likely be sorry for. "And let you get Jonah home."

"You're right," she finally responded in a rushed tone, color tinging her cheeks.

It was all he could do not to reach over and kiss her. "I'll see you later, okay?"

"Yes, later," she said, removing her gaze.

Somehow, Holt managed to get out of the car and walk into his office as though nothing was wrong.

"It's about time you got here."

Vince merely shoved his hat back and gave Holt a slow grin, seeming to take no offense at Holt's short fuse.

"In case you've forgotten," the investigator drawled, easing down into his usual chair, "it takes time to get brakes analyzed."

Holt straightened and drilled him through narrowed eyes. "Ah, so you went by the mechanic shop?"

"Sure did."

"Dammit, Vince, spit it out."

"How do you know I have anything to spit out?"

Holt cursed.

Vince got the message. "All right, I've jerked your chain long enough."

"You got that right," Holt bit out.

"Todd gave the vehicle a thorough going over and said the brakes had definitely been tampered with."

Holt cut another expletive.

"Ditto," Vince muttered.

Holt lurched out of his chair and rubbed the back of his neck. This had not been one of his better days. And from the way it was going, it was getting worse by the second.

"Who the hell cares that much about me, one way or the other?"

Vince removed his hat and scratched his head. "Beats the hell out of me."

"I haven't been here long enough to make any enemies."

"What about the Dodsons? I know they're a long shot, but—"

"What could they possibly have to gain by hurting me?" Holt interrupted, his brows gathered in a frown. "Seymour's dead, which gave them their pound of flesh."

"I'm as confounded as you are," Vince mumbled under his breath.

"So we're back to square one, dammit." Holt paused. "Except for one thing."

"The Sanders case."

"You got it," Holt exclaimed.

"You're thinking the tail and the brakes are somehow related to that case?"

"You have a better idea?"

Vince shook his head. "From where I'm sitting, that's a stretch."

"Why?" Holt shot back.

"I just don't see a tie."

"Let's just think about it for a minute, look at all the angles."

Vince's features came alert. "Perhaps someone doesn't like you representing Sanders."

"Another verse to that is they don't want me getting him off."

"But who?" Vince asked in a puzzled tone.

"That's what I'm paying you for."

Vince bowed up. "Excuse me? Unless I slept through it, I haven't seen a red cent."

Holt almost smiled. "You mean I haven't paid you?"

Vince glared at him. "You son of a bitch, you know you haven't paid me."

"When you leave, tell Marianne to write you a check."

Vince's features brightened. "I'll take you up on that. Just in time to help my girl with an apartment."

Holt rolled his eyes.

Vince snorted. "A wife and children are what you need to settle you down."

"Maybe in another lifetime." Holt rubbed his neck again, feeling it bunch under his hand. "Now back to the subject."

"I know Sanders's wife has a twin brother."

"That certainly adds more flavoring to the gumbo."

"How 'bout I start with him. You know what they say about twins? They're so close that when one farts the other knows about it. Or farts, too."

Holt merely looked at him.

Vince shrugged, then flapped his hand in the air. "Check him out. Who knows what you might dig out of the woodwork."

"I'll also pay another visit to the company where the deceased worked. Maybe someone there doesn't like the fact that we've been snooping."

"While you're at it," Holt said, "go back to the Sanders's neighborhood and take another run at the neighbors."

"Got an idea?"

"If we hold to our theory about Rachel's visitor that night, then maybe someone saw something they didn't know they saw."

Vince rose. "I'll get on it."

"If and when you find the bastard who fucked with my brakes, let me know immediately."

"You're really pissed about this, aren't you?"

"That goes without saying, especially since I had Maci's kid with me."

"I hope you aren't planning on doing anything stupid."

Holt's features turned cold and his voice deadly. "You just do your job and leave the rest to me."

Thirty-Six

Maci felt tired, but it was a good tired, she told herself, making her way into the kitchen. Surprisingly, she was hungry enough to consider making herself something for dinner. But when she reached the kitchen and opened the fridge, she wrinkled her nose in disappointment. Nothing she saw appealed to her, which was her own fault.

Since Seymour's death, the housekeeper had tried to cook for her, but she'd told Annie to please Liz but not her, that she just wasn't hungry. Annie had taken her at her word.

Maci reached for the pitcher of almond tea, poured herself a glass, then sat down in the breakfast nook where she'd laid a folder full of work. She had spent the past few days at the Galloway house and had enjoyed every minute of her time there.

As suspected, Lois Galloway believed in living every moment of life to the fullest. She was a hoot to work for and Maci appreciated her more each day as Lois was such an uplifting person. In fact, she could use another dose of Lois right now.

It had been two days since that scare with Jonah. And though she knew he was well and safe, she'd been unable to concentrate fully. Her mind kept conjuring up the unthinkable—losing her child. Finally, though, she had managed to force those frightening thoughts aside and get a grip on her emotions.

To some degree, that is.

Thoughts of Holt dogged her every waking moment despite the fact that she hadn't seen him since the day of the accident. One evening she didn't think he'd even returned to the mansion, leaving her to wonder where he'd spent the night. But she'd stopped herself from pursuing that disturbing thought, reminding herself that she had no control over him or his whereabouts.

She still couldn't believe she'd fallen in love with him. Having a permanent relationship with Holt would be like trying to trap the wind. He was a free spirit who wouldn't want her and Jonah.

Struggling not to let herself fall into that black hole of despair again, Maci sipped on her tea, opened her folder and flipped though the designs that she'd shown to Lois with the changes penciled in.

"Want some company?"

Startled, she lifted her head toward the door. Holt stood there, his features tight with exhaustion. She fought the urge to get up and fling herself in his arms. She wondered, though, what he'd do if she did.

He wouldn't mind, she told herself. He wanted her. He had made that quite plain. She could turn him on as easily as she turned on a water faucet. While that in itself was exciting, she wanted more.

"Guess not," he said in a rough resigned tone.

"Wait."

Holt swung back around, his eyes unreadable.

"Please, don't go."

He gave her a wary look. "You mean that?"

"Yes. Join me."

"What are you drinking?" Holt asked in a rather strained voice, making his way toward the table.

He was dressed in a casual pair of slacks and yellow sports shirt which looked like dynamite with his blond hair and tanned features. Even with his face scored with lines and his hair overly long and a bit mussed, he had never looked better to her.

Or more dangerous.

"Almond tea. Help yourself."

"I'd rather have food," Holt exclaimed with a semblance of a smile.

"So would I, only I looked in the fridge and found nothing appetizing."

"How 'bout I treat you?"

"Take me out?"

His level gaze challenged her. "Why not?"

"Why not, indeed," she said with more huskiness than she intended. He must never know her true feelings. She must guard her heart at all costs. Still, she couldn't resist the temptation his invitation offered. She wanted to be with him. An innocent dinner sounded so simple, though she knew that with Holt nothing was simple.

"You name it, we'll go there."

Maci stood. “You choose. I don’t want to make any more decisions today.”

“Bad day, huh?”

“No, actually it was good. Just busy.”

She couldn’t believe they were having another normal conversation, that they were not at each other’s throats. Tension hovered over them like an unwanted guest, but Maci hoped this fragile truce would turn into the real thing.

“Let me check on Jonah and tell Liz.”

“How ’bout we do that together?”

She was taken aback and it showed.

“I thought I’d say hello to the little fellow,” he said with a nonchalant shrug.

“Sure,” she responded, trying not to show her shock.

Moments later, they were in Jonah’s room. He was on a pallet playing with Liz.

“Mommy,” he cried, pushing up and rushing to her, his chubby arms outstretched.

Maci picked him up and exclaimed, “My but you’re getting to be such a big, heavy boy.”

“Holt,” Jonah said, pointing at him.

Holt flicked the child on the chin. “Hey, kiddo.”

He sounded both impressed and pleased that Jonah had remembered his name.

“Go, Mommy, go,” Jonah said.

She focused on the wiggling child. “Not now, darling. You stay and play with Liz.”

Jonah seemed content with that. Maci put him down and mouthed to Liz that she would return in a while, to call her cell if she needed her.

All the way downstairs, she felt Holt’s gaze on her.

When she looked up, those blue eyes appeared on fire with suppressed desire.

Feeling her heart leap in her throat she turned away.

"I'm ready, if you are," Holt said in a husky tone.

She dared not look at him for fear of what would happen.

"Have you found out anything about your brakes?"

"Yes."

"I take it it's not good news."

"No, it isn't."

They had just finished eating at a small but upscale restaurant and were lingering over coffee.

Throughout dinner, the conversation had remained civil but impersonal, again leaving Maci dumbfounded at his sudden change in attitude toward her. While she still sensed a reserve in him, there was a difference. She just couldn't say what it was.

"You might as well give me the bad news," Maci said into the silence. "It's not going to get any easier."

"I know, but I didn't want to make you worry." Suddenly color surged into his face. "Not that you'd worry about me, that is."

"You'd be surprised," she said before she thought.

His gaze lingered on her while the tension mounted.

Maci drew her lower lip between her teeth, creating a dewy sheen on her mouth.

A shaft of longing pierced his heart before hitting his groin. He shifted positions then said, "Someone messed with the brakes."

"I was afraid of that." Her voice was unsteady.

"I'm still so damned sorry it happened while I had Jonah."

"Don't go there. I don't blame you. But what is going on?"

"I wish the hell I knew, but trust me, I'm going to find out."

"Could it have anything to do with that case you're working on?"

"Vince and I are leaning toward that." His tone shook with suppressed fury. "But we don't have any proof as yet."

"I hope for your sake it'll be resolved soon."

"Oh, it will."

"Be careful, Holt."

His eyes met hers again with that same fire of desire burning in them. Her breath caught at the same time her lips parted.

"Are you ready?" he asked with rough abruptness.

"When you are."

"Let's get the hell out of here."

They were in the SUV and halfway home when it happened. At first Maci couldn't believe her eyes. The vehicle in the oncoming lane started inching into their lane.

"Holt?"

"I see the idiot." Holt pressed his horn, then muttered, "Get the hell back where you belong."

The vehicle never altered its course. It kept on moving toward them, now in their lane.

"Holt!" Maci cried again, feeling herself give in to the terror building inside her.

"Son of a bitch!" Holt sat down on his horn again at the same time he jerked the steering wheel to the right.

Maci stiffened and looked on in horror as Holt careened onto the shoulder narrowly missing crashing head-on with the other vehicle.

Muttering curses on top of curses, Holt braked suddenly, then yanked open the door and jumped out. Moments later, he got back in, still cursing a blue streak.

"Did you get anything?"

"No, dammit, I didn't. Once he got by us, he kicked it in the butt."

Maci's brows came together in a frown. "That was no accident, Holt."

"Are you all right?"

"I'm…fine. Just a bit shaky on the inside."

"I owe you another apology." His tone was bleak.

"No, you don't."

"After what happened with Jonah, I shouldn't have let you get in the car with me."

"That's crazy."

He didn't respond. Instead, he started the vehicle and drove off.

On the short way home, she glanced over at him. Without fail, his profile appeared as though it was carved out of marble. He was furious. And worried. Holt had made an enemy out of someone. And that someone was out for blood.

Fear tied her stomach in knots. If anything happened to… She couldn't allow herself to think about that. She'd already suffered too many hurts. Surely she wouldn't be made to stand another one.

By the time they made it inside the grounds of the mansion, night had fallen. It had rained earlier, cooling things off considerably. For a midsummer evening, the temperature was quite nice.

Perhaps that was why Holt stopped short of the garage and rolled down the windows before killing the powerful engine. For a moment, neither said a word, listening to the crickets and other nocturnal creatures sing their own special music. Taking a deep breath, Maci inhaled the scents of the night, including the smell of jasmine and roses.

When the back of Holt's knuckles reached out to caress the exposed side of her face, she felt dizzy.

"The moonlight becomes you," he said in a voice that sounded like sandpaper.

She swallowed against the heat spreading through the rest of her body. If she turned and faced him, she knew what would happen. Holt would kiss her.

"Maci, look at me."

His low, guttural plea forced her head around, only to instantly feel his raw, hungry lips devour hers. With a muted groan he then thrust his tongue inside her mouth and began playing with her tongue.

When he placed a hand over her breast, she pressed deeper into the seat, allowing him better access to her body. He didn't waste the moment either. With reckless disregard of the fabric, he yanked the buttons open on her blouse and unhooked her bra.

Her breath came in gaspy spurts as his hands and fingers performed their magic on her exposed flesh, bringing her nipples to turgid points. But it was when his hand delved under her skirt and cupped her mound that she knew she was lost, that she was his for the taking.

And take he did.

Within seconds, he had her skirt hiked around her waist, her panties off and his fly open. "Feel how much

I want you," he rasped, taking her hand and placing it on his erection.

But since she would rather taste him than touch him, she bent over and surrounded the tip with her moist lips. He bucked against the seat before lifting her body onto him.

Once he filled her, he took a nipple in his mouth and began to move her hips, slow at first, then faster until their bodies were pounding against each other.

Feeling as though her heart had sprouted wings, Maci smiled and collapsed against him.

Thirty-Seven

Who the hell was trying to make life miserable for him? More to the point, why? But it didn't really matter that he had no answers for those question. What mattered was that some idiot was messing with the people he loved.

His heart almost stopped beating. *Love?* That word again. Sweat popped out on Holt's brow and upper lip. Had he gone and done the unthinkable? Had he fallen in love with Maci?

If so, what did that mean? God, he didn't want to be hurt. He didn't want the high price tag that falling in love carried either. Hell, he was already taken; he was married to the sea and the freedom that went with it. The thought of being tied down again, confined to land for a given length of time, turned him inside out. On the other hand, the thought of leaving Maci and never touching her again sucked the life right out him.

He suddenly turned cold. Maci had crept up to and entered his heart, without his realization until now.

Stop thinking about her, he told himself savagely. If not, he wouldn't be able to take care of business. He had to find out who was out to get him, because he would not put Maci and Jonah in jeopardy again, which meant he had to stay away from them.

Marianne buzzed him, forcing his mind back on business. "Vince is here with Mrs. Saxton."

"Thanks. Ask Vince to come in first."

He'd given the investigator a description of the vehicle that had veered into his lane with the intention of either killing or terrorizing him. Vince had called and said he had some info and needed to see him. He'd also told Holt he'd revisited the Sanders neighborhood and found a woman who'd said she had seen something. Vince had gone on to say, however, that he wasn't sure she was reliable.

"I want to talk to her myself," Holt had told him.

"Your place or hers?" Vince asked.

"In my office as soon as you can get her here."

There was a long silence. "I'm not sure that's a good idea."

"Why?" Holt demanded impatiently.

"I can't explain it."

"What the hell does that mean?"

"Never mind. I'll see what I can do."

"Good," Holt said in a clipped tone.

And once again, Vince had come through, though Holt still didn't know what all the brouhaha was all about. But he guessed he'd soon find out.

Moments later Vince strode through the door, closed it behind him, then propped himself against it.

"What have you got?" Holt asked without preamble, feeling like ants were crawling through his insides. Apparently that incident on the highway had left him more rattled than he cared to admit. And all because Maci had been involved.

"Why are you frowning?" Vince demanded in an irritated voice.

Holt raised his brows in surprise. He could count the times on one hand that he'd seen his friend out of sorts. "What's eating you?"

"You'll see."

"Is that all you have to say?"

"For the moment." Vince's eyes narrowed. "At least about your guest."

"I wish you'd stop talking in riddles."

Vince ignored him. "Before we get to Mrs. Saxton, I think I might have located the vehicle that did the number on you."

Holt's adrenaline kicked in. "Man, if that's true, you deserve a hug."

"Don't even think about it."

Holt chuckled, then said drolly, "Stand down."

"I will, but only if you keep your distance."

"Tell me what you found out," Holt said, his tone all business.

"Remember I mentioned her twin brother."

Holt nodded his head.

"Well, I spoke with him, and talk about attitude. He sucked big time. In fact, it was all I could do not to punch him in the nose. The jerk's name is Buck Collier."

"So old Buck thinks his brother-in-law is guilty, huh?"

Vince snorted. "That's an understatement, and in his book you're pond scum because you're trying to get him off."

"Ah, so he has a hard-on for me, too?"

"That's also an understatement."

"You're making my day. Go on."

"I tailed him and when I got the chance, I snooped around his place and found a vehicle in the garage similar to the make and model you described."

"Yes!" Holt exclaimed, his adrenaline kicking up another notch. "The only problem is we have to have concrete evidence to nail his ass. I'm hoping the skid marks will help us out."

"I'll get a copy of the police report."

"That's a start." Holt paused. "I guess we'd best turn our attention to Mrs. Saxton."

Vince's lips twitched. "I can't wait to see this."

"There you go, talking in damn riddles again."

Vince merely shoved away from the door, opened it and motioned for the lady.

When she sashayed into the room, Holt was glad he was propped against his desk. Otherwise, he might have had trouble remaining upright. Clara Saxton, who had to be pushing ninety, was a sight to behold with her bird-like head attached to a body that was as wide as it was tall. But it was her maroon hair with swatches of blond in various places that caused his jaw to drop.

This lady hailed from another planet.

"It's about time, sonny boy," she snapped, flapping a hand at him that was covered with rings.

He'd bet his butt they were diamonds, too.

"Close your mouth," she ordered in a crackling tone. "I know I look like someone from outer space, but that's by choice."

Holt cleared his throat and didn't dare look at Vince.

"You're among friends here, ma'am. Have a seat. I really appreciate you coming."

"I can tell you, it's going to cost you."

Holt grinned. "You name it."

One painted on eyebrow cocked along with her head. Holt found himself wanting to lean himself in order to follow her. God, what a character.

"A steak and wine dinner."

Out of his peripheral vision, he saw the shit-eating grin on Vince's face. Ignoring it, Holt said, "I can handle that."

"So what do you want to know?" she asked, sitting down and smiling.

That was when he noticed several of her teeth were missing. Suddenly, he wished Maci were here. She'd think Clara was a riot.

"Have you seen any strange men around the Sanders's house?" Holt asked, seeing no reason to beat around the bush. Instinct told him that she was no dummy. Nor was she senile; his instinct told him that as well.

"As a matter of fact, I have."

Holt tried to tamp down his excitement, but he failed. When a case started to come together, it produced an incredible high. "Do you remember when you saw him?"

"Sure do."

"Was it the night Mrs. Sanders died?"

"Sure was."

"Would you know him if you saw him again?"

"Sure would." Clara paused and squinted her eyes. "At least I think so. You know these old peepers ain't what they used to be. Though mind you, I don't consider myself old."

"Of course, you're not old," Holt said with enthusiasm.

"And you're full of it, sonny boy."

Both men laughed out loud.

"Are you going to be around?" Holt asked, forcing himself back on track.

"Why do you want to know?"

Holt contained his impatience. "Hopefully, we'll need you to make a positive ID."

"Well, that will have to wait. My sister's having surgery, and I'm off to take care of her for a few days. But when I come back, mind you, I'll expect my dinner."

"If we need to get in touch with you before then, is there a number where we can reach you?"

"I suppose so."

Holt looked on as she scribbled a phone number on a piece of scratch paper and handed it to him.

"Thanks," Holt said with a smile.

"You think this guy might have killed Rachel?"

"We don't know yet," Vince chimed in. "That's what we're trying to determine."

Holt leveled his gaze on Clara. "Why are you just now coming forward?"

"Don't you get smart with me, sonny boy."

Holt made an innocent gesture with his hands while fighting to keep a straight face. "Sorry, ma'am, I didn't mean any disrespect."

"I can answer that question," Vince responded. "When I first canvassed the neighborhood, Clara didn't answer her door. I assumed she wasn't home."

"You assumed right, young man. I was visiting my sister in upstate New York."

"What's important is that we found you and you're

helping us out now." Holt kept his tone and smile in place, hoping to get himself back in her good graces.

Clara stood. "You through with me?"

"For now."

"I have to go. It's time to feed my cats."

Holt purposely hid a smile, afraid he might offend her again. He couldn't take a chance on that.

"Don't forget what you owe me, sonny boy."

"Oh, I won't. You can count on that."

"Later," Vince said with his lips twitching as he followed the old lady to the door. Once she was out of hearing distance, he turned and said, "I tried to warn you."

Holt grinned. "Get out of here."

Once he was alone, Holt sat down, leaned back in his chair and swung a foot on the desk. Things were moving right along, better than he'd planned and much better than he'd hoped.

But Lucas wasn't out of the woods yet, he cautioned himself, nor had he found the person responsible for his so-called "accidents." Still, he was optimistic on both counts. Suddenly, he had the urge to see Maci. He peered at his watch. She should be home soon. Maybe she'd like to go out to dinner again. And just maybe the evening would end like it had last night, with them making hot, passionate love.

He groaned, shifting positions in order to ease the sudden pinch behind his zipper. All he had to do was think about her delectable body and he got rock-hard.

He was about to pick up the phone and call her when it rang. "Hello," he said in a distracted tone.

"Holt."

His blood heated. "Hey." That tiny word came out a caress.

"I was wondering if you were free this evening?"

The fact that Maci had called thrilled him. But the husky note he heard in her voice thrilled him even more. "I was about to call you and ask the same thing."

"Oh?"

"I thought we might try having dinner again." He paused and took a breath. "Without incident, I might add."

"That would be okay."

"Except?"

She chuckled. "Except I've made dinner."

This time he said, "Oh?"

She let go of another warm chuckle, and his heart soared. What had this woman done to him?

"Are you interested?"

"Are you kidding?" he said in a low tone.

"Is that a yes?" That same husky note again.

"That's a definite yes."

"It's nothing fancy, mind you."

"Hey, beggars can't be choosers."

"I don't recall you begging."

"You just weren't listening."

A pause of silence.

"We won't be dining entirely alone."

His enthusiasm took a major hit. "So you've invited a friend?"

"No."

"No?"

"Jonah's going to join us."

Her teasing voice sent another shaft of desire shooting through him. "Great. I can't think of anything I'd like more."

Except to knock all the junk off the table and make love to you.

"Really?"

"Really," he said with difficulty.

Another pause of silence.

"Anything new on the car who tried to run us over?" she asked.

He didn't want to talk about that right now. He was enjoying their verbal foreplay too much, something he'd never experienced with her. Hell, that was something he'd never experienced with *any* woman. It was heady stuff.

"We'll talk about that later, okay?"

"Fine."

"Look, can I pick up something? Maybe some wine?"

"Don't need a thing." She paused. "Only you."

He lunged out of his chair, feeling like he'd just been given a free ticket to heaven. "Hold that thought. I'm on my way."

Thirty-Eight

Pete was late.

Holt scanned his watch and noticed that he'd only been at the coffee shop for ten minutes. But today he was impatient. And leery. He had no idea why Pete wanted to see him.

The medical examiner had called earlier that morning and asked if he, Holt, had plans for breakfast. He hadn't even thought about food. He'd been at the office reviewing the Sanders file, looking for something he might have missed.

All in all he still felt good about his client's chances to beat the murder rap, especially if he could cast a shadow on someone in Rachel Sanders's investment firm.

That hadn't happened as yet, though both he and Vince had been working that angle. But no smoking gun as yet. So the sooner he got this impromptu meeting behind him, the sooner he could get back to the office. Then he'd be free to return to the mansion.

To Maci.

Ah, what an evening they had spent together. They had played with Jonah before consuming a goodly portion of the pot roast she'd cooked. Afterward, they had cleaned up the kitchen together, put Jonah to bed, then returned to the study. There, they had indulged in after-dinner drinks.

But the pressure of being in such close confines with Maci and not touching her, had finally gotten to him. "You know I'm slowly dying, don't you?" he'd said in a raspy voice.

She raised startled eyes, then whispered, "What does that mean?"

He knew that was a rhetorical question. She had to know that what had once been a smoldering ember inside him had ignited into a full blown blaze. To worsen matters, she wet her lower lip with the tip of her tongue, as though on purpose, desire flaring in her own eyes.

"You know the answer to that," he muttered with difficulty.

Without taking her gaze off him, Maci sat her glass down, then stood.

Holt stood as well and reached for her. Somehow they made it to his room before they ripped their clothes off and fell on the bed. They kissed; they touched, both aware of his erection hot and hard between them.

Still, Holt held himself in check, wanting to prolong this exquisite madness. He explored every inch of her body with his mouth, kissing her face, her neck, her arms, her lips, her breasts and her swollen nipples. Then he moved down to her taut, concave belly where he laved her navel and perfect skin with his tongue.

He didn't stop there. He trailed down her soft inner

thighs to the heart of her where she was so wonderfully warm and wet. There, he tasted her until she thrashed about and cried his name.

"Sweet, sweet. My sweet Maci…so sweet."

"I want you inside me," she said, her breathing ragged and fast. "Now."

He would love to take the foreplay to an even higher level, but he couldn't. He'd gone as far as he could go. He thrust in her, not with only lust, but with a sincere desire to know more than her body. He wanted to know her mind as well. To possess and be possessed.

A torrent of emotion spilled from his heart at the same time his seed spilled into her.

Love was real.

And he'd found it.

In her.

"Hey, good buddy, how goes it?"

Holt visibly jumped when Pete touched him on the shoulder.

Pete looked taken aback. "Didn't mean to sneak up on you like that, but you were deep in thought."

Feeling a flush steal over his face, he got up and shook his friend's hand. "Got a lot on my mind," was all the explanation he gave.

"Don't we all," Pete responded, sitting down across from him.

Holt signaled the waitress, and she came and took their orders. Afterward, Pete's eyes drilled him. "I guess you're wondering what this is all about?"

"Yeah, as a matter of fact I am."

"How 'bout we enjoy our breakfast—my treat, by the way—then we'll talk."

Holt was becoming more curious by the second but he didn't argue. Besides, it didn't matter. At the moment, he was like Teflon. Nothing could stick to him except Maci. God, he was even entertaining the thought of asking her to marry him.

"You've gone off again."

Holt shook his head. "Sorry, man."

"From the look on your face, it must be damn good."

Holt shrugged and gave him a sheepish look.

"These women are bad about grabbing our balls and holding on without us knowing it." Pete smiled. "Until it's too late, that is."

"Who says I'm thinking about a woman?"

"Aw, hell, Holt, I didn't just fall off a turnip truck."

Holt grinned. "No, I guess you didn't."

He had no intention of offering any more information. But the arrival of the waitress saved him. Without further conversation, both men attacked their food with relish.

It was after the empty plates had been removed and their coffee cups refilled that Holt noticed that Pete's expression had turned somber and that he seemed unwilling to meet his gaze.

"So what's up?" Holt pressed, once again anxious to get on with his agenda. "I know this isn't just a social visit."

"You're right, it isn't."

"Are you in some kind of trouble?"

Pete frowned. "Me?"

"Yeah, you. As in needing an attorney."

Pete gave his head a vigorous shake. "No, no. This is not about me."

"Okay, so it's about me."

"On second thought, maybe we should just chalk this time up to a visit and be done with it."

"Man, if you think I'm going to let you out of here with that crap, you're wrong."

Pete looked as uncomfortable as hell. "My wife told me I should keep my mouth shut."

"It's obvious you didn't listen to her."

"It's not too late."

"Oh, yes, it is." Holt leaned closer. "I don't know what the hell's going on, but hey, just lay it on me and we'll go from there."

"I have to tell you up front that what I'm about to divulge is none of my business."

"Okay, so it's none of your business. I still want to know." Holt's tone brooked no argument.

"Okay, here it is. I was closing out your dad's medical records when something caught my eye."

When he paused again, Holt's gaze nailed him. "What was that something?"

Pete took a deep breath. "That something was proof that Seymour wasn't able to father a child, not since shortly after you were born, that is."

At first, Hold sat there with a dumbfounded look on his face. In a hoarse, disconnected voice he said, "Let me get this straight. What you're saying is that Maci's child is not Seymour's."

Pete didn't so much as blink. "That's exactly what I'm saying. That kid is not and I repeat *not* your half brother."

"I wish you didn't have to go."

Bobbi made a face. "Me, too, but I promised my

baby-sitter I wouldn't be long." She looked at her watch. "And I've already stayed more than my allotted time."

Bobbi had stopped by to leave some fabric samples and ended up staying for two cups of coffee. Maci had been thrilled as it was Saturday morning, and she'd made no plans to go to her office. Her plan was to take Jonah to the zoo and she hoped Holt would go with them.

"I understand," Maci added, "but I still wish you'd stay a while longer."

"Whining doesn't become you, my dear," Bobbi replied with a grin.

Maci giggled.

Bobbi's face turned serious. "You have no idea how good that sounds."

"What?" Maci asked with sincere innocence.

"Your laughter."

"It feels good to laugh, too, though I often feel guilty when I do."

"That's absurd." Bobbi sounded undone.

"I've only been a widow for a few weeks. I shouldn't be happy."

Bobbi gave a disgusted flap of her hand. "Oh, for crying out loud, that's ridiculous. Look what Seymour put you through. I can't believe you didn't leave him—" Suddenly she broke off, looking contrite. "Sorry, I didn't mean to shoot off my big mouth like that and talk ill of the dead."

Maci reached over and gave her a hug. They clung together for a moment. "I know you didn't mean any disrespect. But in my own way, I loved Seymour and in his own way, he loved me."

"I know, and it worked. You were happy. That's why I had no right to spout off like that."

"You can spout off anytime you like."

"Okay, so what's put that bloom in your cheeks and that perpetual smile on your lips?"

Maci gave her an incredulous look.

"Hey, don't pull that innocent act on me," Bobbi said with her mouth curved in a downward turn.

"I never could fool you about anything."

"That's right, so why try now?"

Maci sighed.

"It's Holt, isn't it?"

"Is it that obvious?"

"Probably not to anyone but me."

"Thank goodness."

"Like I said before, you had a thing for Holt. From the start."

"I guess I did, only I honestly didn't figure it out until recently."

"Does he feel the same about you?"

"I don't know, Bobbi," Maci admitted in a troubled tone. "Oh, I know he cares and that he wants me—" she felt her face sting, having said that "—but he's a free spirit who fears being trapped."

"Has he told you that?"

"No."

"Well then, don't jump to conclusions. He's not about to sail off right away, is he?"

"Not until he tries that case."

"Between now and then anything can happen. Meanwhile live for the moment. You deserve it, my friend."

Tears suddenly filled Maci's eyes. She blinked them back, opening the front door for Bobbi.

Bobbi bounded down the steps. "See ya."

Once she'd closed the front door, Maci headed straight for the terrace. Even though she employed a wonderful yard service, she liked to putter with the plants close to the house. She would do that while waiting for Holt.

Thinking of Holt gave her pause. Bobbi was right, she was on cloud nine.

Although she knew she was more than likely setting herself up for a life-altering fall, she couldn't help herself. She loved Holt and while she hadn't quite come to terms with that fact in her mind, she couldn't stop herself from existing in an euphoric state.

Especially after last night.

When she thought about how his lips and tongue had burned over her body, which was every waking moment, she got weak. Now was no different. She eased into a chair and stared over the grounds, though her mind wasn't filled with the cluster of beautiful flowers, but the feel of Holt filling her and their naked flesh pounding against each other.

Oh, dear Lord, she told herself, lifting her hands to her scalding face.

"Maci."

With a jolt, she stood and faced Holt, only to receive another shock. He looked like hell. His face was dark and twisted as though he was in horrific pain.

"My God, Holt, what's wrong?"

Her question was followed by several beats of silence.

"Is Jonah my son?"

Thirty-Nine

Maci stood in stunned silence, feeling the bottom drop out of her stomach. Oh, God, this couldn't be happening. It just couldn't be.

"Answer me, dammit." Holt crossed the terrace, stopping short of touching her. "Tell me if Jonah's my son."

She cringed inwardly. "I don't know—" Her voice came out shrill as she grabbed her chest where she felt a severe tightness.

"You don't know," Holt countered harshly. "That's rich. That's really rich."

Suddenly her anger came to her rescue. "What makes you think Jonah might be yours?"

Holt laughed without mirth. "Ah, now I get it." His voice was as hard and cold as a piece of metal. "Seymour never told you."

"I don't know what you're talking about," she snapped.

"Yep, old Seymour had the last laugh on both of us."

"You're not making any sense."

"Oh, yes, I am, sweetheart. I'm making all the sense in the world."

"Damn you, Holt."

"His medical records showed he'd had a vasectomy after I was born which was a helluva long time before he married you. Only he chose not to share that with you."

No, oh God, no, that couldn't be.

"So you see Seymour couldn't have fathered your child."

The pain was so severe she thought she might die. In fact, she wanted to. Since that wasn't to be, she had no choice but to take her punishment with as much dignity and grace as she could muster.

"Why would he not have told me?" she asked in an aching whisper.

"I'll tell you why. When he found out he couldn't control me, he washed his hands of me. He saw Jonah as his second chance to clone himself."

"I don't...can't believe that."

"Well believe it," Holt said in a bitter, flat tone, "because it's true."

"I...I still don't understand." She felt physically sick.

Several more beats of silence.

"I'll make it real simple for you," Holt spat. "When we fucked our brains out on the beach that night, we made a baby. We made Jonah."

Stunned, Maci groped for something to hold on to to keep herself upright. Then her stomach betrayed her. It revolted, and she pressed an arm against it, hoping to stop herself from throwing up.

"You never intended for me to know, damn you."

Maci peered up at him, groping for something to say that would defuse the highly volatile situation. "I didn't know myself. For sure, that is."

Holt gave her an incredulous look. "Are you saying you suspected I might be the father but never confirmed it?"

"Yes," she admitted in a throaty whisper.

He shook his head, as if trying to come to terms with what she had just said.

"I know you find that hard to believe, to accept," she added with a tremor.

"You're damn right I do."

"I found out I was pregnant shortly after I married Seymour, Holt. Because I was *married* and knew I would never see you again, I saw no reason to—"

"Rock the boat, right?" he interrupted. "To mess up your playhouse by telling your husband that your child might not be his."

"You're wrong," she cried. "It wasn't about me."

"Sure, it wasn't."

His brutal sarcasm cut, but she was quick to defend herself. "It was about Seymour. Why hurt him unnecessarily and wreck our marriage before it ever got started?"

"Why indeed?" Holt demanded in that same sarcastic tone. "Especially if it meant him divorcing you and snatching that trust fund out of your greedy hands, something you weren't about to let happen."

"It wasn't about money, either," she snarled. "It was about saving a marriage and making a home for a child."

"Oh, please, don't insult me."

"Why are you doing this?" she cried again. "Why do you care one way or the other? You never tried to find me."

The color drained from Holt's face and he cursed.

Good. She'd struck a nerve, dented that holier-than-thou attitude he was throwing up to her.

"Whether I tried to find you or not is beside the point," he lashed back. "Shouldn't the truth matter? To yourself, for god's sake?"

Maci gave back as good as she got. "Not when, I repeat, I didn't think I would ever see you again."

"Damn you, Maci. That boy is my son, and I had the right to know."

"I don't agree." She lifted her chin defiantly, though she felt her control slipping fast. Fear had her by the jugular and wouldn't let go. She didn't know where this conversation was heading, much less where it would end.

"If you fight me on this, you'll lose."

"Don't do this, Holt."

"Do what, get to know my son?"

"You don't have any right to Jonah, damn you. He's *my* son."

"A court might see it another way."

Maci sucked in her breath. "You…you wouldn't."

"I'll do whatever it takes to get to know my son."

"God, Holt, you make me sick."

"Then we're even," he said, his tone filled with disgust.

Her conscience bothered her. "I want you to leave. Now. Get out of my house."

He grabbed her by the arm and jerked her against

him. "If I leave, it won't be without my son." He pushed her away then, turned and walked out.

Maci sank back into the nearest chair, deep sobs racking her body.

"Are you sure you're okay?"

"I'm fine, Bobbi. I...we don't need a thing."

"I find that hard to believe since you're on your own without anyone to look after you."

Maci transferred the phone to the other ear. "I didn't grow up in the lap of luxury, my friend, so stop worrying. I know how to be self-sufficient."

"Okay, I'll stop nagging, but if you need anything, anything at all, don't hesitate to call."

"You've done enough already by letting me hole up here in your cabin. It's stocked with everything we need."

"Maci, I just can't believe Holt would try and take Jonah away from you."

"You still think I overreacted, don't you?"

"Yes," Bobbi said bluntly

Maci blew out a deep sigh. She had decided to confide in Bobbi, the main reason being she could no longer keep her pain bottled inside her. She had needed an outlet for fear she would lose her mind.

"If you love him, why not try and work it out?" Bobbi asked into the silence.

"Because he doesn't love me back." Maci's voice caught.

"Do you know that for sure?"

"If he loved me, then why would he threaten to take my son away from me?"

"Maybe because he was hurt and that was his way of getting back."

"Oh, Bobbi, I don't know. I'm so hurt and confused. This all came so out of left field that I'm still dizzy from the aftermath."

"I'm sure that you are. He dealt you a major blow."

"God, that's an understatement."

"Do you still love him?" Bobbi asked.

"With all my heart."

"Then call him."

"Oh, I can't. At least not right now."

"Okay. I won't push. I'll talk to you tomorrow."

Once Bobbi was off the line, Maci peeped at Jonah who was fast asleep in his crib in the great room, then walked out onto the deck. She inhaled a whiff of the muggy air, then let it out, feeling the kink in her stomach uncoil. While lacking amenities, the hideaway was perfect to nurse her broken heart and plan her future.

Without Holt.

What a fool she'd been to think they might have a future, that he might love her enough to stick around and make a life together.

How could she have been so wrong about someone?

The morning after her confrontation with Holt, she'd packed a bag, grabbed Jonah and left the house. In the car, she had called Bobbi.

So far, she hadn't been bothered. Of course, Holt had no idea where she was or how to track her. Sooner or later, though, she knew she would face him again, most likely in court.

While that thought frightened her to the core, she would die before she lost her son.

If only Holt could have loved her like she loved him, then none of this would be happening. Could Bobbi be right? Could Holt have just been so hurt that he'd struck back like a wounded animal? Maybe if her fears hadn't gotten the better of her and she hadn't gone on the attack, perhaps things would've turned out differently.

She would like to think that was the case, but what if she were wrong? Could she take that chance? Could she gamble with her son?

Yes, yes, yes. Maci put her hands over her ears, trying to block out that still small voice that spoke from the heart.

When her ploy didn't work, she turned, dashed back inside, lifted Jonah from his crib and clutched him against her.

"Man, you should be singing the 'Hallelujah Chorus.' Instead, you look like a beaten-down dog."

"I've got a lot on my mind," Holt muttered, rubbing his jaw.

When he thought about Maci and her disappearance, he felt rabid. He could've put Vince on her trail, but he hadn't been able to bring himself to do that just yet. He knew Maci needed space and so did he. But he didn't know how much longer he could stand not knowing where or how she was.

"Well, one thing that should be *off* your mind," Vince said, "is that idiot who tried to run over you."

"He is. And trust me, I'm grateful to you for that."

Once Vince had confirmed that the vehicle inside Sanders's brother-in-law's garage matched the tire prints at the scene, he and Vince had put pressure on Buck Collier until he'd squealed like a stuck pig.

Shortly after his confession, Holt had filed charges, and Collier had been arrested.

"How could that guy have been stupid enough to think he could scare you off the case?"

"Beats me," Holt responded. "But we both know this world is full of nuts like him."

"Guess you're right, but still—" Vince let his words play out with a shrug.

"Now, all we have to do is get Lucas off."

"I think we're close to kicking ass," Vince said with a wide grin.

"I'd rather draw blood."

Vince laughed. "I like your idea better."

"At least we've uncovered the fraud at the company," Holt said, "and proved Rachel knew about it."

"Only because you had a brain fart that paid off," Vince said with a grin. "Way to go."

Vince was right. He had indeed done some fine investigative work on his own, having dug under rocks until he'd turned the right one over, finding a disgruntled employee who was willing to sing his guts out to the tune of several hundred dollars. The beauty of his singing was that his words were backed up with documents he'd kept instead of shredding them.

Rachel Sanders had decided to blow the whistle on the company by going to some of the big investors and spilling her guts. When Dane Melton, her immediate boss, learned of her plans, he'd paid her a visit.

Or at least that was the conclusion Holt had drawn from what he'd learned. But he still needed tangible proof to nail Melton in court.

He eyed Vince, his face serious. "We have to prove

Melton was in the Sanders' house the night Rachel fell down the stairs. Hopefully, Crazy Clara will finger him. Without that smoking gun, we're dead in the water. Get me a photograph of Melton and when I take her to dinner, I'll see if she can identify him.

"If not, then I'll send you back to the house to redust for fingerprints. Somehow we have to get proof that prick was there."

"We're going to have to get the lead out of our asses. Time is running out, right?"

"Right," Holt said, drawing his brows together. "The case is due to go to court in a week."

"I'll sit tight until I hear from you." Vince's grin widened. "Have fun with Clara."

Holt waved his hand. "Get the hell out of here."

After Vince left, he switched his thoughts off work and back onto Maci, plunging him back into dark despair.

What had he done? Why had he felt the need to hurt her when he loved her? If only he could take back the words he'd so harshly, so flagrantly spoken. Since he couldn't, he had to do the next best thing and that was find her and tell her he had no intention of taking Jonah away from her.

What if she didn't believe him?

For an instant, he felt as helpless, as utterly alone, as terrified as he had after his mother had committed suicide. Then it hit him. He'd let his bitter anger over his father's deceit and betrayal poison his life to such an extent that it had spewed onto Maci.

Of course, she had done the right thing by not telling him about Jonah. He could forgive her. At the time, she'd done what she had thought was best.

He knew that now. And he loved her all the more for it. What an idiot he was. He had thrown away the best thing that had ever come into his life. He didn't know if she had ever loved him or not. But if she had, he would turn over heaven and earth to right the wrong.

First he had to find her. Feeling his adrenaline kick in, he vaulted out of his chair and headed for the door just as his phone buzzed.

He wanted to ignore it, but he knew Marianne would simply come in his office. Bounding back to his desk, he picked up the receiver. "Yeah."

"A Bobbi Trent is on line one."

"Who is that?"

"All she said was that she was a friend of Maci's and that she needed to talk to you."

His heart sprang back to life.

Forty

Holt wouldn't take her son. While he might be many things, a kidnapper wasn't one of them. Maci tried to shut down those runaway, morbid thoughts, but she couldn't. They haunted her like a bad dream. In some ways, she saw the last few months of her life as one big unending nightmare.

She and Jonah had just been for a walk through the woods, though it had been hot and muggy. Still, he had enjoyed it, and she had, too. She had made a game of their little hike in order to teach him about nature. He could repeat the name of everything she'd showed him.

Now though, Jonah was down for a short nap, and she was at loose ends. This was the time of day when she hurt the worst, when the pain was hardest to ignore.

Heartbreak.

There was nothing that could compare with it, she decided. Even when her fiancé had left her at the altar paled in comparison to how she felt about Holt. She'd had such high hopes that he really cared about her, that he'd gotten over his contempt for her, that she'd proved she hadn't just been out for Seymour's money.

Apparently, she had failed miserably. If only things had been different, her heart cried. If only he could have loved her and forgiven her for not sharing Jonah with him. But she'd been truthful when she'd told him she didn't think she would ever see him again. Nor had she been completely certain he, and not Seymour, had fathered Jonah.

Even if that hadn't been the case, she wasn't sure if she would have done things differently. Holt had been a complete stranger to whom she'd given her body in a heated moment of passion. To this day, she still felt the humiliation, the shame, of what she'd done.

Maybe she was paying for those sins of the past. But in defense of herself, once she had married Seymour, she had been a faithful, caring wife. She had no regrets, except that she hadn't been able to persuade Seymour to stop using drugs. While she missed Seymour, she wasn't grieving over his death as she would have had he kicked his habit and they had gone on to share many wonderful years together.

Still, she would always hold a soft spot in her heart for him. He had accepted Jonah as his, never letting on for a second that he knew she had betrayed him. It would be a long time, if ever, before she got over the fallout from everything Holt had told her. Just thinking back on it sent a shudder through her.

Holt's life would never be the same either. They had created a baby together. That thought made her giddy with joy and paralyzed with fear.

If only Holt didn't hate her so. Though she ached to

have Holt for herself, she could be content if he would love Jonah and not try to take her son away from her.

Suddenly feeling overwhelmed by her tormented thoughts, Maci turned and made her way back inside the cabin. After checking once again on her sleeping child, she made her way to the kitchen area to prepare a bite to eat. That was when she heard a car door slam. Bobbi. Why on earth had she driven up here? Maci had told her she didn't need anything.

Prepared to chastise her friend for making an unnecessary trip, though she would be glad to see her, Maci hurried out the front door, only to grab the railing for support.

It was Holt.

"Maci," he said, his voice sounding like sandpaper.

"How…did you find me?"

"Bobbi," he said without excuse.

She didn't know what to say.

"Will you let me come in?" He sounded like the words were dug from the depths of his very being.

Her heart turned over. Dare she hope they could make amends, after all? Dare she believe that was why Bobbi had betrayed her? No, she wouldn't get her hopes up. That would only open her up for more hurt.

"Why did you come?" Fear suddenly took precedence over all other emotions. "There's no way I'll ever let you take my son."

His features blanched. "I'm sorry about what I said. It was never my intention to take Jonah away from you."

Relief almost made Maci lose her balance. She gripped the banister tighter for support. "You…you frightened me, Holt."

"I know and once again, I'm so sorry." He was looking at her through his heart. "I would never intentionally hurt you. I love you too much for that. Can you ever forgive me? For so many things."

He loved her? "Did you just say what I think you said?"

Holt didn't pretend to misunderstand. "That I loved you?"

"Yes."

He took several more steps toward her. "No, my darling, you didn't misunderstand. I love you with every fiber of my being."

Maci launched off the steps and flew into his outstretched arms. "I love you, too," she whispered, feeling their tears mingle as they clung to each other.

Epilogue

Six months later

Life couldn't get any better.

Maci and Holt had married immediately. Shortly after, he had started the paperwork on adopting Jonah. Since then, she had come to know the true meaning of happiness and contentment.

He was a wonderful husband—kind, considerate, doting, passionate. The list could go on. But one of the things that most endeared him to her was that he was content to let her be herself. He encouraged her to work, to continue her career, to be her own woman. She didn't exist to please him. He was nothing like Seymour and she loved him all the more for that.

But she loved him most for giving up his freedom for her and Jonah.

For the first time since they had been married, they had boarded his sailboat two days ago for a delayed honeymoon trip. They gave Liz a much-needed vacation and left Jonah with Bobbi. It had been hard to leave him behind, but it was necessary.

She and Holt needed time alone. This trip was important to Holt and long overdue.

However, they had accomplished very little so far. They had spent most of their time below making love, which hadn't given her much of an opportunity to learn about sailboats and sailing, though she was eager to do so for herself and for Holt.

"My, but you're quiet, my love," Holt said, after they finished another marathon of lovemaking. In fact, he was still inside her.

"I was thinking," she said in a sated voice.

"About us, I hope, and how good it feels for me to be inside you," he said on a husky note, rekindled fire in his eyes.

She knew all she had to do was move and he would harden again. "You're right, I was. And more."

"Want to share?"

"I was just thinking how happy you've made me."

"Not as happy as you've made me."

"I hope you really feel that way," she said, looking deeply into his eyes.

"Whatever makes you think otherwise?" He seemed genuinely troubled. "I've told you over and over how wrong I was about you."

"So you no longer think I'm a gold digger, huh?" She was teasing him, but he didn't smile.

Instead, he looked crestfallen. "I was such an ass thinking that trust fund was all you cared about."

"Hey, lighten up. You had no way of knowing that I was using that money for Mother's care."

"I should've given you the benefit of the doubt, though."

Maci caressed his check. "Well, you finally came to your senses and that's what counts." She paused. "And you've never stopped making it up to me and Jonah."

He lifted her hand and kissed her fingers. "And I never will."

"And I love you all the more for your sacrifices. I know how hard it is for you to be land-bound."

"Hey, you stop worrying about that. It was my choice to reopen my practice full-time, so I could spend time with my wife and son."

"And you're not sorry?"

"Oh, sweetheart, I've never been sorry for a second. Waking up next to you every morning, then kissing my son, is heaven on earth." Holt smiled down at her. "Besides, you promised we could spend several months on our boat when time permitted."

"And I aim to keep that promise, though this trip falls far short of it."

"But this is a start, and I'm thrilled. I just want you to get acquainted with the sea and love it as much as I do."

She grinned. "I'm working on that."

"Fair enough."

He leaned over and gave her a hot kiss. She felt his erection stir in her, and she sighed. "Did I ever tell you what a good attorney I think you are?"

"No, as a matter of fact you haven't."

"I thought you were awesome in the courtroom the other day. I've been meaning to tell you that."

"Ever since I got Sanders off, I've been swamped with clients, so I guess I'm doing something right."

"In your defense of Sanders, you were at your best. You and Vince single-handedly brought down a whole company."

"That was deceiving its customers and where management committed murder in order to keep that cash-cow flowing."

"Well, you certainly brought them to their knees in a hurry," Maci said with pride.

He tapped her on the chin. "You think so, huh?"

She stuck her tongue out at him. "I know so. You were brilliant when you accused her boss in open court, then produced the evidence to back it up."

"I couldn't have done it if it hadn't been for Clara's testimony. But you'd best be careful about that," he said, his eyes darkening.

"About what?"

"Sticking your tongue out."

"Oh, really," she said in a teasing voice.

"Yeah, really, 'cause it's going to cost you."

She giggled. "I'm counting on that."

He groaned, then leaned over, his lips closing over the tender flesh of her nipples, tonguing them until they were quivering.

Maci gulped, not daring to breathe, feeling him fully expand in her. The late afternoon sun poured through the porthole, softened the hard angles of his face and smoothed out any of the pain of the past that she couldn't fully understand. "I love you," she said from the heart.

"And I love you," he whispered.

When they were both drained, they stared into each other's soul while the soft night wrapped around them.